Hades' Return

Look for these titles by N.J. Walters

Now Available:

Jamesville Series
Discovering Dani
The Way Home
The Return of Patrick O'Rourke
The Seduction of Shamus O'Rourke
A Legal Affair
By the Book
Past Promises

Legacy Series
Alexandra's Legacy
Isaiah's Haven
Legacy Found
Quinn's Quest
Finding Chrissten
Damek's Redemption
Craig's Heart

Spells, Secrets and Seductions Series
A Touch of Magick
Dreams of Seduction
Love in Flames

Hades' Carnival Series
Night of the Tiger
Mark of the Bear
Pride of the Lion
Howl of the Wolf
Heart of the Serpent
Flame of the Phoenix
Lure of the Jaguar

Salvation Pack Series
Wolf at the Door
Wolf in her Bed
Wolf on the Run
Wolf from the Past
Wolf on the Hunt

Hades' Return

N.J. Walters

Samhain Publishing, Ltd.
11821 Mason Montgomery Road, 4B
Cincinnati, OH 45249
www.samhainpublishing.com

Hades' Return

Print ISBN: 978-1-61923-557-1
Digital ISBN: 978-1-61923-552-6

Editing by Heidi Moore
Cover by Kanaxa

Heart of the Serpent, ISBN 978-1-61922-389-9
First Samhain Publishing, Ltd. electronic publication: January 2015
Flame of the Phoenix, ISBN 978-1-61922-390-5
First Samhain Publishing, Ltd. electronic publication: April 2015
Lure of the Jaguar, ISBN 978-1-61922-567-1
First Samhain Publishing, Ltd. electronic publication: July 2015
First Samhain Publishing, Ltd. electronic publication: February 2016
First Samhain Publishing, Ltd. print publication: February 2016

Heart of the Serpent

Dedication

For all the readers who wrote wanting to know what happened to Mordecai.

Chapter One

Mordecai stood outside the stately old house in the French Quarter and stared up at the apartment on the top floor. She was up there. Jessica Miller, solitary witch and the woman who'd given him his soul back. A dark shadow passed across the closed drapes, and he knew it was her silhouetted briefly before she moved away.

"You coming inside or standing out here all night?"

Mordecai sighed and turned his attention to his friend and fellow immortal warrior. Arand was standing next to him holding a large paper bag filled with groceries. In spite of himself, the image made him smile. Badass wolf bringing home bread, milk and other sundries to the little woman. He envied his friend. Not only had Arand gained his freedom from the curse that had imprisoned them for more than five-thousand years, but he'd also found his heart, the other half of himself in the woman who'd set him free.

"I was out for a walk," Mordecai told his friend. Not a lie, but not the entire truth either. He had taken a walk. He'd followed Jessica home from Café Ledet, the eclectic coffee shop owned by her friend Tilly. The streets weren't always safe for a woman walking alone, and Mordecai was determined that no harm would befall Jessica.

"Come up and have dinner with me and Sabrina," Arand offered. Mordecai knew his friend was genuine with his offer, but he just wanted to be left alone.

He knew his fellow warriors had forgiven him for what he'd done, but he hadn't forgiven himself yet and might never be able to. And even though they understood why he'd done what he had, his relationship with them wasn't the same as it had been before. And how could it be when he'd willingly joined with Hades. Yes, he'd done it to try to save them all, but in hindsight, he couldn't be certain how much good it had actually done.

Trust would always be an issue between them.

"Thank you, but I think I'll sit in the garden for a while." He turned and sauntered off through the iron gate and into the courtyard. It actually encompassed the back of two houses. Arand and his mate had bought one of them and Mordecai had purchased the other.

"If you change your mind, come on up," Arand called after him. He waved his hand in acknowledgement of the invitation but kept on going, needing the solitude.

It was still difficult for Mordecai to be around his friends. There was a darkness in him that seemed to grow larger with each passing day. He sucked in a deep breath and was enveloped by the sweet scent of the flowers and herbs that bloomed in the garden. The space was really rather lovely and quite private. Tall stone walls, an iron gate and a wild explosion of plants made it seem quite isolated, an oasis in the heart of a major city.

Mordecai lowered himself onto a stone bench situated in a dark corner and peered up at the two houses. Both homes stood three-stories high and had been partitioned into apartments years ago. The buildings had been well maintained, and the previous owners had kept much of the original character and details of the homes that made them so unique. They'd needed little updating before he and the others had moved in. In all the years he'd spent dwelling in Hell, Mordecai had never pictured himself living in such a place, surrounded by this kind of beauty.

He was one of the seven immortal warriors who followed the Lady of the Beasts, goddess of all the animals. A war with the Greek gods centuries ago had resulted in the Lady being trapped in Hell and her shapeshifting warriors cursed to remain in their animal forms for long, long years. So much time. Lost forever.

Hades had finally been defeated, but not without some tragedy. Mordecai rubbed his chest over the vicinity of his heart. He had not escaped unscathed.

But all the warriors were alive, and that was what mattered. Roric, the tiger, lived with his mate Aimee in North Carolina. Marko, the bear, was currently residing in California with his mate, Kellsie. And Leander, the mighty lion, was happy with his Araminta in North Dakota.

Of all of them remaining in New Orleans, only Arand was mated. He and his Sabrina lived in one of the houses and the other three apartments were ready and waiting for the other warriors and their mates whenever they wished to visit.

The other two unmated warriors, Stavros the jaguar and Phoenix, lived in the home Mordecai had purchased. Each occupied one of the apartments. With each home having four apartments, that had left one vacant in his building. Mordecai had offered it to Jessica. He hadn't liked the idea of her living alone. This apartment gave Jessica her own space, but she was also surrounded by immortal warriors, all of whom would lay down their life to protect her.

A much better arrangement.

After so many years of imprisonment and torment, all of them were doing their best to adjust to the new world they found themselves in. It was a challenge for most of them. Less so for him as he'd often visited this realm to do Hades' business. Their goddess had taken herself off to explore the world, leaving her warriors to do the same.

Mordecai cocked his head to one side and concentrated. He could feel the steady hum of the Lady's power and knew she was currently in the wilds of Scotland. With his power restored, he could be there in a heartbeat.

Instead, he kicked back, extended his legs in front of him and crossed them at the ankles. Just knowing he could go to her was enough. He was content to simply sit and enjoy the warm evening air and inhale the sweet perfume of the flowers. After years of the stench of brimstone and charred flesh in Hades' domain, this was paradise.

A slight rustling off to his right had him on his feet in the blink of an eye, sword in hand. He'd manifested the blade without even thinking about it. It was a natural extension of his hand.

"Oh, I'm sorry. I didn't mean to disturb you." Jessica hovered in the dim light from the back porch looking like some angel sent from Heaven.

He quickly sent the sword away, not wanting to frighten her. Jessica was everything he wasn't. Where he was the darkest shadow of the night, she was pure light. She was petite and pale, her hair such a light blonde it almost appeared white. It tumbled around her face like a halo, framing her delicate features. Her eyes were a pale blue and her lips full and pink.

His cock stirred and he clamped down on his wayward hormones. She deserved better than his lust. She deserved nothing but respect after all she'd done for him, for all of them.

It was Jessica's grandmother who'd freed him from his cursed imprisonment decades before. The woman had risked everything to help him. It was she who'd come up with the idea to hide his soul from Hades. She was gone now, but she'd lived a long, happy life from what Jessica had told him. It eased his conscience to know she'd not only survived but also thrived.

He'd never felt anything for the woman beyond a sense of gratitude and awe that she would help a creature like him. Everything was different with Jessica. She unsettled him. It was Jessica who'd fulfilled her grandmother's promise and returned Mordecai's soul to him when he'd needed it most. Jessica had risked her life to save him. He owed her more than he could ever repay.

"You are not disturbing me," he assured her. Well, she was, but not in the way she thought. Being around her was pure bliss and the most horrendous torture. His fingers itched to touch her, but he did not dare.

"If you're sure?"

He inclined his head, and she took him at his word, leaving the safety of the light and walking toward him. She was tiny in stature, but she was all womanly curves. The flowing dress she wore was blue and covered in tiny flowers. She was barefoot. Her arms were slender and shapely and a long strand of stones and beads was draped around her neck.

She seemed a woodland sprite, a nymph sent to tempt him. She was totally at home here in the garden. In fact, she was responsible for its upkeep. Jessica had an affinity for plants.

He fought the urge to straighten his T-shirt and rub his damp palms over his pant legs. He'd resided in Hell for decades, tricking the Lord of the Underworld himself, and at no time had he felt as helpless and out of place as he did at this moment.

"Sit." It came out more like a command than an offer. Still, she didn't seem to take offense. She sat on the bench and motioned for him to take a seat beside her.

He sat but held himself stiffly. He desperately tried not to notice how the top of her dress clung to her plump breasts. His perfect night vision was usually a blessing, but tonight it was a curse. He wanted to cup those lush mounds, feel them in his palms. He wanted to rub his thumb over her pert nipples until they beaded.

He licked his lips and wondered what they would look like and how they would taste. His cock surged to life once again, a reminder that it had been a very long time since he'd last had a woman.

That situation was easily rectified. This new world was filled with women who would have sex with him. All he had to do was go to one of the bars downtown and he could have a woman within minutes.

But he'd recently discovered that he didn't want just any woman. He wanted Jessica.

"Are you all right?" she asked. Her voice was slightly accented, almost musical. He could sit and listen to her talk for hours.

"I'm fine." He shifted in his seat, trying to hide his erection from her. He was glad it was dark and she lacked his clarity of vision. She was human, unable to see in the night shadows like he could.

"How was your day?" he asked. Jessica made and sold jewelry in Jackson Square. That's how she and Sabrina Wolfe, Arand's mate, had met.

She sighed and placed her hands on the stone bench, leaning back onto them. Her breasts jutted upward, causing him to swallow a curse. Her fingertips were almost touching him. "I sold several of my more expensive pieces."

"Good. That's good." He cleared his throat, feeling like an idiot. He fought to keep from moving closer so her fingertips would graze his. He longed for her touch.

He shifted away from her.

She slowly sat upright and clasped her hands in her lap. "I'm not sure this was a good idea."

He frowned. "What do you mean?" He tried to think if he'd done anything to offend her and could come up with nothing.

Jessica waved her hand in front of her. "Me living here. Maybe I should have stayed in my old apartment."

Terror grabbed his guts and squeezed them. "No." She couldn't leave him. She was his light. If she left, he was afraid he'd sink into the darkness that threatened to take him daily and never find his way back to the light again. Hades' curse might have been broken, but too many years of living in Hell had marked Mordecai. He was more dark than light, and every day was a struggle to save himself.

Jessica wished she could see Mordecai more clearly, but the surrounding shadows seemed to almost cling to him. She shook off the fanciful thought. Shadows couldn't cling to a person. Still, there was something wrong with him and had been for a while.

When Hades had finally been defeated, she and Mordecai had become friends, spending hours talking about her past and her grandmother. It was strange to think that her grandmother had been the woman to set Mordecai free from his curse, his prison. Her grandmother had been a witch of power, and she and Mordecai had tricked Hades into believing Mordecai had killed her and gone over to the dark side.

Jessica shivered. She wished she'd worn a sweater. The night was warm but her thoughts chilled her to the bone. All those years, her grandmother had kept Mordecai's soul with her, passing it on to Jessica just before she died. It was Jessica who'd completed her grandmother's debt, who'd returned Mordecai's soul, his animal half to him at the right moment during the final battle with

Hades.

She'd thought they'd become friends. But he'd been avoiding her ever since she'd moved in to the spacious apartment on the top floor of his building.

"Have I done something wrong?" she asked. Maybe she'd offended him with all her questions. Maybe she was assuming a friendship when all he felt was an obligation. And didn't that just make her feel lower than a snake's belly.

He seemed taken aback by her question and shook his head. "No. You haven't done anything wrong."

She wasn't so sure about that. Mordecai looked like he always did. Translation—he looked good enough to eat. All the immortal warriors were easy on the eyes, but there was something about Mordecai that drew her. Maybe it was because of the stories her grandmother had told her about him. Maybe it was because she'd always been drawn to bad boys.

Whatever the reason, being around him was exhilarating and overwhelming all at once. He was darkness personified, but not evil.

His hair fell to his shoulders in a dark curtain. His eyes were midnight black and could be as cold as winter or as hot as the Sahara depending on his mood. The seams of the T-shirt he wore strained beneath the muscles of his shoulders and arms. Power clung to him like a second skin, surrounding him.

But it was his face that fascinated her. It could have been carved from stone. He showed little emotion, his dark eyes always moving, always cataloguing his surroundings, searching for an enemy in every corner. His cheekbones were sharp, his forehead high. His skin was deeply tanned.

And his mouth. Dear God, his lips were firm and full and she longed to kiss them. But he didn't seem the least bit interested in her in that way. He was always friendly and polite, always willing to lend a hand if she needed one. There was no denying he was incredibly generous. She was living in a gorgeous two-bedroom apartment she'd never in a million years have been able to afford if she'd been paying the going rent. But Mordecai had offered it to her for dirt cheap. Heck, he'd wanted her to stay rent free, but she didn't want to take advantage of him.

She knew he hated taking money from her. But she had her pride.

It was time to clear the air. "Things have been different between us since I moved in upstairs." It had been a huge decision to leave her tiny apartment and make the move. But she'd wanted to be closer to her friend Sabrina and, if she were being truthful, she'd wanted to be closer to Mordecai.

His entire body stilled beside her. "Nothing has changed." His voice was as cold as an iceberg and as distant as the Arctic Circle.

She'd had enough. "That's not true." Better to air things out between them then to go on like this. "I thought we were friends. We used to talk. You used to hang out with me." And she'd longed for those evenings when he'd come by her little hole-in-the-wall apartment and she'd cook for him. They'd talk about current events and watch movies. "But since I moved in here, you treat me as if I have the plague."

While Jessica liked all the warriors and had become friendlier with Stavros and Phoenix, Mordecai had become more distant with each passing day.

"You're imaging things," he began, but she cut him off.

"No, I'm not." She fisted her hands in the skirt of her dress to keep from reaching for him. "When was the last time we ate dinner together, or had a coffee or hung out?"

"We're hanging out now," he pointed out. She hated his low, reasonable tone.

"Only because I came looking for you," she challenged. "If I didn't seek you out, I'd never lay eyes on you." Her heart ached, but she pushed onward. "If you've changed your mind about me living here, I can find a new place. No hard feelings." It would break her heart to leave him, but she'd do it if she had to.

He sat forward and raked his hands through his long hair. Her fingers itched to touch his hair, to discover if it was as soft as she thought. "I don't want you to move."

"Then what is it?" she pressed. "Am I being presumptuous? I thought we were friends."

A low growl escaped him. An actual growl. It was a reminder he was more than just a human. He was an immortal warrior. A shapeshifter. She'd seen him shift into the mighty serpent, more dragon really, and he was a sight to behold. Deadly and dangerous.

"We cannot be friends."

His words dug into her heart like sharp talons, shredding it. The pain took her breath away. It was quickly followed by a flood of embarrassment. She could feel her cheeks heating. She'd thought they were friends, but obviously she was no more than an obligation.

"I see," she began, doing her best to keep from crying. "I'll start looking for a new place tomorrow." She couldn't stay here. Not now.

"No, you don't see." Mordecai gritted out from between clenched teeth. "You don't see at all." His hands were clasped behind his head and the muscles in his arms bunched and tensed.

She stood, legs trembling, heart pounding. She needed to get out of here before she totally disgraced herself. The last thing she wanted to do was cry in front of him and add to the mountain of guilt he already shouldered over his past. She should have known better than to move into the same building with him. One he owned.

Maybe Sabrina and Arand would let her temporarily move into one of the apartments next door. Just until she found a new place away from Mordecai. Away from all of them. She wasn't a part of their lives. Not really. They were all immortal and she was a simple woman, a human, who wanted to offer her heart.

How silly to think a man like Mordecai would be the slightest bit interested. Talk about fantasy. She'd fulfilled her family's obligation to him, done her duty. It was time to move on with her life.

She took one step away but got no farther. His strong arms banded around her waist and pulled her back. She stumbled and fell onto his lap. He tilted her until her head fell back and she was staring into his black eyes.

"You don't see at all," he repeated.

Then he kissed her.

Chapter Two

Mordecai's lips were firm but soft. His tongue snaked out from between them to trace the contours of her mouth. Jessica's head was reeling. Holy crap. Mordecai was kissing her.

"Open for me," he demanded.

Jessica parted her lips and he slid his tongue between them. She moaned and gripped his shoulders. Everything around them—the garden, the houses, indeed the entire city—disappeared as she lost herself in his kiss.

She ignored the warnings in the back of her mind that were telling her this probably wasn't a good idea. She didn't care. Far too many nights, she'd lain awake in her solitary bed wondering what it would be like to kiss him, to touch him.

And now it was happening.

Jessica let her hands roam over his wide shoulders and thick biceps. He was all hard muscle and sinew. A warrior in body and heart.

He cupped her jaw in his hand and tilted her head to one side. The angle allowed him to deepen the kiss. No, he wasn't just kissing her. She'd been kissed plenty of times before. This was something different. She felt as though he was trying to consume her.

She'd never dreamed he felt the same way about her that she did about him. It was a heady realization. He pulled away, leaving her gasping for air. But he wasn't done. He peppered her face and jawline with more kisses. Then he nibbled on the sensitive skin just below her ear.

Her entire body hummed with arousal. Her breasts ached for his touch and her panties were damp. "Mordecai." His name fell from her lips, a plea, a need.

"I have to stop," he muttered as he caught her earlobe between his teeth and gently tugged. Jessica felt the caresses throughout her entire body, a hot, pulsing need that throbbed in time with her heartbeat.

"No, you don't." That was the last thing she wanted him to do. After weeks of wondering and wishing, Mordecai was finally kissing her. And it was even better than she'd imagined. And she'd imagined plenty.

Heat came off his large body in waves. He was so big and solid. She smoothed her hands over his broad chest, loving the way the muscles jumped beneath her touch.

Sitting in the corner of the yard, lost in the shadows, with the thick perfume of the flowers and herbs surrounding them, Jessica knew if she let him go she might never get another chance. Mordecai might see himself as not as honorable as the other warriors because of the choices he'd made, but she knew differently.

Even though the light barely penetrated where they sat, her eyes had adjusted well enough for her to see his face. His jaw was rigid and she could tell he was trying to pull himself back under control.

She wasn't having it.

Jessica reached out, grabbed his hand and pulled it against her chest until it covered her breast. She sucked in a deep breath when his broad palm covered her. Her nipple beaded against the soft fabric. She wasn't wearing a bra beneath the dress and it was almost like he was touching bare skin. Almost.

And she wasn't the only one who was aroused. His cock was fully erect and pressed against her hip.

Mordecai growled again, his eyes glowing and his entire body tightening. His fingers closed around her breast, and Jessica knew she'd won. He rubbed his thumb over her nipple. Even with the fabric separating them, his touch was devastating to her senses.

Her skin tingled all over her body. She was warm, almost hot. Empty and aching for him to fill her. She felt more alive than she had in her entire life.

Then he reached up and slid his fingers beneath the shoulder strap of her dress. His fingers grazed her skin as he slowly lowered the thin piece of fabric down her arm. It didn't go down all the way, but it was enough to lower the bodice of her dress and expose her bare breast.

Mordecai sucked in a breath, and she could feel his gaze gliding over her uncovered flesh. "Beautiful," he muttered.

He circled the hard nub with his thumb. Her breath quickened and her need grew deeper with each passing second. She wanted this man, this wounded warrior.

He leaned down and flicked her distended nipple with his tongue. She moaned with growing pleasure. His touch lit a fire inside her and it quickly flamed out of control.

She caught his hair between her fingers and held him to her chest. The thick strands slid over her skin. She'd been right. It was soft and silky, such a contrast to the hardened warrior. She kneaded his scalp, loving the way he groaned beneath her touch.

He sucked the tip of her breast into his mouth, laving the bud with his tongue. The sensation shot straight down to her pussy. She gasped and squirmed on his lap, wanting to get closer.

Mordecai pulled back and shuddered. She knew she was losing him. "No, don't stop," she pleaded.

He didn't listen. He slowly, carefully, pulled the strap of her dress back up until her bodice once again covered her.

Mordecai had seen lost souls burning in rivers of molten fire in Hell. He wasn't sure what they suffered was much different from what he was feeling at this moment. His tongue still tingled where he'd touched her pert nipple. His hands itched to caress more of her soft, supple skin.

And her scent. Dear goddess, her sweet scent was making him crazy. He could smell the vanilla soap she favored, but beneath that was the unique perfume of her arousal. Sweet and spicy and all for him.

He wanted to throw back his head and roar, but that would only bring the other warriors running. Not to mention it might also bring the neighbors and the police. At this moment, he hated living in the city. If they were alone on a deserted mountain, he could claim her as his own.

No.

He couldn't claim her. He shook his head and tried to clear his thoughts. There was a reason he shouldn't touch Jessica. He just couldn't remember what it was with her sitting in his lap offering herself so sweetly to him.

Reality slammed down with a heavy thud. That was the problem. She was innocence and light. And he was tainted beyond redemption. She deserved better than him. Even if the thought of another man touching her full breasts, kissing her lush lips made him want to kill, he knew he had to let her go.

His fingers had a mind of their own and stroked over her bare skin next to the strap he'd pulled back up. He couldn't believe he was dressing her. If that didn't nominate him for sainthood, nothing would.

Mordecai buried his face in the curve of her shoulder and simply held her. As if sensing his inner turmoil, Jessica wrapped her arms around him and stroked his shoulders and back. After thousands of years of being alone. After decades of existing in Hades' realm, her touch was a balm to his soul. It was given freely, without cost or expectation. And that made Jessica a gem among women.

She knew he was rich, knew he could give her anything. Yet she asked for nothing. In fact, she was very careful not to take advantage. It still bothered him that she wouldn't take the apartment rent free. Not that he'd cashed the check she'd given him. And if she pressed him to do so, he'd simply set up an account in her name and deposit the money into it. No way was he taking money from her. Not after she'd risked her life to return his other half, his very soul to him.

He owed her everything. There was nothing he could give her that would ever repay her for what she'd given him. He was indebted to her and her grandmother for all they'd done for him. Her grandmother might have released him from the curse, but he'd never been drawn to her, not like he was to Jessica.

"Are you okay?" she asked. Once again, he could hear the concern in her tone and knew it was genuine.

He raised his head, already feeling bereft even though she was still sitting on his lap. "I'm fine. You?"

She studied him before nodding. "I'm good."

She was more than merely good. The scent of her arousal was still wrapped around him, chaining him to her more tightly than the heaviest god-forged steel ever could.

But it was time for him to prove his mettle, to be a better man than he'd been. He lifted her from his lap and placed her on the bench beside him.

"Why?" She touched his bare forearm and his cock jerked against the zipper of his pants. He could only imagine how it would feel to have her soft hand gripping his hard shaft. He shuddered and slid along the bench until she was forced to drop her hand back down to her side.

"This is wrong." He knew if he stated the reasons she'd refute them one by one. But that didn't change the facts. He was immortal and she was human. But he could share his immortality with her, a sly voice in the back of his head reminded him. It was the Lady of the Beasts' gift to the remaining unattached warriors. If they found a mate, they could make her immortal.

He would not submit a woman as pure of spirit as Jessica to a life chained to a monster with a blackened soul. Because that's what he was. No, for once in his eternal life, he had to put someone else first. That meant he had to protect Jessica from himself even if it killed him.

Jessica made a sad sound, drawing his attention back to her. He knew he'd hurt her, and that had never been his intention.

"It's not wrong if we both want it." She hesitated and then stood. "I don't understand your reasoning, but I will respect it."

When she turned to leave, Mordecai felt his heart shatter. That surprised him. He'd thought his heart long hardened. He stood and reached out, clamping his hand over her shoulder. "I'm sorry." Such inadequate words to express what he was feeling.

She turned and faced him. Standing like this, he was reminded of how tiny she was. She had such a big spirit and vibrant personality it was sometimes hard to remember how delicate she was.

"But you won't change your mind?"

He shook his head. "I can't."

She absently rubbed her breastbone like her heart hurt as well. Maybe he was being stupid, but he treasured Jessica too much to drag her into his personal hell. He had to fight his own demons. Maybe somewhere down the road, once he'd come to grips with everything he'd done.

No, that way led to madness. He had to let her go.

Jessica squared her shoulders and straightened her spine. Even then, she only came to mid-chest on him. He expected her to turn around and head back to the house. But, once again, she surprised him. She stepped toward him, reached up and wrapped her arms around his neck and pulled him down.

He went easily and was rewarded when she kissed him.

Her lips were as sweet as honey. They parted easily for him, inviting him to partake of the bounty of her mouth. He was too weak to refuse.

Just one more time. Then he would walk away.

Their tongues tangled and dueled. He let his hands roam down her sides and around to her butt before cupping the full mounds in his hands. He squeezed her behind and then lifted her right off her feet. She gave a startled squeal and tightened her hold around his neck.

Mordecai easily held her weight. In truth, he could carry her around for eternity and never tire. She squirmed in his arms, trying to wrap her legs around his waist, but the fit of her dress was too tight to allow it.

Probably a blessing in disguise.

He eased her back down to her feet and forced himself to release her. The serpent inside him was breathing fire, demanding he keep her. The beast would have him spirit her off to a cave high in the mountains where no one could ever harm her or steal her from him.

But he was more man than beast. After decades of being separated from his serpent, it was no longer as much a part of him as it had been. That saddened him greatly. The two parts of him were together again, but not fully integrated.

Living in such a highly populated area didn't allow for him to shift either.

Another reason it might be better for him to leave. But he couldn't. Some instinct was warning him not to leave Jessica. And if there was one thing he did listen to, it was his instincts. They'd saved his life more than once.

He was finally forced to remove her arms from around his neck. He gripped her hands in his, careful to temper his strength, and gave them a squeeze before releasing her. "You should go inside." His voice was rough, but he couldn't help it. He felt raw. Exposed. Angry.

"You know where to find me," she told him. Then she turned and slowly walked back to the house. She paused beneath the light over the back door and looked back. He stayed deep in the shadows.

She shook her head and went inside, leaving him alone in the dark. He watched, but she didn't return.

He was alone. Just as he was always alone.

Inside him, his serpent snorted, a reminder that he was there. Mordecai didn't think, didn't hesitate. He embraced the serpent, allowing the power of the beast to flow through him, filling every cell, every crevice. His body changed, his limbs contorting and expanding. The top of his head flattened and his jaw elongated. His skin became thick and leathery as armor-like scales covered his entire body. About twenty feet long from the tip of his snout to the end of his tail, he didn't have room to really stretch out and certainly not enough space to walk around.

But it was enough.

He folded his wings over his back and was careful not to breathe fire. The last thing he wanted to do was damage the yard and houses. He closed his eyes and settled in the courtyard. Like some mythical beast from a fairytale, he was content to protect the princess in the castle. No one would hurt her while he lived. No one.

Hades wasn't happy. Years of planning down the drain. Not only had his plan to take over the earthly realm and gain ultimate power over the humans and the gods failed, but he was stuck in a gilded cell on Mount Olympus. Even worse, he was forced to listen to the lectures of his brothers almost ever day. And, really, both Zeus and Poseidon were tedious on their best days.

It had only been a matter of weeks, but it felt like a lifetime. It made him appreciate the Lady of the Beasts all the more. After all, she'd survived five thousand years of imprisonment.

Still, he burned for revenge against the goddess and her warriors, especially Mordecai. The serpent had tricked him for decades, pretending to be on Hades' side when all the while he'd been working to help his fellow warriors. Hades had put up with the arrogant creature for years because he'd needed him for his plan. All the while, the serpent had played him false. Even worse, Hades hadn't realized it.

The serpent deserved to die.

Unfortunately, Hades had given his word as a god that if the warriors broke the curse neither he nor his minions would be able to harm them for eternity. Nor could he enlist another god's help to destroy them. If he broke his word, he'd die. It was that simple. And if there was one thing Hades had no plans to do anytime now or in the future, it was to die.

He leaned back on the wide bed with pristine white sheets and tapped his fingers against his leg. He hated this place. He longed for his own bed with his black satin sheets. He was comfortable enough, but this wasn't home. It smelled of flowers for pity's sake. He could barely stand the scent.

The need for revenge ate at him daily. No one got the better of him without retribution. It just wasn't done. After all, he had a reputation to uphold. They deserved payback for what they'd done to him. He conveniently ignored what he'd done to them because, really, no one mattered as much as he did.

He couldn't touch the Lady or her warriors or the women who'd released them from their animal forms. His fingers stilled on his leg, and he started to smile. The women who'd released the warriors were safe from him. But two of the women who'd helped defeat him weren't part of the curse at all. He wasn't bound not to hurt them.

Hades jumped to his feet and started pacing the confines of his room. His powers had been seriously depleted by the Lady of the Beasts. Another defeat he could lay at her feet. But it was time to stop looking back and move forward.

He might be weakened, but he was not without some resources. No, there was too much greed and evil, not only in the human realm, but in this one as well. It all fed into him, making him stronger.

The door to his opulent prison opened without warning. He turned and came face to face with his ex-wife. He was surprised she'd actually come to see him. "Persephone, my love," he began.

She held up her hand. "Don't *my love* me. That ship sailed a long time ago, Hades."

For a moment, he felt a pang for what he'd lost. His need for power, for absolute control over everyone and everything around him had cost him this magnificent woman. He ignored the pang in his heart. Nothing came without a cost, and he'd paid dearly.

"To what do I owe the pleasure of your visit then?" She really was quite lovely. Her hair was a midnight black that fell in a thick curtain all the way to the curve of her ass. And she had a spectacular ass. He knew that from firsthand experience.

She changed her hair color often, depending on her mood. She was slender but strong, and there was no duplicity in her, which was one of the reasons he'd been drawn to her so long ago. It was also one of the reasons they hadn't lasted. She didn't understand his need to come out on top and his willingness to do whatever it took to obtain it.

Persephone sighed. "It took some doing, but I convinced Zeus to let you go back to your own realm."

Hades hid his surprise. That she would do this for him had to mean she still cared for him. Not that it mattered, he reminded himself, but maybe he could make use of it. "Why?"

She shrugged. "Your demons are getting unruly. Left to their own devices, they might actually break out of Hell and create all kinds of havoc."

Now that made more sense. His brothers and the others wouldn't want to deal with a demon uprising. They were lazy, content to play their small games and enjoy their pleasures. Only he could control his demons.

"But, Hades," Persephone cautioned, "don't make the mistake of thinking they aren't watching you. Push them too far and the others might drain all your power, throw you into Hell with your demons and seal you all in there for eternity." With that final warning, she disappeared, leaving the door to his prison wide open.

Hades strode to the opening and stepped out into the hallway, half expecting a trap. When nothing happened, he smiled and opened a portal. The black circle swirled, growing larger with each passing second. It took a lot of effort to create the portal, something he would have done without thought only weeks ago.

Damn the Lady of the Beasts and her warriors.

Sweat beaded on his forehead, but he persisted. When the portal was wide enough, he walked through it, sighing with relief as darkness surrounded him. When he stepped out of the portal, he was in his private quarters in Hell. The moment he stepped out, the entire realm shuddered and his demons became aware that he was home.

He smiled, knowing many of them were fearful. Such a lovely emotion, and it fed him, making him stronger. Some of them had been very naughty while he'd been away. He'd deal with his unruly demons later. Right now, he had more pressing business.

He went to his throne, frowning when he noticed the dust on it. He waved his hand and the grime disappeared. Hades sat and savored the moment before turning to face the mirror on his left. It was special, magical. It allowed him to see into other realms for one hour of every day.

"Show me the serpent." The glass rippled and a scene appeared. He was just in time to watch Mordecai kissing a woman. And not just any woman, but one of the females who'd help defeat him. As he watched, Mordecai released the woman and sent her away. Hades could all but feel the longing of the serpent to claim her.

He rubbed his hands together. Really, this was too good. He couldn't have planned it better himself. The woman disappeared inside a house, but Mordecai remained outside. Hades was surprised when he shifted into his serpent form. "Impressive." He'd seen the beast before, but it was still quite an imposing sight. Unlike his fellow warriors, Mordecai had power and wasn't afraid to use it to get what he wanted.

That could be a problem. Hades couldn't harm Mordecai because the curse was broken. But the serpent could hurt him.

He waved his hand and the image winked out of existence. Hades rose from his throne and walked to the antique golden sideboard. He picked up a crystal decanter and poured himself a drink. He lifted the glass and swirled the amber liquid around the goblet before taking a sip. Smooth and perfect. Just as it should be.

It would be a challenge, but how sweet would it be if he could kill the woman and steal her soul. He might not be able to harm the warrior directly, but Hades knew that hurting the woman would crush the serpent.

Hades laughed and then called for his demons to attend him. As though several had been waiting just beyond the door for his command, they hurried in. He crooked his finger toward the first one. He'd take their power for his own. Yes, it would kill them and the power would only be temporary, but it was better than nothing.

And he had plenty of demons.

Chapter Three

Jessica closed her eyes, tipped her head back and enjoyed the warmth of the sunshine on her face. It was a beautiful day in Jackson Square. It had been three days since she and Mordecai kissed in the garden, and she could still taste him on her lips. She touched her fingers to her mouth and almost groaned when they tingled with remembered arousal.

"You okay?"

She opened her eyes and smiled at Sabrina. Her friend was now immortal, and how strange was that? But she still came to the Square several days a week to sell her paintings. She'd stopped reading tarot cards and working behind the counter at Café Ledet so she could be home with her handsome warrior every evening, but she still continued to paint and sell her art. Jessica was glad. It was selfish of her, but she'd miss Sabrina if she wasn't here. The two of them had sat side-by-side for several years selling their wares.

"I'm fine." Jessica straightened her display even though nothing was out of place on her jewelry table. "It's just warm today." There was no way she was talking about the kiss to anyone. It was too personal, too private. Plus, it wasn't likely to happen again. Not with Mordecai avoiding her like she had the plague.

"How about I go buy us some lemonade or an iced coffee from Tilly's place." Their friend Mathilda Ledet—Tilly to her friends—owned and operated Café Ledet, which was conveniently nearby.

"Lemonade would be great. I'll watch your stuff for you."

"And maybe sell a painting or two," Sabrina teased.

Jessica only smiled. She often sold more of Sabrina's work than the artist did herself. Jessica had a way with people. It was a gift. Too bad it didn't seem to work on Mordecai. And she had to stop obsessing about the man.

"I'll do my best," Jessica told her friend. Sabrina laughed and headed off toward Tilly's place, leaving Jessica alone. Well, not alone. There were always plenty of people and other vendors around. But Jessica felt very much alone in the crowd.

She sat on her folding stool and watched the people come and go, some of them hurrying, others meandering with no specific destination. She wondered what Mordecai was up to. She had no idea how he spent his days but knew he kept busy. He'd invested heavily over the years and oversaw a vast fortune. Just the idea of it boggled Jessica's mind. She was busy enough just trying to run her small jewelry business. She couldn't imagine the logistics involved in handling and investing billions of dollars.

A tall, blonde woman in a business suit stopped by her table and perused the offerings. Jessica forced herself to forget about Mordecai and pay attention to her customer. Daydreaming didn't pay the bills. "How are you today?" Jessica asked as she stood.

The woman smiled. "How much for this necklace?" She pointed out one but made no move to pick it up.

Okay, so the woman wasn't chatty. No crime in that. Some folks liked to get right down to business, especially if they were in a hurry. "That one is sixty dollars."

"Hmm." The woman looked at a few more. "Can I see it?"

"Absolutely." Jessica picked up the necklace and held it out to the woman.

The blonde reached out but didn't touch the jewelry. Instead, she ran her fingers over Jessica's exposed wrist. Under her breath, the woman muttered some words in a language Jessica didn't recognize.

She jerked back her arm, but it was too late.

A burning sensation engulfed her wrist. She dropped the necklace. It bounced off the table and landed on the pavement. She grabbed her injury with her other hand and held on. Tears filled her eyes as the pain worsened.

The blonde smiled and it wasn't a particularly pretty thing to see. No, it was sly and vicious. "Hades sends his regards." With that, the woman turned on her four-inch heels and walked away, leaving Jessica in utter agony.

The pain heightened, and Jessica was afraid she was going to pass out. She concentrated on breathing in and out, one slow breath at a time. She was in big trouble. Hades was supposed to be powerless and imprisoned. But obviously the god had a long reach.

Jessica tried to chant a healing spell, but the pain made her catch her breath. She heard someone call her name, but it sounded as though it was coming from a great distance.

"Jessica?" She managed to raise her head and found Sabrina watching her, concern on her face.

She opened her mouth to reassure her friend, but nothing came out beyond a low moan of pain.

"What happened?" Sabrina's arm came around her. "Sit down." She eased Jessica down onto the folding chair. It seemed like it was a long way down. Jessica doubled over, still clutching her arm, trying to breathe through the pain.

She heard her friend talking to someone in the background but only heard one voice. The phone. Sabrina must be on the phone to Arand.

"It's okay," Sabrina told her. "Everything will be just fine."

Jessica didn't want to disagree with her friend but knew she was mistaken. Whatever Hades' minion had done to her wasn't good. Gritting her teeth against the burning in her wrist, Jessica made herself remove her hand from the injury and study it. It wasn't a big mark, just a small burn. But instead of being red, it was as black as midnight.

"What's that?" Sabrina asked. "How did you get it?"

"Hades," she managed to get out through her clenched teeth.

"What?" Sabrina yelled. Then she was back on the phone talking quickly with someone. Jessica was locked in her own hell and unable to make sense of anything. There was a flurry of activity around her and Jessica realized that Sabrina was packing up their stands and storing their gear for transport.

Jessica closed her eyes, bowed her head and concentrated on trying to breath through the pain. She didn't know how much time had passed, but the air around her shifted and changed, becoming denser and more charged. She knew without looking that Mordecai had arrived.

"Let me see."

Jessica opened her eyes to find him kneeling in front of her. His dark hair shimmered like silk in the sunlight. His black eyes were filled with concern and banked anger.

She licked her dry lips and tried to speak, but nothing would come out. She raised her arm, wincing as the pain shot up to her elbow.

"I've got you." His deep voice calmed her, soothing her like a cooling balm. The minute he touched her, the pain moved from critical to manageable.

He gently removed her hand from her injured wrist so he could see it. He cursed beneath his breath. "How did you get this?"

"A woman," she began.

Arand suddenly appeared. "We should take this back to the house. I don't like being exposed here. I've got the car waiting at the curb."

Mordecai didn't waste any time. He lifted her into his arms and started toward the vehicle. Jessica caught a glimpse of a stony-faced Arand walking next to him, carrying her belongings. They were attracting quite a lot of attention. And why wouldn't they? Both immortal warriors were gorgeous in a dangerous way, both exuding an animal magnetism that had every woman around them very aware of their presence.

"Don't look at them," Mordecai instructed. "Concentrate on me."

With pleasure. It was too bad she was finally fulfilling one of her fantasies—being carried by Mordecai—and she was too ill to really enjoy it. Her stomach roiled and she swallowed hard, afraid she might throw up on him. And wouldn't that add to her misery.

The car was waiting at the curb. Sabrina was already in the front seat. Arand threw her belongings into the trunk and slammed it shut. Mordecai eased into the backseat with Jessica still clasped in his arms.

She was glad he didn't release her. There was something about being in his arms that helped lessen the pain. Car doors shut and then they were moving. The city passed in a blur. She stopped looking out the window as it was making her nausea worse.

"Someone tell me what the hell happened?" Mordecai demanded.

Jessica gave a small laugh and then groaned in pain. "You answered your own question. Hades happened." Her voice was shockingly weak. She felt almost faint.

"You said a woman did this?" Sabrina prompted.

Jessica nodded and licked her lips.

"Here." Sabrina passed Mordecai a bottle of water. He held the open bottle to her lips and let her have several sips.

"Stopped to look at jewelry. Tall. Blonde."

"Take your time," Sabrina told her.

"Asked to see a necklace. I held it up for her to take. Instead, she touched my wrist." Talking about it was making the small burn throb. "Pain. Fire. Said Hades sends his regards."

Mordecai swore long and lurid. Jessica wasn't sure she'd even heard some of the inventive combinations that came out of his mouth. It made her want to laugh in spite of the dire situation.

The car came to a stop. Jessica peered out the window and heaved a sigh of relief, grateful to be home. Mordecai pushed open the back door and climbed out. Sabrina ran ahead, but before she could reach the door, Phoenix opened it.

"What's going on?" the red-haired immortal asked.

"Hades." Mordecai's succinct reply made his friend swear.

Mordecai eased past him and carried her up the stairs to her apartment. He didn't have the key, but that didn't stop him. With his immortal powers, a lock was nothing.

Jessica was sweating profusely by the time he laid her down on her bed. By then Stavros had joined them, looking as concerned as the others. "Tilly," she managed to get out. "Call Tilly. Danger."

"Shit." Sabrina turned to Phoenix, but the warrior was already on his way out the door.

"I'll get her," he promised.

"Don't bring her back here. She isn't safe either," Mordecai reminded them.

"I'll protect her." With that final pronouncement, Phoenix strode away.

"I thought Hades couldn't attack us." Stavros paced the bedroom, obviously distraught.

"He can't attack us." Mordecai removed her shoes and tossed them onto the floor. "Nor can he attack the women who released us from our captivity." He grabbed the cashmere throw off the end of the bed and spread it over her.

Jessica was shivering from the cold but burning up at the same time.

"But while Jessica and Tilly both helped us defeat Hades, neither of them is exempt from his ire." Mordecai sat next to her on the bed and eased her injured arm onto his lap. "I should have thought of this. But I honestly thought Hades would be too busy with his own problems to bother with us."

"Shit." Arand raked his fingers through his hair. "What do we do?"

"I don't know."

Mordecai's stark reply sent a frisson of fear down her spine. "What is it?" she asked. "You know what this mark is, don't you? You know what it means?"

He nodded.

"Tell me." She had to know.

"A death mark." Mordecai's words fell with the force of a hammer on an anvil, shattering her hope for an easy solution.

"What exactly is a death mark?" Sabrina asked. She sat on the other side of the bed and pushed a stray lock of hair off Jessica's fevered brow.

"Exactly what it sounds like." Mordecai wrapped his long fingers around her wrist just above the mark. The pain didn't disappear, but at least her stomach didn't feel like it was going to turn inside out any longer. "Unless Hades removes it, Jessica will die."

"How long do we have to find a way to fight this?" Sabrina demanded.

"I don't know. Hours. Days. There's no way to know." Mordecai's voice hardened. "But we'll fight it, fight him."

"We need to make her more comfortable." Sabrina slid off the bed and returned a few moments later. She placed a cool cloth on Jessica's forehead. The relief almost made Jessica cry.

"She has a fever." Mordecai gently stroked his fingers up and down her arm.

"She can also hear you," Jessica pointed out. "I may be sick, but my ears are working just fine." She needed to think. There had to be a way to fight this. She pushed upright in bed.

"You need to lie down," Mordecai told her.

Jessica shook her head. "I need to get a cool shower, change into something that isn't covered in my sweat and I need to think. I'm a witch for goddess's sake. I can fight this.

"Let me help you." Sabrina offered her hand, but Mordecai eased the other woman aside.

He lifted Jessica off the bed and carried her into the bathroom with Sabrina close on his heels. He carefully set her on the counter. "I'll be right outside the door if you need me."

She stared into his dark eyes and drew on his strength. "Thank you."

He closed his eyes and heaved a deep breath. "Don't thank me. You wouldn't be in this mess if it weren't for me." With that, he turned on his heel and stalked from the room. Sabrina closed the door behind him.

Mordecai wanted to descend into the fiery depths of Hell, find the vindictive god and beat the crap out of him. Only knowing he'd have no way out and that would leave Jessica even more vulnerable stopped him. Anger the likes he'd never experienced engulfed him. Smoke actually began to rise from his skin until he took several breaths to calm himself.

The last thing anyone needed was for him to burn the place down around them. He needed to find control. He'd finally found his way into Jessica's bedroom, but it was under circumstances he could never have imagined. The space reflected Jessica's personality. It was bright and airy, filled with books and chunks of semi-precious stones and other treasures. Several plants stood in a stand by the window, lending their fresh scent to the air.

Arand's hand fell on his shoulder. "We'll find a way to defeat this."

But Mordecai wasn't so sure. "Why? Why is Hades doing this?" He gave a dark laugh. "No, don't answer. I know why he's doing this. He would have left her alone but for me. I lived in his domain for decades, tricking him. He can't attack me because the curse is broken, but he figured out how to hurt me anyway."

"I'm sorry." Arand's words were like stones in his belly.

"There has to be a way." Mordecai wouldn't rest until he found it. "Maybe the Lady?" He reached for his goddess with his mind and found…nothing. "I can't feel her." This was exactly the way it had been while they were cursed and the Lady had been trapped in Hell. It was like being cut off from a part of himself.

That was shocking. Ever since the curse had been broken they'd been able to sense where their goddess was at any given moment.

"I can't feel her either." Arand pulled out his cell phone. "I'm calling the others. Maybe they can find her." He walked away to place the calls.

"This has to be another trick of Hades." Mordecai wanted to wring the god's neck. Why couldn't he leave well enough alone? "He's not harming us, just interfering with communications."

"Why isn't he imprisoned?" Stavros asked. The jaguar was restless, pacing back and forth in the small space. "I thought after the Lady drained his power that Zeus imprisoned him."

"The gods don't see things the same way we do. You can't trust them." Mordecai had seen well enough how they worked. "They might consider a few weeks punishment enough for his misdeeds."

"Even though he'd planned to overthrow them, steal their power and imprison them?" Stavros seemed incredulous. And while Mordecai could understand his friend's point of view, Stavros didn't know the gods as well as he did.

"One of the other gods or goddesses may have spoken up on Hades' behalf if he or she wanted a favor from Hades now or at some time in the future. They're always bartering and playing games." And he'd hated it.

The shower came on in the background and Mordecai's entire body tightened. His serpent roared at him to go and see to Jessica. He could easily imagine the cool water running down over her smooth skin. He envied the water. It got to touch every inch of her delectable body.

His cock was hard and swollen, but it was about more than just sex. His arms ached to hold her as well. He wanted to kiss her and make everything better.

"None of the others can connect with the Lady either." Arand strode back into the room, tucking his phone back in his pocket as he approached. "They wanted to come, but I told them to stay away and keep vigilant. I don't think Hades will go after them. To do so would end in his destruction. But I'd rather we not all be in the same place just in case."

Mordecai agreed.

Stavros stilled. "I'll go look for the Lady."

When Mordecai started to object, Stavros shook his head. "I'm the logical choice. Arand should be with Sabrina, and Phoenix is protecting Tilly." He gave Mordecai a knowing look. "And I don't think you'd willingly leave Jessica."

"Where will you start?" Mordecai asked his friend.

Stavros stilled and seemed to look inward. "Scotland, where she was last. If she's left there, I'll try the mountains in Washington State, the Rockies in Canada and then the rainforests of South America. After that, I'll try Asia and the Middle East. I won't stop searching until I find her."

"Thank you." The words were inadequate, but they were all Mordecai had.

"We are brothers. There is no need for thanks." Those words were a balm to Mordecai's dark soul. His fellow warriors had believed for far too long that he'd betrayed them. And in many ways, even though his intentions had been good, he had betrayed their trust. He knew that most of them still didn't trust him, and he didn't blame them for that.

Stavros closed his golden eyes and his entire body shimmered before he disappeared. Having all their powers back meant they could easily move from one place in the world to another with nothing more than a thought.

The water in the bathroom shut off and Mordecai swallowed hard. "I'm going to get her something cool to drink." He hurried out of the bedroom and into the kitchen before he did something stupid. He couldn't afford to think with his dick, not now, not when Jessica's life hung in the balance.

Like the rest of the place, Jessica had managed to put her stamp on the kitchen in such a short time. His own apartment was spartan. But he didn't need much. Her place was homey, inviting.

A pale green bowl filled with apples sat in the middle of her kitchen table. Bright yellow curtains hung at the window and the walls were painted a pale cream. He opened her refrigerator and pulled out a bottle of water and another one of ginger ale. He knew from spending time with her that she enjoyed the carbonated beverage. He heard the bathroom door open and hurried back into the bedroom.

Sabrina hovered next to Jessica, a worried frown on her face. Jessica wore a loose cotton dress that floated around her calves. No, not a dress, a nightgown. That's what it was called. Her hair was damp and it was obvious that the shower had tired her. He set the drinks on her nightstand and went to her side. "You shouldn't be walking. You need to conserve your strength."

"I'm okay." Her voice was weak but filled with determination. "I need that bag." She pointed out one on the shelf, and he got it for her.

"What can I do to help?" Sabrina asked.

"Incense." Jessica motioned Sabrina toward the door. "Middle drawer in the cabinet in the dining room."

"On it." Sabrina hurried from the room.

Jessica sat on the bed and took the bag from Mordecai. She opened it and dumped the contents on to her lap. Stones of all shapes, sizes and colors fell out. She studied them and then picked out several, holding them tight in her hands.

Mordecai quickly gathered the rest and put them back in the bag. "You need to rest," he told her. She was naturally pale, but now her skin appeared almost translucent.

"Maybe for a minute." She leaned back, settled on the pillows and released a sigh. She placed the stones she'd chosen around her and then gripped her wrist once again. Lines of pain bracketed her mouth and eyes.

He covered her bare legs with a throw and tucked the edges in around her. He felt more helpless than he had since the early days of the curse that had imprisoned him for five thousand years. He hated feeling this way.

Behind him, he heard Sabrina moving around. It wasn't long until the scent of sage and sweet grass filled the air.

Jessica's eyes had closed and her breathing was even. She'd fallen asleep, exhausted by the pain and the physical exertion of getting a shower.

"She asleep?" Sabrina asked.

Mordecai nodded.

"I can sit with her."

He shook his head. "I'll sit with her for now. You check on Tilly. Maybe she knows something that can help." He'd once underestimated the strength, wisdom and resilience of humans, but never again. He'd seen too much, been through too much to doubt them.

"Call if you need us or if her condition changes." Arand squeezed his shoulder and led Sabrina from the room.

Alone with Jessica, he studied her features. When had this human woman become so precious to him? Was it solely because she'd given him back his animal half, his soul? He didn't think so, but he couldn't be certain.

What he was sure of was that he'd do everything in his power to defeat this latest curse of Hades and see her well again.

Nothing else mattered.

Chapter Four

Jessica woke slowly, aware of another person lying next to her. Mordecai. She'd know his earthy scent anywhere. But why were they in her bed together? And they were in her bed. She could smell the herbs she'd planted perfuming the space and the scent of incense on the air. Feel her soft sheets against her skin. She opened her eyes, surprised there were shadows in the room.

She frowned. The sun had been shining only moments ago. Hadn't it? Now it was going down. She remembered sitting in Jackson Square and tipping her head back to enjoy the warmth on her face.

She turned her head slowly and studied Mordecai. Even in sleep, there was no softness to his features. Tough and uncompromising. Those were the two words that sprang to mind. And, okay, ruggedly handsome. His dark hair fanned over her pillowcase and long black lashes were swept downward. It should be a sin for a man to have hair that silky and eyelashes that long and thick. But it didn't diminish his masculinity in the slightest bit.

As if he sensed her regard, his eyes popped open and he was totally alert. He started to reach out to touch her face but abruptly pulled his hand back. She tried not to let her disappointment show. Obviously nothing of a sexual nature had occurred between them because they were both fully dressed.

"How do you feel?"

She frowned and automatically did a mental check of her body. It was only then she realized her left arm was throbbing from wrist to elbow. "My arm." She went to touch it, but he caught her hand.

"Don't." His fingers were warm and strong against hers. "Do you remember what happened?"

Now that her brain wasn't so foggy with sleep, she did remember. "The woman in the Square."

"Yes. Hades has found a way to harm us without directly attacking."

"Tilly." Jessica sat up in bed and threw aside the covers.

"Phoenix has her," Mordecai assured her.

"But is she okay?"

"I haven't heard any news, so I assume that's a good thing."

"I need to talk to her." Jessica would rest better if she knew Tilly was okay.

Mordecai reached over and turned on the bedside lamp. Several of her healing stones sat beside it. She had a vague memory of holding them in her hands at some point.

He plucked his cell phone off her nightstand. "Call her." He handed her the phone and she quickly placed the call. It rang and rang and rang again. Jessica began to worry but, thankfully, it was answered on the fourth ring.

"Mordecai? How is Jessica? Is she okay?" Tilly's voice and her concern soothed Jessica like a healing balm.

"It's me, Tilly."

"Why are you using Mordecai's phone?" She could hear the suspicion in her friend's voice.

"Because I don't know where my phone is and he's sitting with me." That seemed to satisfy her friend.

"What happened, Jessica? Phoenix said something about a woman, a minion of Hades, burning your arm."

Jessica winced as she studied the circular wound. It was black in color, raw and inflamed at the edges with tiny steaks of red running up toward her elbow. She described it to Tilly. Her friend was quiet for quite some time. "I'm not sure about this, Jessica. This is bad."

"I know." Jessica knew in her heart that Hades wanted her dead. She'd helped Mordecai defeat him and she was completely human and without protection. Easy prey for a vengeful god.

"I'm coming over. I should be with you."

As much as she wanted her friend with her, she wanted Tilly safe even more. "No. Stay with Phoenix. Hades may be after you too. No sense in all of us being in one space and making it easier for him."

"What does the Lady say?"

Jessica wondered the same thing herself. "Just a second and I'll ask Mordecai." She didn't need to ask him. With his preternatural hearing, he'd been listening to her entire conversation.

"We can't reach her." She sensed his growing frustration. Not that you'd ever know it by looking at him. As always, he seemed calm and self-contained. No, it was only because she'd come to know him so well over the past few weeks that she realized just how agitated he was. "It's as though Hades is doing something to block our communication with her. Stavros is searching for her but that will take time."

What went unsaid was it was time Jessica didn't have. She filled Tilly in on what Mordecai had told her.

"Shit." Tilly echoed all their sentiments.

"I'll be okay," Jessica told her friend, even though she didn't really believe it. "Maybe you should leave town or something."

"I'm not sure that would make a difference."

"But you can't know that." The more she thought about it, the more she liked the idea. "It might be safer for you to go away. Just until this blows over."

"What if it never does?" Tilly asked. "What if it only ends when we're both dead?"

Mordecai frowned and reached for the phone. She moved out of his reach. "We'll figure something out." Jessica had to believe that. "In the meantime, stay safe."

"I will. If I think of anything, I'll call you." There was a long pause. "Love you, Jessica."

She closed her eyes and swallowed hard. "I love you too, Tilly." She pressed the button to end the call and handed the phone back to Mordecai.

"You are not going to die." Mordecai emphatically pronounced each word as he dumped the phone back onto the nightstand.

"You can't promise that. No one can." The last thing she wanted was for him or her friends feeling guilty about this. "Whatever happens is on Hades. There's nothing you or anyone could have done to prevent this."

"Bullshit." Mordecai rolled off the bed and began to prowl around the small room. "I should have left weeks ago. If I'd been off living by myself, Hades might have left you alone."

Jessica shook her head. No way was she allowing him to go down this road. "No. It might have taken him longer to remember I existed, but he would have remembered. It was my grandmother who set you free, who helped you trick the devil himself. For that alone, he'd have come after me."

There was a question she'd wanted to ask for weeks but hadn't dared. Now with death staring her in the face, she figured she had nothing to lose. "Were you attracted to my grandmother?" Her grandmother had been quite the looker back in the day. It was all too easy to imagine Mordecai attracted to her. Jessica didn't like the dark jealousy that gripped her when she thought about him and her grandmother together, but the image just wouldn't go away.

"What?" He stopped pacing and stared at her like she had three heads.

"It's a valid question," she pointed out. "Considering the last four warriors released from the curse all ended up mated to the women who released them from the curse."

"Why do you even care?" he countered.

She would not let this go. She couldn't. "Because I do. Just answer the damn question."

He stood, hands on his hips, legs spread, scowl on his face, looking every inch a warrior. "I admired your grandmother. She was a brave and clever woman."

Jessica felt her heart sink. Her grandmother had been tall and curvy, not short and slender like Jessica was. Her color had been darker, more striking as well. Jessica was blond and pale. She hated feeling so inadequate and knew her grandmother wouldn't like her feeling that way. She'd lecture Jessica about it.

She could practically hear her grandmother telling her that any man would be lucky to have her.

A muscle twitched beneath his eye and his jaw tightened. His eyes darkened, becoming deep pools of midnight. "But, Jessica, she wasn't you."

It took her a moment to process what he'd said. When she did, she threw herself off the bed and into his arms, ignoring the pain that rocketed up her arm.

He caught her easily. "What are you doing? You need to rest."

No, she needed something more than that, something only he could give her. "I might not make it," she began.

"You will." He tightened his arms around her briefly before he set her back on the bed. "You have to."

She shook her head. "But I might not. I don't know how much time I have, but I suspect not long." In fact, she was surprised by the reprieve. "If I'm going to die, there is one thing I want to do before that happens, and only you can give it to me."

"What is it? He sat on the bed, his arms braced on either side of her body as he loomed over her. "Anything you want. You have only to ask."

She reached up and touched the side of his face, marveling at his hard, smooth jaw. "You, Mordecai. I want you."

Not much had taken him off-guard over the course of his long lifetime, but Jessica had managed to do just that. Oh, he knew she was attracted to him. But he'd certainly never expected her to say the only thing she wanted before she died was to have sex with him. No, not have sex. He knew she wanted him to make love to her.

He wasn't sure he could, didn't know if he truly understood what love was. Hell, he hadn't even been certain this thing called love had even existed until he'd seen what the warriors and their women had been willing to do for one another to survive. Such selflessness still amazed him.

"Mordecai?" Her soft voice brought every cell in his body humming to life. He wanted her so much his teeth ached with need. But he wouldn't take advantage of her, not when she was wounded and clearly not thinking straight.

"Jessica," he began.

She shook her head. "If you don't want me, that's okay. But don't lie to me or to yourself. I want you. I want to have your lips on mine, feel your hands on my body while your cock thrusts deep."

Holy crap, Mordecai was surprised his dick didn't explode after that pronouncement. It was certainly hard and read for action. "You're not yourself." He had to do the right thing even if it killed him.

"No, on the contrary, I know exactly what I want." The smile she gave him was filled with tenderness and an underlying sadness. "All my adult life, I've known I'd eventually have to do my part to pay my grandmother's debt. She knew it too. That's why I never got involved in any serious relationship. I didn't seem fair when I knew I was facing a potential death sentence."

The thought of some other male having the right to touch Jessica, hold her, love her, made him crazy. But was she saying she'd never been with a man? He swallowed heavily and his cock twitched. "Are you saying?" he began and broke off, not quite sure how to ask. "Are you saying," he started again, "that you've never had sex?"

She smiled then, so brightly it made his heart ache. "No, that's not what I'm saying."

Mordecai wasn't sure whether to be disappointed or relieved. On one hand, he couldn't bear the thought that she'd been alone all these years without someone to look out for her. On the other hand, he didn't like the idea of any man touching her. His hands were fisted, and he made himself relax his fingers. No, he didn't like that idea at all.

"I've been in relationships," she continued. "But I always knew going in they were short term. And once I moved here to New Orleans, I didn't bother with anything other than a casual date." She touched her chest over her heart. "I always knew that my family's debt would be paid here, in this place."

"A debt. Is that all it is?" He didn't like hearing her talk about her returning his serpent half, his soul, as nothing more than a debt.

"In the beginning, that's all it was. Then I met Sabrina, and it became about keeping my friend safe.

He tried not to let her words hurt him. It amazed him that a puny human had the power to make his chest ache and his soul cry out in pain.

She licked her lips, and he tried not to notice how lush and pink they were. It was impossible. Everything about Jessica called to him.

"Then I saw you." She shook her head. "I don't know. It was as though I'd known you in another lifetime." Her blue eyes grew soft as she gazed at him. "Then it became as much about saving you."

"You can't save me," he blurted. "No one can."

He tried to move away, but she wrapped her uninjured hand around one of his wrists, chaining him to the bed with her gentle touch. "Why would you say such a thing?"

Anger bubbled up from the well of darkness that dwelled deep within him. "Why?" He leaned down until their noses were almost touching. "Because I am tainted. After so many years residing in Hell, I am filled with the stench of Hades' realm. It changed me."

She stroked her hand up his arm. Shockingly, he began to tremble beneath her touch. "The core of you is unchanged, Mordecai. You are a man of honor and courage. A man who did what was necessary to protect his friends and his goddess."

Mordecai shook his head. He could not allow her to believe such lies. "No, I knew I couldn't defeat Hades in battle and I wasn't ready to die." There, he'd laid his greatest shame out in front of her. "I was a coward." There was such self-loathing in his words and he deserved every ounce of mistrust and anger his fellow warriors felt toward him. He didn't deserve their trust. He had betrayed it. "I wasn't even certain until the last minute I was going to try to save Roric and the others. I was tired of fighting the darkness after so many years."

He shook his head and sat back, feeling bereft when her hand fell away from him. "It was easier with Stavros and Phoenix. It was early days then and I still had hope." He'd been so fired with noble thoughts of saving them all.

Arrogance was his curse. "But it was long years after that before Roric was released. I was teetering on the edge by then."

And Hades' lies were seductive. The offer of power and freedom had begun to look good after so many years of being alone. But that was no excuse.

Jessica sat up in bed and smacked his arm. The slight sting brought his attention back to her. "How dare you say such a thing?"

He rubbed his arm, trying to absorb her touch even if it was an angry one. "It's the truth, Jessica." He would not lie to her or to himself.

"It doesn't matter." She crossed her arms and he tried not to notice the way it pushed her breasts up against the thin material of her nightgown. He almost lost his mind when he saw the outline of her dark nipples against the pale lilac material. His pants grew uncomfortably tight. She was killing him and his good intentions.

"In the end, you did what was right. No one can blame you for having doubts."

"Roric wouldn't have had them." And that's what was killing him. Mordecai had always felt he should have been the leader of the immortal warriors of the Lady, not Roric. But, in the end, he wasn't worthy of the title. He was too distrustful, too dark in nature. Roric was a much better man.

"That's a load of crap," Jessica retorted. He was so surprised at her vehemence all he could do was stare at her. "Anyone locked in Hell for decades would have had doubts. It would be impossible not too. The devil is seductive, offering what you most want."

He let his head drop forward, unwilling to look at her any longer. Her faith in him was astounding. "Jessica," he began, not quite sure what he wanted to say. She deserved so much better than being marked for death by Hades. She was human, yet she hadn't hesitated to throw herself into the middle of their war with the god to save Mordecai and her friend.

"No. Don't say anything more. I'm tired of talking." She caught his face between her palms and raised his head until he was forced to look at her. "You're a good man, Mordecai. And I'm proud to call you my friend."

Something inside him shattered and the light of her belief filled him. At that moment, he could almost believe he was the man she thought he was—honorable, loyal, worthy. He'd give anything, well, almost anything—no sense in tempting Hades to make a return and offer a new deal—to be that man.

She brushed her fingers lightly over his jaw. Her touch ignited a firestorm inside him. The serpent roared and breathed fire. He would kill Hades if anything happened to Jessica, even if he had to descend to the very bowels of Hell once again in order to find him. The god was as good as dead the moment Jessica took her last breath.

The thought of that moment was like a sword thrust to his heart. He didn't know if he could bear it. She was the only person who'd ever looked at him as though he was something special, something more than a traitor or an immortal warrior. Jessica treated him like he was a man and a friend.

"We both know I might not make it."

"No." He wouldn't believe that.

"Mordecai, if I'm going to die, I don't want to do so without ever knowing what it's like to come apart in your arms. Don't deny me. Please."

Fury and passion rolled together inside him like thunderclouds. Once he unleashed the storm of his passion, there would be no going back. "Be certain, Jessica." His willpower was all but lost beneath her plea. How could he deny her anything?

"I've never been more sure of anything in my entire life." She pulled him closer. "Kiss me."

Mordecai knew he was lost.

Chapter Five

Jessica didn't know what she'd do if Mordecai walked away from her. She knew she was dying. Her body was getting weaker with each passing hour. At least the pain in her arm was manageable. It was as though the mark was somehow draining the very life from her body.

She didn't know what to do to fight Hades' curse. While she was skilled in many ways, she was in no way equipped to deal with something this nasty and powerful. The incense, healing stones and wards she'd set around her apartment helped, but they wouldn't defeat this plague Hades had sent to her. She could only trust her friends would come up with a way out. But she wasn't hopeful. In war, there were casualties. The rest of them had gotten away, if not unscathed than at least alive. She was collateral damage.

Ever since she was young, she'd known she wouldn't grow old. It was a knowing she'd felt deep in her heart and soul. Truthfully, she hadn't expected to survive the battle with Hades, so she'd gotten a reprieve of sorts. Just when she'd relaxed and started to believe maybe everything would be okay, Hades had struck.

There would be no happy ending for her.

But Mordecai could make her passing easier by giving her what she wanted. She hated how he saw himself. No one was harder on him than he was. The other warriors were slowly getting past what he'd done, even beginning to understanding it. But he wasn't ready to take the overtures of peace they offered. He didn't even see them, he was so caught up in his guilt.

Right now, she wasn't certain if he was going to walk away from her or give in to the passion that simmered whenever they were in the same room together. She'd tried being just friends, but she wanted much more than that.

She pulled him closer. "Kiss me."

She felt the tension running through his big body, the slight resistance as she eased him closer. Then he groaned and touched his mouth to hers. His lips were soft and warm. It was all she could do to keep from giving a cheer and a fist pump of victory. She had him now and wasn't letting him go.

Maybe it wasn't fair to him. After all, she was dying and he was immortal. But they both needed the healing that making love would bring them. Mordecai needed to understand his worth, that he'd done his best and done the right thing in the end. She needed to feel the heat of passion rushing through her veins, to understand what had been missing in her previous relationships.

She loved Mordecai. It had happened so suddenly and so completely that she'd worried about it at first. Was it a trick of Hades? A way of torturing her? Maybe it was, but it was also a gift. Sharing her body, her love with Mordecai was a way of healing them both from old wounds.

Mordecai moved his lips over hers, traced his tongue between them before dipping inside to taste. She tugged on him, wanting him on top so she could feel his weight blanketing her.

He was too strong for her to move. His muscular arms were braced on either side of her, veins prominent, muscles taut with the effort it was taking him to keep his distance.

He touched his tongue to hers, stroking it, twining with it. He tasted hot and male with a tinge of coffee. Of all the immortal males, he was the only one who'd developed an appreciation for that particular beverage. Not surprising since he'd had years to cultivate a taste for it when he'd been traveling the human realm on Hades' business.

She cupped the back of his head, not wanting him to ever stop. Her toes curled and her skin tingled. In spite of the mark draining her, she felt a surge of energy within her. Was there anything more life-affirming than making love with the man she loved? She knew the effects were only temporary, but that was okay. She'd take whatever she could get and be grateful for it.

"Jessica." He pulled away from her, his chest rising and falling rapidly as he sucked air into his lungs. She was no better. Totally breathless, all she could do was stare up at him in wonder. His kisses were better than most men's lovemaking.

He shook his head, not saying anything more than her name. But there was so much emotion in that one word. She heard all his doubts as well as a tinge of hope.

She stroked a hand across his chest. "Take off your shirt."

He shuddered and then grabbed two handfuls of material, yanked the garment from his body and tossed it aside. Jessica licked her lips when his bare skin was exposed. His chest was broad and muscular with just a sprinkling of dark hair in the center that dissipated as it traveled down his abs of steel. Just looking at him made her pussy wet.

She reached for him, but he caught her hands in one of his and shook his head. "No, you relax and let me take care of everything." He tenderly pushed her hands over her head.

He stared at her until she nodded her compliance. Then he smiled. It was filled with such masculine satisfaction it made her entire body clench with anticipation.

Mordecai trailed his fingers down the front of her nightgown. She sucked in her breath when he stroked between her breasts. Her nipples tightened to the point of discomfort. She needed him to touch her.

He sat up on the side of the bed, unlaced his boots and discarded them and his socks. Next, he stood and his hands went to the button of his jeans. There was no mistaking the bulge in the front of his pants. He was very aroused.

He unzipped the jeans and his cock fell forward. He wasn't wearing any underwear. Her entire body heated. She felt feverish and wasn't sure if it was coming from the death mark or from her growing need for Mordecai.

He shoved the jeans down his thick thighs and kicked them away, leaving him totally naked. He took her breath away. He was hard everywhere. The muscles of his legs and arms rippled as he tensed. Dark curly hair surrounded his groin. His cock stood at attention, hard and ready.

She moaned and her legs moved restlessly against the sheets. She was on fire for him. "Mordecai." She was practically panting. The scent of her growing arousal permeated the air, and she knew he could smell her need.

"You are fucking perfect," he told her. He knelt on the bed next to her. Heat poured from his big, fit body. He slipped his fingers beneath the straps on her shoulders. Then he frowned. "You're feverish."

"For you," she told him. Maybe it was partly a lie, but not totally. He was responsible for an enormous amount of the heat coursing through her veins.

He looked concerned, and she was afraid he was going to stop. Then a second later, she felt the coolness of a sharp talon against her skin and realized he'd partially shifted his hands. The fabric at her shoulders dropped away and his hands were normal again when he tugged her nightgown down to expose her breasts.

His gaze practically scorched her skin. Her nipples puckered even more beneath his perusal.

He reached out and touched one perky nub, rubbing it lightly. Jessica moaned and arched her hips. She'd never wanted a man the way she wanted Mordecai. "Yes," she hissed.

Mordecai growled and tugged the nightgown lower. "Lift your hips." She did as he asked and he whisked the ripped gown away, leaving her naked. He shifted position, kneeling between her spread thighs. "Tell me if I hurt you."

She shook her head. "You won't." Of that, she was certain. He might look big and scary, might be a total badass, but she knew he would never harm her.

"Promise me."

Afraid he might stop if she didn't, she nodded. "I promise."

Mordecai now knew if such a place did exist that this must be what Heaven was like. Having Jessica naked in front of him, but even more than that, having her trust was intoxicating. Not even Hades with all his power and promises could give him this. Only Jessica could. He didn't feel worthy of her trust, but he would do everything within him to earn it.

Her arms were still lying over her head, her elbows slightly bent. The position thrust her breasts upward. They weren't too big or too small. They were firm and full and perfect for her. She was so delicate, so fine. Her skin paler than cream.

The mark on her arm caught his attention. It worried him even though she didn't seem to be in any pain at the moment. She moaned and arched her back, pushing her breasts toward him.

He had to taste her. He leaned over her and dragged his tongue over one of her tempting nipples. She rewarded him with a gasp of delight. Parting his lips, he sucked the tip into his mouth, savoring the sweet bud.

She tangled her fingers in his hair, holding him to her. Liquid seeped from the head of his cock, a reminder that he was close to the edge. He pressed his erection against her smooth stomach as he continued to suck and tease her. After he'd enjoyed one breast for a while, he switched to the other one.

Jessica made little inarticulate sounds of pleasure. She massaged his scalp before her nails gently grazed it. He growled, wanting more of her touch. A thousand years wouldn't be enough time for him to sate himself with her warmth. He wanted to bathe in her sweet scent, lick every inch of her body, hear her moans of passion, feel the bite of her nails scoring his skin and watch her as she came.

But time was something they had little of. The clock was running out for them.

Mordecai dragged his tongue over her nipple one final time before pulling back. He sat between her thighs, missing the feel of her fingers tangled in his hair. Her eyes were partially shut, her lips parted, her nostrils flared. The pulse in her neck was beating a rapid rhythm.

He lifted her legs over his forearms and pulled her up to meet his descending mouth. The smell of her arousal had his balls drawing up tight. Her pussy was swollen and pink and wet with arousal. He lapped from her opening to her clit.

She cried out and dug her fingers into the sheet beneath her.

"I'm going to eat you until you come," he promised. Her eyes widened with surprise, and then she moaned in anticipation.

Mordecai rubbed his face against her smooth inner thigh, savoring every moment. Each one was special and he committed them all to his memory. Keeping one eye on her face, he slowly inserted a finger into her tight channel. It gripped him hard. His cock almost exploded. It would be a tight fit for him and it would feel so damn good.

But that wasn't going to happen until she found her release.

Her clit was swollen, the taut little bud peeking out from its protective hood. He couldn't resist the lure and leaned forward and stroked the nub with the flat of his tongue. Jessica moaned his name. He'd never heard anything so fine.

He wanted to hear it again so he captured her clit between his lips and sucked. She cried out, her hips rising to his touch. He released her and licked his lips. "Say my name," he ordered.

"Mordecai." Her voice was thick with arousal. Mordecai shuddered as his cock jerked, wanting inside her sweet pussy.

He inserted two fingers into her wet channel, pushing deep. She moaned his name again and he almost lost it. "Come for me," he demanded. He needed her to find her release so he could get inside her before he disgraced himself.

He licked and sucked her sensitive clit. He used his fingers to tease and torment and arouse. A low wail broke from her lips. He felt the walls of her pussy spasm around his fingers. He surged upward, capturing her lips in a kiss while he worked her with his fingers.

She moaned and thrashed beneath him. The perfume of her orgasm washed over him. He'd never felt so satisfied by another's pleasure before. Making Jessica come made him feel like a king, a god.

He knew she could taste herself on his lips. Goose bumps raced down his body and his scrotum tightened when she licked at his mouth. He reared back. "I have to have you." He felt half-crazed with need.

He was grateful the house was empty. Both Phoenix and Stavros were gone. Arand and Sabrina were still next door, but he wasn't about to wait any longer. If someone interrupted them now he wouldn't be responsible for what he did to them.

"I need you." He'd never wanted anything more in his life, not even his freedom. That should scare him, but he was too horny to care.

"Then take me." She wrapped her arms around his neck and kissed him.

Mordecai shoved one hand under her ass and lifted, angling her body until the head of his cock was pressed against her opening. He took a deep breath and reminded himself to go slow. The last thing he wanted to do was hurt her.

He pushed forward. It took some effort for him to get the head of his cock past her tight opening. They both shuddered. Sweat coated his body as he forced himself to ease his shaft forward one inch at a time. Only concern for Jessica could have compelled him to slow down when all he wanted to do was pound his cock into her until they both came.

Jessica had had sex many times, but she'd never made love before. She knew that now. Her entire body was covered in a light sheen of perspiration. Every cell in her body hummed with energy and anticipation. Her nipples ached to feel his touch again. Her lips tingled where he'd kissed her.

For such a big, brutal man, he was so gentle with her. Even now, he loomed above her, one strong arm supporting his weight while the other one angled her body against his. She loved the feel of his hand on her behind. The way his finger splayed over the taut globes.

Her pussy was wet and swollen after her explosive orgasm. As satisfying as it had been, it still wasn't enough. She was still empty and aching for him. And now he was filling her, pushing his cock into her hot, wet channel. His thick shaft stretched her in the most delicious way. He was bigger than her previous lovers and she enjoyed every hard inch of him.

He groaned and pressed his hips inward, not stopping until he was buried to the hilt. They both shuddered. Jessica felt complete. It was a strange way to feel. She was an independent woman who'd never needed a man before. But having Mordecai joined to her like this fulfilled her in a way she'd never imagined.

Being with Mordecai felt right. Having his cock inside her, their bodies joined was like fitting two pieces of a puzzle together.

"Am I hurting you?" he gritted out from beneath clenched teeth. His jaw was tight and the muscle beneath his left eye jerked.

"You're not," she assured him.

She stroked her hands over his chest and rubbed her fingertips over his flat nipples, drawing a deep groan from him. "You have to stop touching me."

"Why?" she asked.

"I'm barely holding on to my control. I don't want to hurt you."

He was sweating and his entire body was tense to the point of snapping. She knew it wouldn't take much. "You won't hurt me," she promised him. "Love me."

It was as close as she'd get to telling him she loved him. It wouldn't be fair to him to do otherwise. She was most likely going to die. And even if she lived, she didn't want him to feel obligated to her. She wanted his love. But if she didn't have that, she at least had his passion.

He fell on her like a starving beast. He pushed both arms under her and clasped his hands around her shoulders. Then he began to thrust. His hips hammered against hers, harder and faster than she thought possible. He kissed her everywhere he could reach—her lips, her jaw, her neck. He muttered words in a language she couldn't understand.

She was powerless to do anything more than cling to him as passion flared between them. Each stroke of his powerful body brought her closer to another orgasm. Each time his cock retreated, she tried to bring him back again, moaning in relief when he filled her.

He shoved one hand under her left knee and pushed it up and out, opening her wide for his thrusts. He fucked her harder and harder, both of them gasping for breath.

Her pussy quivered around his shaft. She threw her head back against the pillow and cried out. It was too much, but it would never be enough. He called out her name and she felt the hot spurt of his release fill her. Her pussy spasmed around his cock, squeezing every last drop out of him.

Exhausted, Jessica let herself collapse against the mattress. Her entire body felt like jelly. Her limbs quivered and shook. Closing her eyes, she tried to catch her breath.

"Jessica." Hard hands cupped her jaw. She managed to open her eyes and stare up at the man she loved. His dark eyes were filled with concern. She smiled at him and was rewarded when he smiled back. He looked so different than he usually did. More carefree. Younger in spite of his great age.

"That was amazing," she told him, sensing he needed reassurance he hadn't harmed her. Her warrior worried so much. That's how she thought of him. Hers.

He slowly withdrew and lay down beside her, pulling her against him. She snuggled close, enjoying the after-sex cuddling. He stroked his fingers up and down her spine. She didn't even think he was aware he was doing so. It felt nice.

Fatigue washed over her and it was suddenly too much trouble for Jessica to keep her eyes open. Like a balloon being deflated, she felt all the energy from their lovemaking dissipate, leaving her weaker than she'd been before.

Mordecai sensed the change and rolled her over until she was lying on her back. She could feel him staring at her, heard him call her name, but it was too much trouble for her to answer. The darkness inside her was growing thicker, blocking out her inner light.

Hades' death curse was growing stronger, and she was afraid her battle was almost at an end.

Hades reclined on his throne and watched the image in the mirror with glee. This was even better than he'd hoped for. He'd known the serpent cared for the human, but he'd had no idea just how much. It made his victory all the sweeter. It was only a matter of hours now before Jessica succumbed to his curse and he was able to claim her soul. He planned on spending eternity taunting

Mordecai with what he was doing to the woman deep in the bowels of Hell.

It really was delicious.

His entire body hummed with the power he'd stolen from a dozen of his demons. It was nothing compared to his usual strength, but it was better than feeling totally helpless as he had when the Lady of the Beasts had stripped him of his own power. He was using quite a lot of it to hinder communication between the Lady and her warriors, not to mention the amount of energy it had taken for him to create the death mark. It would soon be time for him to refuel.

He'd enjoyed walking through the ranks of his demons and picking some at random to kill. He had to take his fun where he could get it. It would be quite some time before he dared personally step into the human realm. Maybe decades or longer. His brothers were watching his every move. He could feel their spying eyes on him from time to time, and he played weak and pathetic whenever he sensed their presence.

They would lose interest in him over time. All he had to do was wait and slowly regain his power.

The picture in the mirror winked out the moment he sensed the presence of another god outside his door. He waved his hand at the entrance and it opened. He half expected it to be one of his brothers or at least one of their flunkies.

The sweet scent of wildflowers preceeded her as she strode into the room like she owned it, put her hands on her hips and glared at him. "What are you up to, Hades?"

Chapter Six

Mordecai didn't know what in the hell to do. He should never have made love with her. No, scratch that. He couldn't bring himself to regret something so beautiful. He just hated feeling so fucking helpless.

After Jessica had passed out following their lovemaking, he'd carried her into the bathroom and tenderly bathed her in the tub. Once she was clean and dry, he'd taken her back to her bed, found another one of those sleeping gowns in a dresser drawer and put it on her. Then he'd dressed, aired out the room and disposed of the nightgown he'd ripped off her earlier.

That was hours ago. Dawn was almost upon them and she hadn't stirred. He was beginning to fear she never would. He sat on the bed, simply watching the slow rise and fall of her chest, silently willing her to live. Arand and Sabrina had come and gone several times, checking on her. If they'd noticed Jessica was wearing different clothing, they didn't comment on it. Perhaps they thought she'd simply bathed and changed herself.

Mordecai didn't care what they thought about his constant presence by her bedside. He wasn't leaving her.

Roric, Marko and Leander had all called, but Stavros hadn't contacted them. Neither had Phoenix. That was worrying. But the phoenix would have to take care of Tilly on his own. All Mordecai's concern was for the pale, slight woman lying so still in the bed beside him.

"Open your eyes, Jessica," he begged. "I need you." He, who had never needed anyone in his immortal life, not even his fellow warriors, needed this fragile human. If it wasn't so tragic, it would be laughable. Brought to his knees by a woman.

He feared that when she died, what little light remaining inside him would dissipate and the threatening darkness would consume him forever. If that happened, he'd have to go to the Lady and ask her to destroy him. There was no other way. He didn't want to live in the darkness any longer. He longed for the light, for Jessica.

The dawn light filtered in through the window, the beam falling on Jessica's still body. After a moment, she turned her head toward it, as if seeking the warmth and light.

"Jessica." He held his breath and willed her to open her eyes.

Her eyelids fluttered and finally opened. "Why is it so dark?"

Mordecai's heart sank. Hades' curse was getting worse. His darkness was overtaking her.

"It's dawn. It will get lighter now," he promised. He reached out and took her hand in his. Her skin was hot to the touch. She was running a fever again. Her usually vibrant eyes seemed dull and lifeless. Hades' cursed mark was literally draining the life from her.

She licked her lips. "Is there something to drink?"

"Of course." He lifted a glass of freshly squeezed orange juice from the bedside table, glad Sabrina had brought it with her the last time she'd stopped in to check on her friend.

He put one hand behind her head and lifted her up to meet the rim of the glass. She was so weak she could barely take a few sips before she was done. Mordecai wanted to rage at the world and at the capricious gods. Why was this happening to someone as good as Jessica?

But he knew the answer. Goodness had little to do with it. The gods played games with all of mankind, and sometimes fate was a bitch.

He gently lowered her head back to the pillow and set the glass on the table. She licked her lips again and offered him a weak smile. "Is there anything I can do?" He wanted to do something. Anything.

She nodded. "Can you—" She broke off and her cheeks turned a charming pink.

"What is it?" He brushed a damp lock of her sunlit hair off her forehead.

"Can I see your dragon once more?"

Of all the things she could have asked him, he never would have guessed she'd ask him this. "You want to see my tattoo?"

"For starters."

He stood and dragged his shirt over his head. Jessica watched him so intently it almost made him smile. He turned, presenting his back to her. Her murmur of awe had him flexing and tightening his back muscles.

"He's so fierce." He heard the slight rustle of the bed covers, and then she stroked her fingers over the beast's wing. Mordecai arched his back into her touch.

"The serpent is just like you," she continued. "Wild. Untamed. Unpredictable." She continued her exploration, touching the serpent's flat head. Mordecai bent his head to the left, feeling her caress just as the beast did. When she caressed the beast's flanks, his cock roared to life.

He lowered his head as his breath came faster. He knew he should object, should make her lie down and conserve her waning strength. But her tiny, capable hands felt so right against his skin. That she accepted his serpent as readily as she did him astonished him. Most people feared his beast.

Even when they'd roamed the world in days long past, the other warriors had garnered the awe of the people. Mordecai was feared and, in some cases, reviled. His lip curled and he sneered. Humans should be afraid of him. He was an immortal warrior.

He was so caught up in Jessica's tender touch that he didn't sense anyone around them until the door opened. Instinctually, he shifted. His dragon burst from inside him. His head changed shape, flattening and elongating. His body lengthened and thick, protective scales took the place of skin. Tough, leathery wings burst from his back. Long, vicious claws sprang from the tips of his fingers. The room was too small to contain him and he was forced to curve his twenty-foot long body. But that wasn't a bad thing. His large form provided a shield for Jessica.

He knocked Jessica back with his tail, being as gentle as possible. She gasped and cried out, but it was quickly lost in his battle roar as he faced the intruder.

Arand stood outlined in the doorway, his mate shoved behind him. "What in the name of the Lady are you doing?" his friend yelled.

Mordecai calmed his racing heart. It was only Arand. It wasn't Hades come to attack Jessica. He huffed and a billow of smoke was released from his nostrils. At least he'd remembered not to breathe fire.

"Jessica," Sabrina yelled from behind her mate. "Are you okay?"

Had he scared her? Mordecai didn't know if he could live with himself if he had.

"I'm fine," Jessica called back. "Isn't he cool?"

Mordecai gave a chuff of laughter. Only Jessica found him cool and not ugly. His body was a combination of browns and greens. Earth tones that easily blended with the wild forests of the world.

"You can stand down now, big guy," Arand told him. Smug bastard was laughing at him, but Mordecai didn't care. Jessica thought his serpent was cool.

He morphed, taking his human form once again. His chest was still bare, but he conjured pants so as not to embarrass either woman. Sabrina peeked around Arand's shoulder and grinned at him. Then she looked at Jessica and gave her a thumbs up.

Mordecai shook his head. Would he ever understand these modern women?

"How are you feeling, sweetie?" Sabrina rushed over to the bed, the bangles on her arm jangling.

"Okay," Jessica replied, but he could hear the fatigue she tried to hide.

He returned to her side and inserted his body between her and Sabrina, practically muscling the other woman out of his way. He picked Jessica up and shifted her to the head of the bed, propping her against the pillows. She smiled her thanks. But he wasn't done. He tucked the covers around her and smoothed them once again. Then he snagged the juice and held it to her lips until she had several more sips. Once he'd done everything in his power to make her more comfortable, he turned to her visitors.

"Any news?" he asked, dreading the answer. He could see the answer in the bleakness in Sabrina's eyes.

"No. Stavros hasn't been in contact and neither has Phoenix. Roric and the others have joined the hunt to find the Lady, but this is a big world. Without the connection to her, she's going to be difficult to find." Sabrina tried to offer them hope. "While their men are gone, the women are researching possible ways of breaking the curse."

It was such a blessing for the warriors to have their powers back, to be able to jump from place to place with only a thought. But Sabrina was right. The world was a large place. As for fighting the curse, Mordecai wasn't sure that was even possible. Hades, even at his weakest, was a formidable opponent.

Jessica started to speak but grabbed her throat and began to wheeze. Heart pounding in his chest, he caught her by the shoulders and forced her to look at him. "Breathe. Look at me, Jessica." He waited until her blue eyes met his black ones. "You can do this. Breathe with me." He inhaled and exhaled slowly, willing her to follow his example.

He heard Sabrina and Arand behind them but had no idea what they were saying. Only Jessica mattered. Her eyes bulged slightly. She grabbed his wrists and squeezed tight. He could feel and see her panic. Her skin began to take on a bluish cast.

He was losing her.

"No. He can't have you. Do you hear me, Jessica? Breathe," he commanded.

She managed to suck in a small amount of air. It whistled into her lungs. Just as quickly, the air passage was cut off. It was as though the devil himself was choking her.

Arand sat on the bed opposite him. Sabrina was on the phone, urgently speaking with someone. He heard her say Aimee's name and knew she was trying to find out if Roric's mate had discovered anything that could help Jessica.

Fear. It was something he'd known intimately in his years with Hades, but nothing he'd ever been through compared to this. "Jessica." He tried to infuse every ounce of his determination into his voice. "You will breathe. Do you understand?"

She tried, but she was so weak. Her hands fell away from his wrists, flopping back to her sides. The mark on her arm seemed to pulse with dark power. Her eyelids slowly lowered. He roared when he lost sight of her blue eyes. Was it the last time he'd ever see them?

"No, you can't die. You must live." He shook her. Her body flopped around like a rag doll, lifeless and boneless.

Arand touched his shoulder. "There is nothing more you can do."

"There has to be," he snarled. He'd taken on Hades and beaten him. He could defeat this death curse. "There has to be a way to save her."

His friend went still beside him. Mordecai pinned him with his black gaze. "What is it?"

"You could share your life force with her. That might be enough to drive out Hades' darkness."

For the first time since he'd come into being, Mordecai wished he'd been more like his fellow warriors. But his soul was dark and stained. "I fear I have only darkness to give her." He saw the growing understanding in Arand's eyes. "It might only hasten her death."

"She's dying anyway," Arand pointed out.

"Do it," Sabrina demanded. She'd tucked away her phone and now climbed onto the bed next to her mate. "Save her."

"She'll be tied to me forever," he warned.

"Better that then dead." Sabrina's bluntness drove the point home. What did it matter as long as Jessica lived? And if he had to give her every last drop of his life force, he would. Because he'd already decided he didn't want to live without her.

He only prayed he didn't taint her with his darkness.

She was lying on the bed, her skin damp with perspiration, her face pale, her lips turning blue. Mordecai leaned down and gently touched his mouth to hers. "I won't let you die," he promised her.

He closed his eyes and placed his hands over her heart. Digging deep, he searched for the light of his goddess. It was a rainbow of color, hidden beneath layers of shadow. It tried to conceal itself from him, but he ruthlessly yanked it from its hiding spot and shoved it into Jessica. As though sensing more light energy, it flowed eagerly from him into her.

Good. That was good. The heat was intense, even more so than the bowels of hell. But Mordecai held firm. Jessica's life was in the balance.

His serpent roared, lending its strength to the battle. Like him, the beast didn't care if he lived or died as long as Jessica survived.

Darkness swarmed around him. It poured into him until he could no longer see or sense the world. He was blind and deaf. It was the same sensation he'd gotten every time he'd stepped into one of Hades' dark portals. It was like being imprisoned in a void of nothingness. Staying here for long would drive him mad, would make him pray for death.

Still, he held on. There was nothing he wouldn't do for Jessica.

It dawned on him as the darkness consumed him that he loved her. He'd never understood the emotion, wasn't even sure he'd believed in it. But this had to be what it was. He put her well-being above his own, willing to do whatever it took to make her healthy. He wanted her happiness above his own. Even if that meant his death.

She belonged to him and he would take care of her.

As the last of the light streamed from his hands, he prayed to the Lady to save her.

Jessica wasn't sure if she was dying or if she was already dead. She couldn't breath. The suffocating feeling enveloped her despite Mordecai's attempts to help her. She felt so bad for him. He was so alone. He needed her to love him even if he didn't realize it.

But time had run out and Hades had won this round. She wondered what Hell would be like, because she had no doubt the god would be coming for her soul.

The light faded, leaving only darkness. Fear gripped her. She fought through the thick black, searching for a light. She centered herself and concentrated, not without, but within. The light wasn't outside her, she carried it with her.

It began as a mere difference in shade. A pinpoint of black became gray. She imagined a circle of power around her, blocking out the negative. It grew brighter. Hopeful, Jessica concentrated on the point until the faintest glow emerged.

She nurtured the ember and it grew bigger and bigger until it surrounded her. She was the sole light in the pitch black. Then the world went supernova. As though a star exploded, the world around her lit up in a rainbow of color. It poured in, driving out the blackness. The dark could not survive in the face of such beauty.

The light was alive and it was more powerful than anything she'd ever imagined. It chased the darkness, opening up and swallowing it whole. It was destroying the death curse.

Hope filled Jessica and the glow grew even brighter. It was like being in the middle of the sun. She closed her eyes but could still see the light. She laughed and spun in a circle. Mordecai and the others must have found a way to defeat Hades' curse.

She held out her hand to the light and it skipped over her palms, tickling them. It was a playful energy. It swirled in front of her and began to take a shape. A sense of anticipation filled her as the light coalesced.

It was a serpent. But not any serpent. It was Mordecai.

She frowned, not quite understanding.

Voices pulled at her attention. They seemed to be coming from far away. They were distracting her. There was something important she needed to know, needed to understand. But the voices wouldn't go away.

Finally, she was forced to open her eyes. The first thing she saw were the faces of Arand and Sabrina leaning over her, both of them worried. She offered them a smile to let them know she was okay. The light still filled her and she had a feeling it always would. She felt great. Better than great. She felt invincible.

Everything inside her stilled. Invincible.

"Where's Mordecai?" Why wasn't he here with her? He never would have left her.

Arand shook his head and glanced to her side. She followed his gaze and cried out when she saw Mordecai's lifeless body lying next to her on the bed. She surged upward, filled with purpose and determination. "What did he do?"

"He gave you his life force so you could live." Tears rolled down Sabrina's cheeks.

"No. It doesn't have to be this way. Why did he give it all to me?"

"I think there was too much darkness in him," Arand began.

"I don't believe that," she shot back. Really, she was tired of Mordecai and the others treating him as though he were defective.

She took a deep breath and centered herself. She muttered a quick protection spell and was shocked when it slammed down around her like a titanium shield that nothing dark could penetrate. "I'm not letting you go that easy, serpent." Placing her hands on his chest, she concentrated. The light hesitated, but she wielded it ruthlessly.

Jessica sang a healing chant as she surged into Mordecai along with the light. The serpent was right alongside her, protecting her. The darkness surrounded her, trying to suffocate her. But she was stronger than the encroaching shadows. And she had something that could stand against all darkness.

I love you. She said the words, not aloud but inside her, as she chased the darkness through his body. Like it had in her body, the light began to consume the blackness. *Mordecai, hear my voice and come to me.*

The shadows went deep and she followed them. There was no way she was turning back. Better she be lost in the depths of Hell forever than to leave Mordecai to such a fate.

Laughter, sly and masculine, seemed to come from all around her. "You cannot beat me." She recognized Hades' voice before he stepped forward. The devil had come to claim their souls.

Then she did the one thing she knew he'd never expect. She turned her back on him. Fighting him would only increase his power. What she needed was something to counter it.

Love.

Mordecai. If you can hear me, I need you. I love you. Hades has come for me. Help me. Jessica threw the plea out from the depths of her heart and waited. It was their only hope.

Mordecai knew he was already lost to madness. He was hearing Jessica's voice calling to him. He tried to turn away from it, but it was impossible. Even if it was nothing more than a figment of his imagination, it was her voice.

He traveled toward the sound. It grew louder and clearer the closer he got until he understood her words. Hades had come for her and would not let her go. *No!* He would not let that happen.

Giving a fierce battle roar, Mordecai surged forward, pressing through the pitch black that fought to surround him. Nothing would keep him from Jessica.

He stumbled from the black void into a circle of light. Jessica. She was truly here. How had that happened?

As if sensing his presence, she turned and smiled at him. Behind her, Hades loomed, like the demon god he was, waiting to snatch her soul.

Mordecai snarled and pushed forward, ready to fight. But Jessica stopped him. She stepped into his path, blinding him with her radiance. He threw up his arm to block the light so he could see.

"Get behind me," he roared. She was between him and the vengeful god. He tried to move her but couldn't. She was shockingly powerful.

"No, my love. Fighting will only empower him. If you want to defeat him, there is only one way. You must trust me."

Trust. It was the one thing he'd always had trouble with, even with the Lady and his fellow warriors. But Jessica he would trust even if she led him to the very depths of Hell for eternity.

"What would you have of me, my lady?"

Her eyes widened at his manner of address. The Lady might be his goddess, but Jessica was the lady of his heart.

"Do you love me?" she asked.

"With all of my being," he freely offered.

Behind them, Hades gave a frustrated roar. "I will have your souls."

Jessica turned and smiled at the god. "No, you won't. Be gone from here. You cannot harm us now or ever. I am part of Mordecai now. I share his life force. If you try to harm either of us you will die. That was the deal you agreed to with the Lady."

Hades' roar practically deafened them. Darkness swept around them like a whirlwind, swirling madly. But it didn't touch them. Their love anchored them.

More certain now, Mordecai poured all his love into Jessica. If that's what it took to protect her, he would give it his all.

"You are the light in my dark world," he told her.

"And you are the light in mine," she returned.

The thought of being anyone's light astounded him, but he didn't doubt her sincerity. A rainbow of light swirled around them and through them until no hint of darkness remained. He felt his serpent rise within him, more powerful than ever before.

"You did it," he told her. "You drove away the darkness."

"No, Mordecai, we drove back the darkness." She took his hand and led him upward. "Now it's time to return to the real world."

He followed her. He who had grudgingly followed Roric for an eternity, followed this slight female without hesitation. She was his salvation.

But would she still want him when they returned to the real world?

Then it was too late for questions. The bright light receded and he felt his body lying on the bed, cradled by the soft covers. He sat up and looked around. Arand slapped him on the back. Sabrina was laughing and crying at the same time while she talked to someone on the phone. But he only had eyes for Jessica, and she was smiling at him.

Hades roared with fury as he landed back in his body. He hadn't physically left Hell. He couldn't. Not with Persephone watching him so closely. He'd imagined having problems with his brothers, not with his estranged wife. But he'd managed to send his spirit into the void created at the moment of Jessica's death in order to claim her soul. It astounded him that she'd had the power to fight him. Even more incredible was the idea that the serpent had given the woman all of his life force, sacrificing himself for her.

Now the woman was lost from Hades and, along with her, his chance at vengeance against Mordecai. The serpent had been clever enough to discover the loophole in his plan. If the warrior shared his life force with a woman, she became a part of him. He'd honestly never expected Mordecai to do such a thing. It perplexed him.

Why anyone would give up power to another was beyond his comprehension. The goal in life was to be the most powerful of all. He curled his lip. The weak got trampled by the strong, and no one was going to walk on him. Not while there was life in his body.

He strode over to the gold-lacquered table and poured himself a drink. He tossed back the expensive liquor without a thought, enjoying the burn as it traveled to his stomach. He was ridiculously weak after expending so much energy. It was time to sacrifice a few more demons and recharge.

He set the crystal glass back on the sideboard and considered his options. There was still another woman he could go after. The corners of his mouth drew up in a smile. It wouldn't be quite as satisfying as stealing Jessica from the serpent, but beggars couldn't be choosers. Her friend, what was her name? Tilly, yes, Tilly. She would have to do.

Chapter Seven

Jessica knew something was wrong. It had only been a matter of hours since they'd defeated Hades' death curse. She was immortal now. That was hard to wrap her head around. She was filled with an abundance of energy and more alive than she'd ever felt in her life.

The only problem was that Mordecai seemed more distant than ever.

Of course, he'd been through a lot. She should probably give him time to come to grips with everything that had happened. But she feared if she did, he might disappear somewhere to the far reaches of the world. Not that she wouldn't be able to find him. With his life force coursing through her veins, she could easily sense the serpent within him. She knew he was down in the yard even now.

Freshly bathed and dressed in a simple sundress, her hair hanging around her shoulders, Jessica walked barefoot down the stairs to the garden. Arand and Sabrina had retired to their home a few hours ago. Darkness now shrouded the world. She stepped out into the fragrant night and peered up at the sky, wishing she could see more of the stars shining there.

Like the last time she'd sought him out here, he was seated on a bench in the far corner, hiding in the shadows. It was time for him to step into the light.

She knew that he sensed her presence. He straightened, his shoulders tensing, but he didn't turn to face her. With her new immortality, she was able to see him clearly even though the darkness clung to that corner of the yard. A handy skill for sure. Solar lights were scattered throughout the space, lending their glow to the thick foliage, but she no longer needed illumination in order to be able to see in the night.

She paused beside him and waited.

"You should be resting." His low, rough voice gave her shivers, the good kind. She was naked beneath her dress. Her skin was sensitive to the brush of the fabric against it. Her breasts swelled and her nipples puckered.

"I had a long nap." In truth, she'd slept most of the day away and had awakened totally invigorated. "If I should be resting, then you should be too." She tentatively touched his shoulder and felt the muscles bunch beneath her fingertips. He was so wary, her dark warrior. "I feel fine. Better than fine."

"Good." He inhaled sharply and slowly released his breath. "That's good."

"There's still no word from either Stavros or Phoenix. I'm worried about Tilly." She wished she knew her friend was okay. Tilly hadn't answered her phone and Jessica's concern grew with each passing hour.

"No news is probably good news. If Hades had Tilly, Phoenix would have contacted us immediately."

"I suppose so." Still, she hated not knowing. Taking a chance, she sat alongside him. Her arm and leg touched his. So close but so far. "What's wrong?" She had to know.

He shook his head, the distance between them a growing chasm.

"I won't let you do this," she told him. She reached out and took his hand in hers. "I won't let you turn away without talking to me."

He slowly turned. His face could have been carved from stone. Gone was the man who'd professed his love in order to save her. In his place was the implacable warrior who'd spent decades in Hell.

"What is there to talk about? You're safe. You're free. And you're immortal." He tried to pull away from her, but she tightened her grip on his hand. "You have your entire existence ahead of you."

That sounded like a goodbye if she'd ever heard one. Her heart sank and her stomach clenched in fear, but she fought it back. She'd come too far to give up now. "And you, Mordecai. What do you have?"

The laugh he gave was not the least bit pleasant. "Me, I have eternity as well."

"You don't sound happy about it," she pointed out. She had to get him talking. Had to find out what was going on in that complex brain of his.

He shrugged. "It is what it is."

The man was maddening. She was tempted to smack him but refrained. "Do you know what I want?" Better to lay it all out even if that meant he might break her heart. She really didn't have any other choice.

He looked at her then, really looked at her. His eyes glowed in the darkness, their blackness so deep and compelling. "What do you want?"

"You, Mordecai. I want you."

Mordecai had come out to the garden to contemplate his next move. He liked it out here, mostly because it had been created by Jessica. Her touch, her stamp was everywhere. He felt closer to her here even when he was alone.

How utterly pathetic.

He'd know the moment she'd stepped into the yard. Her presence filled the space like the sunrise drove back the night. Now she was sitting right next to him and it was all he could do not to grab her and take her away somewhere no one would ever find them.

But she deserved better than him.

Yet for some unknown reason, she wanted him. Her words reached deep within him, filling him with hope. He trampled the sensation, not quite believing in it even after everything that had happened.

"Did you mean what you said?" she asked him.

"When?" It was hard to concentrate with her sitting alongside him. The sweet scent of her soap and the natural muskiness of her skin combined to create the most delightful perfume known to mankind. He felt the press of her arm and leg against him and his cock responded eagerly. Every cell in his body hummed with recognition and his serpent was beside itself, demanding Mordecai claim her.

"When you said you loved me?"

There it was. The stark truth thrown down between them. He could lie. He should lie. He looked into her pale blue eyes and knew he could not. She trusted him. And, as he'd learned, trust was the most precious of commodities. Once lost, it was never truly regained.

"Yes."

She caught her breath and then she smiled. By the Lady, she was the most breathtaking creature on the planet when she smiled. Her entire face lit up as if by some inner light. Her pale hair formed a halo around it.

"I love you too. I meant that."

"I know you did." He cupped her fragile jaw in his big, powerful hand. She didn't flinch from him. Instead, she leaned into his touch. Such trust almost broke his heart. If he still had one. And he must, because it ached so much. "I'm not good for you, Jessica." There, he'd said it. "You deserve better."

She covered his hand with hers. "You're a very good man. Better than you believe. And I deserve to get what I want. And I want you."

He wanted to believe her so badly. "You don't know the darkness that resides inside me."

She shook her head. "No, Mordecai. It's you who doesn't know yourself. We drove the shadows from Hell out of you when we fought Hades. Look inside and see that I'm telling the truth."

He curled his fingers around her and brought her hand to his lips, laying a tender kiss on each knuckle. "I don't need to look. I know it is gone. But there is a natural darkness inside me. One the others don't have."

"Are you so sure of that?"

Her simple question caught him off-guard.

"There is dark and light within all of us. There must always be balance. And darkness is not always a bad thing." She placed her free hand on his chest and caressed him through his shirt. "Take now, for instance. The night is hiding us from view of the neighbors. We could do whatever we wanted and they wouldn't see us."

Her philosophy of life, her belief in him was staggering. "Do you truly believe I am worthy of you? You trust I will not hurt or betray you?"

"Oh, Mordecai." She slipped from the bench and knelt before him, her hands on his thighs. "You are more worthy than anyone I've ever met. You've been tested far more than anyone has a right to be and you emerged victorious." She pulled the straps of her dress down, exposing her firm, round breasts. "And I know you'll never hurt me. I know for a fact you'd give your life for me. And you said you loved me. What more can a girl ask for?"

Mordecai's head was spinning. So many beliefs he'd held about himself lay shattered around him. And all because of the woman kneeling before him. He plucked her off the ground and into his arms. "You are too good for me. But I'm keeping you," he pledged. "It's too late to back out now."

He needed her more than he needed air to breathe. Her delighted laughter pushed away the remaining shadows until there was only the two of them surrounded by love. He buried his face in the curve of her neck. "Goddess, I love you."

Her hands threaded through his hair. "I love you too. Now. Always." It was a vow and it sealed both their fates.

He became very aware of the press of her breasts against him. He pulled back and yanked off his shirt, needing to feel her skin to skin. "You're sure you're feeling better?"

She clasped his head in her hands so he was looking straight at her. "I'm sitting half-naked in your lap. Are you really asking me that?"

He chuckled. It sounded rusty, but it was a slight laugh. Jessica smiled at him as she ran her hands over his biceps and shoulders and down to his pecs. "You're really wearing too much clothing."

He stood and placed her on her feet in front of him. "We can't have that," he told her. He shoved her dress down her hips, and it fluttered to the ground around her feet. "You are exquisite."

"And you're still wearing too much clothing," she teased. She reached for the opening of his pants, but he was too impatient. He yanked them open and shoved them down his legs and off. Naked, he stood before her.

"Mmm. Now this is what I've been dreaming of for the past few hours." She reached out and cupped his sac, lightly massaging his balls. Every muscle in his body tensed, but he didn't move. He wanted more of her touch.

She released him and slid her hand up his shaft from the root to the bulbous tip. His cock jerked toward her and liquid seeped from the slit. She rubbed her thumb over the top, spreading the moisture. "So hard. So strong. I love how you feel inside me."

He growled and reached for her, but she took a step back. "Not yet. This time I get to touch you."

"You are touching me," he pointed out. His hunger for her was almost out of control.

"Sit." She gave him a little push and he reluctantly sat back on the bench. When she knelt back in front of him, he thought his cock might explode.

His breathing was labored and he curled his fingers around the edge of the stone bench to keep from grabbing her. He needed to be inside her, to have her pussy squeezing him tight.

But Jessica had other ideas. She lowered her head and blew on the slick head of his cock. His balls pulled up tight. "Jessica," he growled in warning.

"I just want to play for a while." How could a woman who looked like an angel be so sexy. Like a nymph, she sat at his feet, her bare skin pearly white in the moonlight. Her rosy-pink lips got closer to his cock and he gritted his teeth.

Then she took him to Heaven. She licked the head of his shaft, swirling her tongue around and around, teasing the slit at the tip. He groaned when she opened her mouth and finally took him inside. Wet heat closed around his cock. She teased up and down the hard length with her tongue.

He gripped the stone bench tighter and swore when two pieces broke off. He held up his hands, each holding a piece of stone. He could see the laughter in her eyes and suddenly he was laughing too. He tossed the stone pieces behind him and heard them *thunk* on the ground when they landed.

Then she took him deeper and sucked. Laughter fled and he threaded his fingers through her hair, holding her closer. She gave a little hum of pleasure. He could smell her arousal and knew she was getting turned on by touching him.

But he didn't want to come this way. Not this time. He needed to be joined to her once again, to feel a part of her.

He eased her head back and she released his dick with a wet pop. She stared quizzically.

"I need to be inside you." Even as he spoke, he was lifting her. He sat back on the bench and positioned her so she was kneeling over him, her thighs on either side of him. "Take me, Jessica."

She gripped his cock in her small, capable hands and shimmied closer until the head of his shaft was pressed against her opening. Their eyes met and she smiled as she pushed downward. Her pussy swallowed his cock, undulating around it as he went deeper and deeper. This was where he wanted to be. This was home.

With his hands on her hips, he guided her all the way down until he was fully inside her. He liked having her this way. It allowed him to easily cup her breasts. Her nipples were taut red berries waiting to be tasted.

Mordecai took one nipple into his mouth and suckled. Jessica rocked against him and that slight movement sent him over the edge.

Jessica had won. Happiness filled her to overflowing. Sexual need thrummed through her. It was all too much. They would have problems in the future. Of that she was sure. But what couple didn't have them? And unlike most couples, they had eternity to figure things out.

Touching Mordecai, tasting him, bringing him pleasure had sent her temperature spiking. Her pussy was swollen and damp and she easily took him when he seated her on his lap.

He made a deep sound of pleasure as he sucked one of her nipples. The intense sexual pull shot down to her core. His cock pulsed within her. He was big and thick and stretched her pussy. The sensation was delicious. It also wasn't enough. She had to move.

She rocked her hips and he groaned. She bit her bottom lip to keep from crying out. More. She needed more. She rose up slightly and then lowered herself.

Mordecai pulled away and threw back his head, exposing the long, thick column of his neck. He was panting hard, but so was she. "Now," she implored him. "Hard."

He moved so quickly, the world was a blur. One second they were seated, the next she was flat on the bench with him over her. He hooked her legs over his thighs, cupped her ass in his big hands and began to thrust.

Jessica gripped the edges of the bench, needing something to hold on to. His thrusts were so hard and deep she would have slid off the bench if he hadn't held her so tightly. Each time he retreated she wanted him back. And each time he filled her was even better than the last.

His dark hair hung around his shoulders, his lips were parted and his nostrils flared. He looked as dark and dangerous as he was. And he was all hers.

With a growl, he fell on top of her. He gripped her shoulders and fucked her faster, short, hard thrusts that made her gasp. She was so hot. Her body on the edge of ecstasy.

He shoved one hand under her, angling her pelvis so her clit rubbed against him with each thrust. Her nipples grazed his chest.

Lost in the sensual pleasure of his touch, she came. He took her mouth, capturing her cry as her orgasm washed over her. He stiffened above her. His cock jerked inside her as he found release. The warm rush of his pleasure made her pussy spasm again.

Her heart pounded in her chest and she sucked in the warm night air, tasting their passion and the perfume from the surrounding flowers. Mordecai slumped over her and she wrapped her arms around him, savoring the quiet moment between them.

Eventually, the sounds of the night came back into focus. A bird flitted in the trees. A car drove down the street. A dog barked a few doors down.

Mordecai raised his head and lifted his body from hers. She didn't have enough energy to move and lay sprawled on the bench. He chuckled and lifted her into his arms. She lolled against him and rested her head on his shoulder.

"I owe you a new bench." His dry comment made her laugh. Sure enough, two large chunks were missing from the stone bench where he'd ripped them off.

"I don't know about that. I kind of like the way it looks."

He kissed her and she tasted his love, his commitment.

She patted his chest. "Everything will be okay. You'll see."

"I believe you." She could see the truth in his eyes and it warmed her heart.

"I'm taking you inside to bed before the neighbors discover us." He started walking to the back door, not bothering with their clothes. She closed her eyes, trying not to notice they were both stark naked as he walked past the solar lights and onto the porch. "Although it might be too late for that."

"What? Who saw us?"

He opened the door and carried her up the stairs to her apartment. "I doubt they watched, but Arand and Sabrina probably heard us. Preternatural hearing and open windows," he reminded her.

She should be appalled. Really she should. Instead, all she could do was giggle. She was still laughing when Mordecai unceremoniously dumped her on the bed.

"You think that's funny, do you?" he asked.

She nodded and then pulled her pillow over her face to smother her uncontrollable laughter. She just felt so good. So right. Her nightmare was finally over and their future was bright.

He pulled the pillow off her face and tossed it aside. "You can't hide from me. I'll always find you."

She linked her arms around his neck and smiled up at him. "I like that."

"I think you'll like this even more." Fully erect once again, he slid inside her. She gasped as he filled her. That gasp turned to a moan when he kissed her. He began to thrust and he was right. She really enjoyed what they did next.

Epilogue

Jessica shivered and pulled her coat closer around her. She'd thought Mordecai was crazy when he'd handed her a parka and a pair of snow boots to put on. After all, it was summer in Louisiana. "Where are we?" There was snow and mountains as far as the eye could see. It was breathtakingly beautiful and extremely cold.

Mordecai had used his powers to transport them here in a blink of an eye. One minute she'd been standing in the middle of her living room, the next she was on a snowy ledge way up high on a mountain. The only sound was the relentless howl of the wind.

"Nepal."

She blinked. "You're serious."

He grinned and it made him look younger, more carefree than he normally did. He pointed off in the distance. "Katmandu is that way."

She was really having a hard time wrapping her head around this one, even after everything she'd seen and been through. "Are we on Mount Everest?"

He nodded. "Although it wasn't called that when I first came here. It had no name back then." He placed his hand against the snow-covered rock. "All I knew is that it called to me."

This was a special place for Mordecai. The way he spoke about it with such reverence in his voice gave her heart a hitch. He was sharing this special place with her. She slipped her mitten-covered hand into his bare one. He didn't seem to feel the cold like she did. He was wearing leather pants and boots and a long-sleeved waffle-weave shirt. She was still figuring out what she could and couldn't do now that she was immortal. Controlling her body temperature wasn't one of her new talents, at least not yet.

The wind whipped around them and blew snow into her eyes. She gave a startled shriek as the cold pelted her face and turned her head away from the bitter bite.

"Let's get you inside."

"Inside?" She scrubbed the snow off her cheeks. "The mountain?"

He guided her down a narrow pathway and stopped in front of a wall of white.

"Um, I hate to tell you this, but there's no doorway there."

Mordecai threw back his head and laughed. "I don't need a doorway." He waved his hand over the snow and it instantly disappeared, exposing a rock-hewn corridor. "Come."

She followed, trusting him implicitly. The cold died away and she was able to remove her mittens and stuff them in her pockets. She lowered the hood of the parka and stamped her feet to remove the snow that clung to her boots.

As they walked along the corridor, torches sprang to life at regular intervals, lighting their way. It was amazing, like something out of a fantasy book. It was so quiet here. Peaceful.

"The serpent is a part of me," he began.

"I know." She caught his hand in hers and gave it a squeeze. "I'm rather fond of all of the parts of you."

He kept his gaze forward and followed the path when it veered off to the right. "I am the basis for the legend of dragons."

"Get out." She stopped, forcing him to halt or drag her behind him.

He shrugged. "People thousands of years ago had never seen the likes of me before."

"I got news for you, my love. People today have never seen the likes of you either," she teased.

One corner of his mouth turned up. "You may be right." He continued down the path and she followed once again.

"I needed a place to be by myself. To think. The others loved the camaraderie of the group, but I needed space."

"I can understand that." She thought about it. "I enjoy my friends, but I need solitary time as well." She paused. "You don't need to show me this if you don't want to," she added gently. "It's okay if you want to have a special place that's yours alone." She understood and respected that.

He shook his head as another torch sprang to life. So much power and he wielded it without thought or effort. She might be immortal and share his life force, but she had nowhere near the power or skills Mordecai had.

"I want you to see." He took a step away from her. "Watch and follow."

She wasn't sure what to expect until his body started to change. His clothing vanished and the air around him shimmered. His head elongated and grew, flattening on the top. His arms and legs grew, his body morphing until there was no sign of a human male. In his place was a huge dragon-like creature. Her serpent.

He turned and slithered down the path. She had to hurry to keep up with him. He turned left and ducked through a giant archway. She stilled as torches sprang to life, illuminating the cavernous room.

The entire space glittered and sparkled. She blinked, practically blinded by the rare gemstones that were piled and scattered on every available surface. "Wow. This is incredible." Mordecai had stopped in the center of the room, surrounded by his treasure. She understood her dragon well. In human form, he'd started a company—Dragon's Holdings—building massive wealth for himself and the other warriors. Oil, minerals, technologies, he had his fingers in a lot of pies. He not only needed the challenge, it was in his very nature to acquire.

The light reflected off him when he moved and Jessica caught her breath. She walked forward, hand out in front of her. "You look different than you did before." She touched the hard scales on his side. Where they'd been a muddy green and brown before, now they sparkled like emeralds and bronze.

He tilted his head in question. "You shine. You shimmer just like the jewels around you." She began to laugh.

Mordecai shifted back to his human form, not bothering with clothing beyond a pair of pants. He didn't feel the cold at all. But he worried about Jessica, who was bundled in an arctic parka he'd purchased for her. They both had a lot to learn about what being immortal meant for her.

She jumped into his arms and he caught her easily. She twined her arms around his neck and her legs around his waist. "You're so pretty now. You were fierce in your serpent form before, but now you're gorgeous too."

He frowned. "I'm not pretty. I'm ferocious."

She patted his cheek. "Of course you are, baby."

No one else in the entire world, or in any realm, would talk to him in such a way. Nor would he allow it. But when Jessica did it made his heart melt. He shook his head. "You know I'm feared the world over and in Hell itself."

She grinned. "I know. That's pretty cool too."

He gave up and spun her in a circle. "The darkness from Hades' realm dimmed the light inside me, and thus my serpent's as well. Now that you've chased it away I am finally myself again."

He kissed her then, tasting the love on her lips. Her touch satisfied him in a way that all the diamonds, sapphires, opals, emeralds and rubies of the world could not.

He eased his mouth from hers, loving the way her eyes clouded with passion and her lips were moist from his kiss. "It's in my nature to collect," he began. "I don't know why, but it's instinctual, much like a bear might hibernate in winter."

"You've got a pretty awesome collection." She twisted in his arms, taking in the entire space. "This place is incredible."

"I'm glad you approve. But unlike the legends of dragons, this serpent doesn't mind sharing." He wanted her to understand that all he had was hers now as well.

"Oh, Mordecai, I know that." She stroked her fingers over the side of his face. "After all, you made certain all the other warriors got a piece of the company you built over the decades. None of them ever have to worry again because of your generosity."

She was everything to him. Sheer perfection. This tiny woman held his fate in her hands. There was nothing he wouldn't do for her. "But there is one thing I will not share. In fact, I would kill anyone who dares to try to take it from me."

She frowned and leaned back in his arms. "What is it? I have to know so I don't accidentally take it."

Just when he'd thought he couldn't love her more. He sat in the center of his jewel cache high in the mountains, holding her tight in his arms. "You," he told her. "You, Jessica Miller are my greatest treasure, and I will annihilate anyone who tries to take you from me."

Jessica hugged him. "Never going to happen. You're stuck with me for eternity."

Eternity. The word had never sounded so good.

Mordecai surrounded them with his power, and in the blink of an eye they were sitting on her living room floor back in New Orleans. Jessica looked around and frowned. "Hey, if you can do that, why did I have to bundle up in a parka and stand on the side of a mountain?"

He shrugged. "I wanted to impress you."

Laughing, she threw her arms around him. "You certainly did that."

He leaned forward until her back rested on the floor and he loomed over her—big, naked and gorgeous. "Now you're wearing way too many clothes.

"I'll have to do something about that." She pulled on the zipper and quickly shed the heavy coat. "Can you check to make sure no one called while we were away?" There'd still been no word from either Stavros or Phoenix, and he knew she was getting more worried with each passing second. He was getting concerned himself.

Hades had lost Jessica, but Mordecai knew the vengeful god wasn't done. Not while Tilly was still out there.

Mordecai grabbed his phone off the coffee table and checked his messages. "Nothing yet," he told her as he tossed the phone away. He grabbed one of her boots and pulled it off. He could have her naked with a wave of his hand, but he enjoyed undressing her. It was like unwrapping a present every time.

"All we know is they're no longer in the city," he continued. "Tomorrow, we will start searching the world for the Lady. Maybe she can help, if we can find her."

"What are we going to do until then?" Jessica asked. She batted her eyelashes, looking as innocent as ever. But he knew better. She was a sensual woman with the heart of serpent. She was his heart.

"I'm sure I can think of something," he told her. Then he swept her into his arms and carried her into the bedroom.

Flame of the Phoenix

Dedication

For all of you who wanted to know what happened to Phoenix.

Chapter One

Mathilda Ledet—Tilly to her friends—moved her hips to the jazzy music pumping out of the stereo speakers while she poured two large coffees with cream to go. It might be hot outside, but people still wanted their coffee. Good thing for her since she owned Café Ledet. Well, she and the bank. Every piece of mismatched furniture, the layout, the colors, the logo and more had all been chosen by her. And she loved every square inch of the place.

It was only a small hole-in-the-wall on Chartres Street, but it was a great location within easy walking distance of Jackson Square. She got a lot of locals and tourists who wanted their shot of java and one of the delectable pastries and treats the café offered for sale. They also had tarot readings several nights a week, which brought in quite a few customers.

Only a handful of the tables in the place were currently filled, but that was okay. A lot of their traffic was takeout. Tilly eyed the glass display case, which was half empty. Time to refill. She let her counter staff continue serving customers while she went back and forth from the small kitchen, ferrying more treats to fill the space.

When she was done, she took a deep breath and slowly released it. Then she rolled her neck from side-to-side to work out the kinks. She'd been up and at work since the crack of dawn and it was time for a break. Too bad Sabrina, one of her best friends in the world, had stopped in earlier to pick up two lemonades to go, otherwise Tilly might be tempted to fix their favorite drinks and stroll down to the square to visit. Sabrina and her other best friend, Jessica, both sold their wares in Jackson Square. Sabrina was an artist and Jessica made incredible jewelry.

She'd have to settle for an iced coffee alone in her office. "I'll be out back if you need me," she told Marcia, her senior staff member. The short, perky redhead gave her a wave and kept filling orders. The woman was like the Energizer Bunny and Tilly was lucky to have her as an employee.

Tilly started to head to her office to deal with paperwork but suddenly changed her mind. The sunshine blazing through the big picture window beckoned to her. "Marcia, I changed my mind. I'm going to sit out front instead. It's too nice a day to stay inside."

"Go on, boss." Marcia grinned and shooed her away. "I've got it covered."

Tilly laughed. The café ran like a well-oiled machine, but it had taken a lot of hard work and sweat to get it to this point. Running a small business wasn't for the faint of heart, but Tilly loved the challenge. Each day brought a different set of problems and dramas to deal with.

She stepped outside and breathed in the thick air. The sun was beating down on the city, and it would only get hotter as the day went on. But Tilly had been born just outside New Orleans and was well used to the weather. She sat at one of the small tables outside the café and shaded her eyes against the brilliance of the sun.

The street was filled with people talking in many languages. English, French, Cajun and a smattering of what she thought was German. Some of them were on their way to work, others were obviously on holiday. Some hurried despite the heat, others ambled, taking their time. There was a vibrancy and energy about the city that she loved, and she was grateful to call it home.

Tipping her face back, she soaked in the sun's rays. It recharged and invigorated her. This was exactly what she needed.

Phoenix hurried down the cracked sidewalk, moving as fast as he could without actually running. Most people would think it was a hot day, but if there was one thing he didn't mind, it was the heat. Even wearing jeans and a T-shirt, he felt quite comfortable. It would have to get a lot hotter than this for him to even notice.

He could raise his arms and shoot fire from his fingertips, all without breaking a sweat. He was the mythical phoenix, after all.

He could feel many eyes on him as he headed down the street, but he was becoming used to attracting attention. His great height and distinctive red-and-gold hair always garnered unwanted notice from both men and women alike. It made him uncomfortable, but he was learning to ignore it.

As one of seven immortal warriors who followed the Lady of the Beasts, goddess of all the animals, he was capable of great feats of strength and courage. But right now, he was afraid. Not for himself. All his fear was for one particular human woman—Tilly Ledet.

Tilly was the most beautiful woman he'd ever set his eyes on, and he'd seen many in his long immortal life. She was tall and slender, her smooth skin the color of light toffee. He wanted to lick her entire body to see if she tasted as sweet as she looked.

He groaned as his cock stirred to life. He ignored the unruly appendage and quickened his pace. He was a shapeshifting warrior, one honed by the fires of war. He would not allow his sexual attraction for Tilly to distract from his mission.

A bloody battle with the Greek gods centuries ago had resulted in the Lady of the Beasts being trapped in Hell and her warriors cursed to remain in their animal forms for thousands of years. Now they were all free and the curse was broken. Hades had been defeated and stripped of most of his power. They thought he'd been imprisoned.

But now the god was back.

He'd targeted Jessica Miller, the woman that Mordecai had feelings for. A shiver raced down Phoenix's spine as he pictured the round burn on Jessica's arm—a death mark. Unless they found a way to get rid of it, Jessica would die.

Both Jessica and Tilly had gotten dragged into their war with Hades. The god could no longer harm the warriors or the women who'd freed them from the curse. To do so would bring about his own demise. Even the gods had rules, and Hades had agreed to the terms, never once believing he'd lose the war and have to abide by them.

That left two human women for Hades to vent his anger on. Phoenix could do nothing for Jessica, but he could protect Tilly.

The café was in sight and the constriction in his chest area eased when he saw her sitting outside her shop at one of the tables sipping a cold drink. She was wearing a long, flowing skirt in a flaming-red color. The fabric had slid up her crossed legs, giving him a wonderful view of smooth, supple calves. She'd topped the skirt with a bright yellow sleeveless tunic. No, it wasn't called a tunic. A tank top. That's what it was. The garment clung to her full rounded breasts and exposed her strong arms.

He growled low in his throat when he noted he wasn't the only man in the area noticing how good Tilly looked. Unfamiliar feelings of possessiveness welled up within him. The great bird inside him fanned the flames of jealousy, but he ruthlessly quenched them. He couldn't afford to be distracted. Not now. Not with Hades causing trouble.

As if she could sense him staring, Tilly glanced in his direction. The moment their eyes met, she smiled. Her lush pink lips parted to expose straight white teeth. Tilly had the kind of smile that invited others to join her. She held out her hand to him as he approached. "Phoenix, I wasn't expecting to see you today."

He took her hand but didn't sit, forcing her to tilt her head back in order to see him. Her long black hair was pulled away from her face and wound into a thick braid. Her dark brown eyes went from welcome to worry in a heartbeat. "What is it? What's wrong?"

The woman was extremely perceptive. Uncannily so. Phoenix wondered if she was a bit psychic or just incredibly attuned to the world around her. "We need to talk."

"Inside." She stood, grabbed her drink and led the way. He tried not to notice the gentle sway of her hips as she walked into the café, but he'd have to be dead not to. Tilly was all woman—sensual and confident. Was there anything sexier than that? Phoenix didn't think so. Some men might be put off by her height and forthright nature, but not him. She'd fascinated him from the first moment they'd met a few weeks ago.

He stayed close behind her as she led him down the short hallway and into her office. Like the café, the walls were colorful, these ones painted a vivid combination of green and blue. A laptop sat on a small desk and several file cabinets and shelves lined the wall behind it. It was a tiny space but ruthlessly organized.

Tilly perched on the corner of her desk and set her drink to one side. Phoenix closed the door behind him and took a moment to gather his thoughts. He didn't want to scare Tilly, but she needed to know what was going on.

"What is it? What's wrong?" She reached into her skirt pocket and pulled out her phone. "It's Sabrina and Jessica, isn't it? Something happened to them?"

He reached out and stopped her from dialing. "They're home."

Tilly shook her head. "No, they're not. They're in the Square this time of day."

He wanted to ease the growing fear making her eyes darken, but he would not withhold the truth from her. "Hades has cursed Jessica."

Her eyes widened. She crossed her arms over her stomach and leaned forward as if in pain. "No." The word was little more than a gasp. "Hades was defeated. The Lady drained his power from him." He could see her growing anger was quickly driving out her fear. Tilly dropped her arms by her side and stood to face him. "Zeus imprisoned him."

"That is all true, but for some reason, Hades is free. Or at least free enough to send a minion with a death curse."

Tilly rubbed her hands up and down her arms. In spite of the heat, he could see the chill bumps on her arms. "What's a death curse?"

Phoenix raked his fingers through his hair. He hated not being able to do anything to help Tilly's friend. He was strong and a brutal fighter, none of which helped in this situation. "All I know is that if we can't find a way to counteract it, Jessica will die, and soon."

Tears welled in Tilly's eyes, but she blinked them back. "I have to go to her." She started to go around him, but he moved in front of her, blocking her path to the door. She looked up at him. "Get out of my way."

Phoenix shook his head. "I can't. She doesn't want you there."

"I don't believe you." Tilly placed both hands on his chest and shoved. He didn't budge. "Move it," she demanded.

"It's not safe for you to be with her." He carefully gripped her shoulders and eased her back a step. "Putting the two of you in the same place makes it easier for Hades to get to you too."

She froze, her body becoming totally still. She swallowed heavily. "Hades is coming for me?"

Phoenix cursed under his breath. He hated having to be the bearer of such news, but she needed to be aware of the danger stalking her. "Hades cannot touch us or the women who freed us from the curse."

Tilly slowly nodded, quickly following his line of reasoning. "But Jessica and I aren't included in that no-touch ban. We're just two humans who got caught up in this whole mess."

That was the unvarnished truth. Phoenix nodded.

Tilly took a deep breath. "I have to call Sabrina." She took a step back and he dropped his hands down by his sides. His fingers tingled from where he'd touched her. His cock was swollen and full, which was totally inappropriate given the circumstances, but he couldn't control his body. Not around Tilly.

He inhaled and almost swore again. Her exotic perfume, a combination of sandalwood and jasmine with just a hint of sunshine and warm skin, was driving him crazy. While he tried to bring his unruly body under control, she dialed her friend's number. Fortunately, his enhanced sense of hearing allowed him to listen in on her call.

"What's going on?" Tilly demanded. "Phoenix is here and he said Jessica is cursed."

"Yes," Sabrina replied. "Mordecai is with her now."

"What happened?"

"Some blonde chick came to her table in the Square and pretended to look at jewelry. She asked to see one of the pieces, and when Jessica handed it to her, the woman touched her wrist. It burned her somehow. But it's more than that. It's like it's draining the energy from her body."

"Son of a bitch." Tilly glanced his way but he didn't move. No way was he leaving her alone. "What does the Lady say?"

"They're cut off from her. They think it's something Hades is doing."

"How is that even possible?" Tilly demanded.

"We don't know, but we're going to find out. Stavros has gone in search of her. I've contacted the other warriors. Everyone is either searching for a cure to this death curse or scouring the world looking for the Lady of the Beasts."

"What can I do?" Tilly nibbled on her bottom lip. "I could ask Granny Ledet if she knows anything."

"No," Sabrina practically yelled. Tilly yanked the phone away from her ear before carefully moving it back. "No, don't do that. You don't want to draw Hades' attention to your granny." There was a long pause. "I think you need to get out of town."

"But Hades can find me wherever I go, can't he?" The last thing Tilly wanted to do was leave her friends.

"At this point, we don't know how much power he has. What he can and can't do. We're all safe from Hades, but you're not. You need to go away somewhere and take Phoenix with you for protection."

"I can take care of myself."

The great bird inside him squawked with displeasure, and Phoenix scowled at Tilly. No way was she going anywhere without him. Because he was lost in his own thoughts, he missed the last exchange between the two women. Tilly was tucking her phone back in her pocket.

"Well?" he asked her, prepared to fight if she tried to send him away.

She straightened her shoulders and met his gaze straight on. "Looks like we're getting the hell out of Dodge."

Chapter Two

Tilly tossed several tank tops into the open bag on the bed. She hoped she wasn't forgetting anything. Who knew how long she'd be gone. Thankfully, her business would still be here when she got back. Once she'd claimed a family emergency, Marcia and the rest of her staff had gladly accepted extra shifts. It had taken Tilly several hours to figure schedules and do the payroll, which was due in two days. Then she'd written checks for any outstanding bills and called her suppliers to let them know they'd be dealing with Marcia for the foreseeable future.

Phoenix had hovered nearby, clearly impatient. But Tilly had to do this. If she survived this latest fiasco, she at least wanted to have something to come back to.

If she lived, she'd have to give her staff a bonus.

Luckily, all her home bills were paid directly from her bank account and she had enough money in there to cover several months if necessary. She rubbed her arms against the sudden chill and glanced around her bedroom, wondering when she'd be able to sleep in her own bed again. Her bedroom was small, but she loved it. The walls were a vibrant orange and the hardwood floors gleamed. The furniture was all family pieces her granny had given her or thrift-store finds lovingly restored. Each piece unique and to her taste.

This home, this sanctuary belonged to her. Yes, the house was tiny, but that didn't matter. She didn't need a lot of room. No, what she needed was something far more elusive—peace and safety. Those things had been missing from her childhood and she'd sought them both when she became an adult.

"Everything okay?" Phoenix filled the doorway, ducking beneath the jamb so he didn't hit his head. He really was a big man. He seemed to gobble up all the remaining space in the room.

"As good as it gets," she muttered. Why couldn't Hades leave her the hell alone? She almost laughed at her unintentional pun, but there was nothing funny about the situation.

"We need to get going. We have no idea how long it will be before Hades turns his eyes your way."

"Why you?" Tilly asked. She zipped the leather tote bag and turned to face Phoenix. "Why are you the one to guard me?" She wanted to know if he'd volunteered for this or if he'd been conscripted. Call it pride, but she didn't want a man around if she was nothing more than a chore or a job.

He frowned. "I don't understand."

Tilly tried not to notice how sexy Phoenix looked standing there with his hands on his hips, glaring at her. Honestly, the way the man filled out a pair of jeans should be illegal. All the warriors were hot, but Phoenix shot the needle right off the scale. His hair was his most distinctive feature. It was reddish in color with gold tips. Women would kill for hair that color. But it was his eyes that drew her. They glowed like emeralds glistening in the sunlight.

Of course, his broad shoulders, muscular arms, wide chest and rock-hard abs didn't hurt any either. She'd known plenty of good-looking men in her lifetime. Okay, none as hot as the immortal warriors she'd come to know, but none of them had made her body come alive the way Phoenix did whenever he entered a room.

For a woman who prided herself on her independence, on not needing any man, it was disconcerting. And it made her lash out.

"I mean, why not Arand or Stavros. Why you?"

His dark brows lowered and frown lines dented his forehead. "You would prefer Stavros?" He shook his head. "You do not need the jaguar. I will protect you."

"But why? Am I an obligation? After all, you don't owe me anything."

The walls of the room actually vibrated when he growled. The deep, powerful rumble was unlike anything she'd ever heard in her life. The air surrounding him crackled with electricity. The silky strands of his hair began to rise, blown back from his face by some unseen wind. His eyes began to shimmer as though fire danced behind them.

He stepped toward her and put his hands on her shoulders. She was surprised his touch didn't burn. She swallowed hard but faced him. She had to look up at him, which was rare for her as she was a tall woman.

Phoenix towered over her.

Maybe it would have been smarter to placate him or run. But Tilly didn't placate any man, and she sure as hell didn't run. She'd watched her mama do that with her daddy when she was a child. The results had never been pretty.

"I will protect you." He leaned down until their noses were almost touching. Heat rolled off his big body in waves and surrounded them.

Tilly felt the loose strands of hair around her face rise as though they were filled with static electricity. "Why does it matter so much to you?" She had to know. She wanted to be more than an obligation to this man.

They'd become friends over the past weeks, talking and sharing the occasional meal. They'd even gone out to a movie one evening when Phoenix had mentioned his desire to visit a theatre. He was smart with a dry sense of humor. Best of all, he seemed to like her just the way she was. Without even trying, he'd reached inside her and touched her heart. An organ she'd guarded all her adult life.

He framed her face between his large, powerful hands. "Because you are mine." After making that proclamation, he kissed her.

His lips were warm and firm, and the moment they touched hers, her mouth began to tingle. Tiny bolts of pleasure shot from her lips, down to her breasts and then lower.

Holy smoke. She fought the urge to fan herself. She knew he was attracted to her—she was an intelligent woman after all—but not once in all their time together had he ever made a move. She'd convinced herself he never would and, because of that, it had been safe for her to fantasize about him.

He deepened the caress and slid his tongue into her mouth. He found her tongue and rubbed against it. Tilly moaned and creamed her panties. Oh yeah, Phoenix was dangerous to her well-being, but she didn't care. She wanted more, wanted to drown herself in the sensual pleasure of his kiss.

If he affected her this much with such a simple caress, how would her body react if he did more? Sweat broke out on her forehead. She was playing with fire and she didn't care.

Phoenix knew he should stop. This wasn't the time or the place to give in to his physical longings. Tilly was in danger from Hades and it was his job to protect her. But hearing her talk about the other warriors, especially the unattached Stavros, had made him see red. Jealousy had surged through his veins and it had taken all his strength not to burst into flames. It was either risk setting her house on fire or kiss her. He figured this was the best choice.

Besides, he'd wanted to know what Tilly's lips tasted like since the moment he'd first set eyes on her. Unlike the other warriors, he'd never really met the woman who'd freed him from the curse. It had been reflex for him to grab her and go up in flames. He'd been reborn, but it had taken him decades to rejuvenate because he'd been so weak. As for the woman who'd freed him, she'd survived unharmed. He'd put all his energy into assuring that. He'd never told the others, but the woman had walked free exactly a day after he'd been released.

While he was grateful to the woman, he'd never felt anything more for her than gratitude. Tilly, however, brought out protective instincts in him he'd never experienced. She made him yearn for things he'd never wanted before.

She made a little sound in the back of her throat and he pulled her close. Her breasts pressed against his chest and her curvy ass filled his hands. Paradise. He was in paradise. Her lips tasted sweet, but he could also taste the iced coffee she'd had earlier. It added some spice to the kiss.

Her tongue stroked his and then boldly drove into his mouth. She was confident. He liked that about her. He lifted her so he didn't have to bend down. Her feet dangled off the floor, but not for long. She wrapped her long legs around his hips, pressing her hot core against his erection.

He took the one step necessary to bring him next to the bed and then knelt on the mattress. He lowered Tilly down, never breaking their kiss. She stroked his shoulders, his biceps and down his chest, her hands leaving ribbons of heat in their wake. Her legs were still wrapped around him, and he rubbed his cock against her mound. They were both clothed, but that didn't seem to matter. Every touch, every kiss was more intense than the last. He wanted to toss up her skirt, shove aside her panties and fuck her.

He fought the urge, knowing they shouldn't be doing this here or now. It was too dangerous, but Tilly was far too seductive for him to resist.

He had to get her naked.

Phoenix shoved a hand under her top. Her stomach was soft and smooth, such a contrast to his calloused hands. He slowly moved his hand up until he touched the band of her bra. He traced along the lacy edge, savoring the moment before he went any farther.

Tilly plowed her fingers into his hair and yanked him back. He didn't want to break their kiss and did so with great reluctance. Tilly was panting hard, her expressive eyes as tempting as thick, rich chocolate. He'd recently discovered a weakness for dark chocolate.

"We should stop." She spoke the words he didn't want to hear.

He nuzzled her neck and nipped at the lobe of her ear. She was wearing a pretty gold hoop in it, so he tugged on the delicate piece of jewelry. Tilly moaned and arched her lower body, rubbing her mound against his swollen cock. "We should," he agreed. Then he kissed her again.

Tilly opened for him, inviting him to taste her sweet mouth. He nibbled her lips, enjoying their texture and taste before delving inside. His entire body quivered and the phoenix inside him roared to life. The creature stretched its wings and shrieked a warning. This was his woman and he'd destroy any who tried to take her from him.

Yes, Tilly belonged to him. He shoved her top and bra up, exposing her breasts. He broke away from the kiss and looked at his prize. Her skin was light brown and creamy. Her breasts were firm and full, her nipples a dusky rose.

He wrapped a hand around one firm mound and gently squeezed. Tilly's moan turned to a gasp when he drew the pad of his thumb over the puckered tip. She was so responsive to his touch.

Unlike most of his brethren, he hadn't been drawn to the woman who'd released him from the curse. And since he'd managed to rejuvenate his body, he'd spent all his time searching for the Lady and his fellow warriors. He'd taken no time to indulge in carnal pursuits. Hadn't even been tempted.

Not until he'd met Tilly.

She was so self-contained and self-assured. He knew she was independent and determined to be so. She didn't need a man. He respected and admired that. But he wanted to be her man. Wanted her to want him enough to let him into her life and her bed.

If he could bind her to him physically, it would be the first step to inserting himself permanently into her life. With that goal in mind, he leaned down and drew his tongue across her taut nipple. She whispered his name, and he worried he might disgrace himself by coming right there and then. He wanted her to whisper his name for a million nights to come. To hear her scream it as she came.

Phoenix drew the tip between his lips and sucked. Tilly dug her fingernails into his scalp as she pulled him closer. He wanted to tell her she didn't have to worry. He would never leave her. Instead, he sucked her nipple and flicked the tip with his tongue, wanting to give her so much pleasure she would never want him to go.

The rough heat of Phoenix dragging his tongue over her breast made every muscle in her body clench. Had she ever been this hot before? Wanted a man so much she'd throw caution to the wind?

His hair was warm and silky between her fingers as she drew him closer. He made a low sound of pleasure that vibrated against her skin. She knew this wasn't smart but she didn't want to stop. Ever since she'd first laid eyes on Phoenix, she'd wondered what it would feel like to have his mouth and his hands on her.

Reality was far better than anything her fertile mind had conjured.

She shoved her hands under his T-shirt, needing to touch him. He reared back long enough to rip the shirt off and toss it aside. Tilly licked her lips and gently scraped her fingernails over his broad chest, flicking his flat nipples in the process. He hissed out a breath. His eyes narrowed and his jaw tightened.

Oh, he was a sight to behold. His hair hung around his shoulders like a living flame. His biceps bulged and his abdominal muscles tensed. She'd never seen a man this physically fit outside the covers of a magazine. He was perfect.

He traced the contours of her waist and hips before moving his hands back to the waistband of her skirt. "I need to see you naked." His voice was rough but his hands were gentle as he tugged the elastic waistband down. "Lift your hips," he instructed.

They really should leave. It probably wasn't safe to stay here.

Tilly lifted her hips.

Phoenix moved lower on the bed and pulled her skirt away. While he was doing that, she yanked her tank top and bra off. She was left wearing nothing more than a pair of lacy beige panties.

He wrapped his large hands around her ankles and stared down at her. He was so big, so powerful, yet she felt utterly safe with him. Tilly knew he was a protector by nature. All the warriors were. She liked all of them, but Phoenix made her feel all kinds of emotions she hadn't felt in a very long time, if ever.

It was crazy really. He was an immortal warrior and she ran a coffee shop. An unlikely pair, but the chemistry between them couldn't be denied. Not any longer. Maybe it was the threat of death hanging over her that allowed her to reach out and take what she wanted.

She hadn't believed in true love. Not until she'd seen Sabrina with her warrior. Arand loved Tilly's friend and had been willing to die for her. Tilly's father had claimed to love her mother, but it had been a possessive love, the kind that hurt. As a child, she'd watched her father physically abuse her mother and seen her mother fade from a vibrant young woman to a shell of herself as the years passed. When she'd finally found the courage to take her young daughter and run, Tilly's father had come after them.

Tilly silently gave thanks to her granny for saving them. Granny Ledet was a force to be reckoned with and a respected practitioner of voodoo. She'd put a curse on Antoine Robert. If he wanted to avoid the curse, he had to leave Tilly and her mama alone. He was a superstitious man who feared her granny. He'd run, leaving both wife and daughter behind. Tilly's mom had quickly divorced him and taken back her maiden name for herself and her child, but she'd never regained the vitality he'd bled from her.

Tilly had embraced her sexuality as a grown adult but she'd never opened her heart to a man. And she had no plans to start now. No matter how tempting the man was. She could enjoy him physically. She could like and respect him. But she'd never entrust her heart to him.

Phoenix slid his hands up her calves and over the inside of her thighs. "What are you thinking, sweet Tilly? You seem so far away."

It wasn't often a man was that perceptive, especially with an almost naked woman in front of him. She wasn't sure if she should be pleased by the fact he was paying such close attention to her emotional mood or insulted he wasn't totally distracted by her mostly nude body.

She chose to be pleased, especially when he grazed his fingers over the crotch of her panties, running them up and down the seam in the most tantalizing manner. Gasping, she arched into his touch.

"That's right." He stroked both thumbs over the damp fabric. "Stay with me." He eased his fingers beneath the leg bands and teased her heated flesh. "No one or nothing exists but you and me."

She believed him. It was impossible to think with him stroking her slick pussy. Her skin tingled and her body ached for his touch. She licked her lips and watched his green eyes darken with desire. She glanced down at the bulge pressing against the front of his pants. Phoenix was a big man, and she couldn't wait to see him. To touch him.

She curled her fingers inward, her palms itching to hold his cock. "You're wearing too much clothing."

His slow smile made her skin sizzle and her pussy clench. He pulled his hands from beneath her panties and stood, all animal grace and power. His fingers went to the waistband of his jeans and he unsnapped them before carefully lowering the zipper.

He wasn't wearing any underwear.

Tilly moaned when his cock sprang free, full and thick and long. Her pussy spasmed and cream slid from her damp core.

Phoenix shoved the material down his strong thighs. He kicked off his shoes and removed his pants. When he was naked, he let her look her fill.

She licked her lips again, wishing it was his tanned skin she was tasting. "Turn around." Her voice was husky with arousal. "I want to see all of you."

Phoenix slowly revolved away from her until she was faced with his impossibly wide back and tight ass. She bet she could bounce quarters off his behind. It made her insides hum.

But it was the tattoo that made her lose her breath. She'd almost forgotten that all the warriors had a tattoo of their animal on their back. The creature on Phoenix's back wasn't one that was readily recognizable. It was a wild beast of myth and legend.

The phoenix.

It rose from a bed of flames, a proud bird with a powerful beak and six-inch talons that could rip a man apart. The bird's wings were spread wide, encompassing the entire width of Phoenix's back. Like his hair, the bird's feathers were reddish in color and tipped in gold.

Incredible.

She'd moved before she realized she'd even planned to. Kneeling up on the mattress, she reached out and touched the creature's wing.

Chapter Three

Phoenix's entire body jerked when he felt Tilly's fingers slide across his bare skin. Inside him, the phoenix screeched and preened, pleased that she seemed so taken with his tattoo. She'd never seen it before and he was very interested to see what she would do next.

She slipped her hand lower, caressing the inner part of the wing. He shivered and his cock hardened in reaction. He fisted his hands, forcing himself to remain still when every instinct he had was clawing at him to fuck her, to stake his claim.

When her fingers grazed the bird's stomach, his own stomach muscles clenched. She stroked his left wing and his left shoulder trembled. He groaned and her hand stilled.

"The phoenix is alive inside you, isn't he?" He loved the low timbre of her voice—the husky quality never failed to make his balls clench. Tilly's voice was made for sex.

"Yes." He swallowed back a groan of pleasure when she ran her fingers from the tip of the bird's wings all the way down to his legs. "Wherever you touch the tattoo, I feel it in the same place on my body."

"Really?" She teased a path over the bird's stomach.

Phoenix growled and whirled around, unable to take her sexual teasing any longer. Her gaze went straight to his cock and he wondered if he hadn't been better off facing away from her. After so long without sex, his control was precarious at best.

Tilly gave a low hum of pleasure, reached out and wrapped her hand around his thick shaft. "Come closer."

Her willing slave, he did as she asked, stopping when he was standing directly in front of her. She smiled and leaned inward, kissing the center of his chest. His entire body clenched. "Tilly." He wasn't sure if he was warning her to stop or begging her to continue.

She ignored him and licked at his abs, her tongue following the delineation of each band of muscle. Her hand was busy as well. It moved up and down his cock from base to tip and back again.

Phoenix's breath grew more rapid. His lungs worked to pull air into his starving body. When her mouth was within inches of his cock, he stopped breathing altogether.

She blew softly on the turgid length, sending a shiver of pleasure through him. Like the ripple in a pond, it grew and spread until his entire body felt as though it was one stroke away from imploding.

He fisted his hands and dug for every ounce of discipline he possessed. No way did he want to stop Tilly now, not when he was so close to heaven.

She dragged her tongue over the broad head of his cock and swirled it around and around. "Mmm, you taste spicy and hot."

Surely there must be steam rising from the top of his head. "Tilly," he growled, his voice barely human now.

She paid him no heed. Instead, she opened her mouth over him. Phoenix arched his hips and pushed his cock deeper. He gripped her long, thick braid in his hand, wrapping the length around his fingers, chaining her to him. She retaliated by grazing her teeth over his shaft. He threw back his head and gritted his teeth as pleasure unlike any he'd ever experienced threatened to consume him.

Tilly used her mouth, tongue and hands to please him. She stroked and sucked and licked at his shaft. He rocked his hips, pushing his cock deeper with each stroke. Tilly accepted all of him, making a purring sound of satisfaction that almost made him come.

And he didn't want to. Not yet. Not until he'd pleasured her.

He stared down into her beautiful face. She was aroused but she was also in control of herself and of their lovemaking. It occurred to him in a flash of insight that she was used to being in charge during sex, didn't like to be out of control.

He wasn't having it. He had to have her trust, and that meant she had to let go.

As much as it pained him to do so, he pulled back, forcing her to release him. She gazed up at him, an unasked question in her eyes. Most men would think him insane for stopping her. But Phoenix wasn't most men.

And he wasn't angling for one time in her bed. He was playing for keeps.

He pushed her back onto the bed. She laughed as she tumbled down onto the mattress. He knelt on the floor, grabbed her thighs and pulled her forward until her ass was perched on the edge of the bed.

She was still wearing her underwear. As lovely as they were, hinting at the treasure hidden beneath, she'd look even better without them. He gripped the band of lace at the waistband and slowly lowered the delicate fabric. He held his breath, anticipating seeing her for the first time.

There was nothing lovelier than the female form. Hollows and curves, shadows and light. Women, even strong, independent women, were physically weaker than men. It took a lot of courage for a woman to lower her guard and allow a man into her bed. It was a privilege, and one he planned to make the most of.

He glided the fabric down her long, toned legs and whisked it off. He brought her underwear to his nose and inhaled her scent, imprinting it in his memory for all time. The phoenix went wild, squawking and flapping his wings. Phoenix knew just how the creature felt. Tilly had become the most important thing in his world.

There was nothing he wouldn't do to protect her.

She opened her mouth to speak, but he wasn't ready or willing to answer any of her questions. Not now. Not with the sweet, spicy scent of her arousal teasing him and making him crazy. He had to taste her.

He licked his lips, savoring the sense of anticipation that filled him. Then he carefully spread her thighs wide and nuzzled her smooth, toffee-colored skin. She looked good enough to eat. Her pussy was wet, plump and inviting.

Phoenix stroked the flat of his tongue over her damp folds. Her spicy flavor exploded in his mouth. He made a sound of pleasure as he lapped at her, ignoring the stinging of his scalp where she dug her fingernails into him.

"Phoenix," she gasped and bucked against his mouth.

He decided he very much liked the sound of his name falling from her lips when she was frantic for his touch. He shoved his hands beneath her firm ass and lifted her, making it easier for him to lick and suck every delectable inch of her.

The inarticulate sounds that fell from her lips made him feel like a god. He lapped at her clit, teasing the tiny nub of nerves until she was practically yelling his name. Liquid seeped from the head of his cock and his balls ached, but he ignored them. All that mattered now was making Tilly come.

He found her sweet opening and circled it with his tongue before plunging it as far as it would go. Tilly wrapped her legs around his head and dug her heels into his back. He pulled his tongue out of her core and swept it over her clit once again. She tightened her thighs around his head, telling him just how close she was to finding her pleasure. Her back arched and this time she did yell his name. He felt her coming, knew she was rocketing over the edge.

He surged to his feet, flipped her over until she was on her hands and knees and drove into her from behind in one hard, long stroke. She was so tight and gripped his cock so hard he went blind for a moment, unable to see anything.

Tilly was in the center of a hurricane. And having grown up in Louisiana, she was very familiar with violent wind and rainstorms. Every cell in her body screamed for release as Phoenix worked her body, making it sing for him.

She'd always had trouble reaching orgasm with her former partners. She knew it came down to trust, and she had little of it for men. She usually enjoyed her bed partners and saw to her needs after they were gone.

But Phoenix wasn't allowing her to hold back. He blasted through her defenses and laid her bare until she was a writhing mass of need beneath him.

She wanted to push him away. She wanted to pull him closer.

Her entire body trembled when she came. Hot liquid pleasure flowed through her like warm chocolate sauce over ice cream. But she didn't even have time to enjoy it before he'd flipped her onto her front and pulled her up onto her hand and knees. He did it so fast and so easy, she was reminded that he was more than just a man. His strength was enormous, his speed unmatched.

Then he was inside her, his cock buried to the hilt. Her pussy spasmed around him, trying to adapt to his invasion. It didn't hurt—she was so wet he slid in easily—but he stretched her slick channel, his hard shaft rubbing against her sensitive inner muscles.

She glanced over her shoulder. He was behind her, his head thrown back, the cords of his thick neck standing out as he struggled for control. She was glad she wasn't the only one whose self-discipline had fled.

His hands shaped her ass, kneading and rubbing.

She let her head fall back down and concentrated on just trying to breathe. Even though she'd just orgasmed, her body felt tight, her skin incredibly sensitive, as though it was climbing toward the peak once again. It should be impossible, yet it was happening.

He leaned down, and the motion pushed his shaft even deeper when she hadn't thought he could go any farther. A low moan escaped her lips. There was no room for any thoughts with him filling her so completely. All she could do was feel.

His warm lips grazed her nape. "I'm sorry I couldn't wait." He nipped at the sensitive curve of her neck. Goose bumps raced down her back.

He kissed and licked a hot path down her spine. "You are so beautiful. I want to taste every inch of you."

Her pussy spasmed hotly around his cock. She wouldn't mind him tasting every inch of her either. In fact, it sounded like a good plan to her.

His hands seemed to be everywhere, stroking her back, her hips, her ass and down the backs of her thighs to her knees. Who would have thought the backs of her legs would be an erogenous zone? Not her. Not until Phoenix touched her in a way that made her pussy clench.

"I can't wait. Not this time." He eased her forward and knelt on the mattress between her legs. Then he wrapped his arms around her and lifted her so she was upright in his arms with his cock still buried deep inside her from behind. He clasped one of her breasts in a big hand and slid the other between her legs.

Then he began to move.

He flexed his hips, driving into her with short, hard strokes. He played with her nipples and her clit. He surrounded her. His arms chained her to him as surely as if they'd been forged of steel. Pleasure bombarded her from all angles at once. There was no escaping it. And she didn't want to.

Then Tilly did something she'd never done before. She let go. She stopped thinking, stopped trying to be in control and simply lost herself in the moment.

As if sensing the change in her, Phoenix drove deeper, his thrusts grew faster and harder. They both gasped and moaned. His cock rippled deep within her and she knew he was close. She reached behind her and wrapped her arm around his neck. He buried his face in the curve of her shoulder and groaned.

He pressed his thumb against her clit at the same time he lightly pinched her nipple. On the next stroke of his hard cock, she came. Her pussy tightened around his shaft. He cried out and it sounded like the combination of a screech of a hawk and roar of a lion. His cock seemed to grow larger inside her, and it sent her pussy into another round of spasms.

His shaft rippled and she felt the warm flood of his release as he came. The moment seemed to last forever when she knew it had to be a matter of seconds. She felt every inch of his body where it touched hers, smelled his musky, male scent mingling with the perfume of her own skin and tasted his unique flavor on her lips from when she'd gone down on him. The echo of their groans seemed to reverberate around the room like living things.

Had she actually screamed his name? She probably had. Her loss of control should have appalled her, but she was feeling too damn good to worry about it.

Phoenix held her suspended in his warm embrace. The sun was streaming in through the bedroom window, which meant it was midafternoon. The day was quickly passing and they should have already left.

But Tilly couldn't find it in herself to regret what they'd done. If Hades was coming after her, there was a good chance she might not make it through this alive. She was nothing if not a realist.

That's what had probably prompted her total loss of control. That and Phoenix's incredible lovemaking skills. Still, it was time to get things back to normal.

As if sensing her change of mood, Phoenix slowly withdrew from her, but not before he placed a gentle kiss on the back of her neck. The soft caress went straight to her heart and tears filled her eyes. She quickly blinked them away.

"We should get dressed." She did better when she had a plan.

"We should," he agreed. He turned her so she was facing him, cupped her face between his large palms and touched his lips to hers. "Thank you for giving me such a great gift."

Tilly didn't know what to say. What did you say to something like that? "I should get a shower." Better to change the subject and get things back on an even keel.

The corners of his mouth drew up in a sexy smile. "That is a good idea." He climbed off the bed and scooped her into his arms.

She wrapped both hands around his thick forearm. "Alone. I need to shower alone." His smile turned into a frown. She almost caved and asked him to join her. "We need to leave as soon as possible, and that won't happen if we shower together." There was no point in pretending it wouldn't happen, not with every cell in her body still doing the happy dance. It wouldn't take much to convince her to go another round.

No, what she needed was some alone time to regroup. The fact that she'd lowered her guard around Phoenix was shocking enough. That she wanted to keep it lowered was downright frightening.

He slowly released her until her feet touched the floor. "You're right." He raked his fingers through his hair, looking totally disgruntled. She wanted to hug him but made herself take a step away instead. "Go and shower. I will wait here."

"I won't be long." She gathered her clothing quickly, pausing at her dresser to grab some fresh underwear and a clean tank top. She desperately tried not to notice the way he watched her, like she was some delectable morsel he was waiting to pounce on and gobble down whole.

Her body was screaming at her to relent and invite him to shower with her. And so was her heart.

Tilly didn't look back as she hurried into the bathroom and shut the door behind her. The woman in the mirror was wide-eyed and frightened even though her body still hummed with pleasure. Without even trying, Phoenix had slipped past the barriers surrounding her heart. He was her friend, of course he was, but now he was something more.

"Stupid," she muttered to her reflection. "How could you let this happen?" Then she stopped talking, fearful Phoenix would hear her even though he was in the next room. All the immortal warriors had enhanced senses.

She took a deep, calming breath. Big mistake. Her skin still smelled like sex, like him. Her pussy spasmed and she gripped the vanity for support. She carefully set her clothing down and pushed away from the countertop. She needed a shower. A cold one.

Tilly staggered to the enclosure and ruthlessly cranked the cold water tap, making sure the spray was chilly before she stepped beneath it. She clenched her teeth to keep from yelling and shivered as she washed all remnants of their lovemaking away.

But she had a feeling she wouldn't be able to wash away the memory as easily as she did the physical reminder from her body.

Phoenix stood outside the bathroom door and listened. The shower was on, which meant water was spilling over Tilly's gorgeous body. He wished he was in there with her, running his soapy hands over her warm skin, seeing the water cascade over her.

He shuddered and turned away. He grabbed his pants and pulled them on but didn't button them. He'd take a quick shower as soon as Tilly was done.

Now that he was alone in her room, he took a better look around the space. It was vibrant and warm, just like Tilly. It was uncluttered too. There was a book on her nightstand, but there was no clothing lying around, no clutter except for the top of her dresser. He wandered over and examined some of the jewelry scattered there. Tilly did seem to like jewelry, but it wasn't diamonds or rubies she wore, but colorful vintage pieces. Bakelite, he'd heard it call it once before. He put down the bracelet he was holding. Whatever she called it, it suited her.

He went to the window and peered out. The day was quickly waning. It had taken her a fair amount of time to organize her business before she'd been able to head home to pack. And after that…well, they'd gotten distracted, to say the least.

They should have been gone from here hours ago, but Phoenix didn't sense any evil around them. Not yet. He figured Hades would concentrate on Jessica first, wanting to punish Mordecai most of all. The immortal warrior had lived in Hades' realm for years and had tricked the god into believing he'd won Mordecai's soul. All the while, the warrior had been playing Hades false and doing his best to help the remaining warriors. Still, it didn't pay to underestimate the God of the Underworld. As soon as he showered, they were out of here.

Right on cue, the water went off. Phoenix turned, crossed his arms over his bare chest and waited. He knew Tilly was feeling off-kilter. Knew she was disconcerted by the way she'd lost control with him. He'd seen it in the way she'd tried to distance herself as soon as their lovemaking was finished. He'd also heard her muttering to herself in the bathroom.

She could build her defenses as much as she wanted. He'd beat them down again. If he'd learned anything over the long years of the curse, it was patience, especially when there was something or someone worth waiting for. He already knew how to fight. The two traits combined would allow him to win Tilly's heart. He would accept no other outcome. For whether she knew it or not, she already held his heart in her hand.

Chapter Four

Tilly insisted on stopping at a restaurant on the way out of town. Neither one of them had eaten much today, and she knew he had to be starving. Or maybe not. She wasn't quite sure how much food he actually needed to consume in order to survive. But she was hungry.

"This isn't smart," Phoenix said for at least the tenth time since they'd left her home. She'd driven for twenty minutes before pulling into a family restaurant.

"Noted, but I'm hungry." She opened the door, grabbed her purse and climbed out. It was a warm evening but she wore a thin summer sweater over her tank top, anticipating the air conditioning inside.

He frowned but got out of the car and walked around the front and met her. He followed her toward the building, one hand riding low on her back. "Besides," she continued, "if Hades is strong enough to find me here, he can find me anywhere. If he's weak, he'll only be able to check the places he knows I usually am," she pointed out as she opened the door and walked inside.

Phoenix grumbled. "The problem is we don't know what we're dealing with."

And that was a huge worry. She knew Hades had been stripped of *most* of his power, the operative word being most. There was no point in worrying about it. What would be would be. Right now, she wanted a huge dish of shrimp gumbo and this was the place to get it.

The delicious smells filled her nostrils as soon as she entered. This was a place any working person could bring their family for a meal. Crowded and loud, people laughed and talked while music was piped in over the stereo speakers. The hostess bustled up to them with menus in her hands. The woman looked right past Tilly to Phoenix and plastered on her best smile.

"Good evening." The pretty brunette batted her eyelashes. Really? Tilly was tempted to ask the other woman if she had something in her eyes. Like a sledgehammer whacking her in the gut, Tilly realized she was jealous. It wasn't a comfortable feeling. She never got jealous. Never gave any man that kind of power.

"Table for two." Tilly's voice was sharper than usual, but the hostess barely glanced at her. She only had eyes for Phoenix. And, okay, Tilly could understand that. The man was drop-dead gorgeous with his amazing hair, mile-wide shoulders and washboard abs. He might be wearing a T-shirt, but it clung to his torso like a second skin, hiding nothing.

"Right this way." The hostess started to lead them into the busiest part of the restaurant when Phoenix stopped.

"Can we get the table in the corner?" he asked.

The brunette's fingers tightened around the menus and she licked her ruby-red lips. "You can have anything you want." Her voice was low and intimate. The double entendre more than obvious. Tilly felt like waving at the woman to remind her she was standing right here.

"That would be great." Phoenix smiled and Tilly was surprised the woman didn't drop to the floor at his feet. As it was, her eyes widened and she gave him a sultry smile.

Tilly tapped her foot, growing increasingly impatient. Phoenix put pressure on her back and she began to walk toward the table in the corner. Made sense to sit there. Less people around. They'd be able to talk.

Phoenix pulled out a chair for Tilly and she sat, refusing to be charmed by his manners, even though she kind of was. He sat across from her and the hostess put menus in front of them. Tilly could tell the woman was reluctant to leave. But there was nothing left for her to do. "Your waitress will be with you in a minute." She chewed on her ruby-red bottom lip for a moment and then left.

"She wants you." Tilly couldn't help but point out the obvious.

"Who?"

She studied Phoenix and realized he had no idea what she was talking about. He really was oblivious to the attention the other woman had given him. Tilly waved in the direction of the hostess. "Her."

Phoenix frowned. "You must be mistaken."

She sat back in her seat and stared at him. Huh. In her experience, all good-looking men knew when a woman was sending out signals and took advantage of that. But not Phoenix.

He shrugged. "It does not matter. I have no interest in her."

Before Tilly could follow up, their waitress bustled up to the table. "Hi, I'm Gail and I'll be your server tonight. Can I get you something to drink?"

Gail had her order pad and pen in her hand ready to jot down their orders. Then she looked at them for the first time and her pen fell to her feet when she got a load of Phoenix. Tilly sighed, rested her elbows on the table and buried her face in her hands.

"Are you all right?" he asked her, concern deepening his voice.

Tilly slowly raised her head. "I can't take you anywhere, can I?" Phoenix gave her a quizzical look. The waitress scrambled to pick her pen off the floor and shot Tilly an apologetic smile.

"Sorry about that," Gail said. "What can I get you?"

Tilly ordered the shrimp gumbo and sweet tea and Phoenix did the same. But he also added some fried catfish, red beans and rice, jambalaya and crab cakes. When the waitress left, Tilly smiled at him. "But you weren't hungry at all."

Phoenix reached across the table and took her hand. His was broad and large. She shivered remembering just how that hand felt on her body. "I could have gone without, but since we're here I might as well eat." His voice dropped an octave lower. "Although I would have much preferred to eat you."

Holy hell. How in the world was she supposed to respond to that? She gulped in air, practically hyperventilating at his sexual suggestion. Her breasts swelled, her nipples pebbled against her bra and her panties were getting damper by the second. She cleared her throat. "You really shouldn't say things like that."

"Why not?" he asked. He slid his fingers through hers and then withdrew them so his calloused skin dragged over hers. Chill bumps raced down her arms.

"Because." That was it. That was all she had. She couldn't think of a single reason, not with him looking at her like she was a gourmet feast and he was a starving man. In spite of the air conditioning, sweat pooled at her nape and a single drop rolled down her spine.

Just when she thought she might do or say something really stupid, her phone rang. She tugged her hand away and reached into her purse. She frowned when she noticed whose number was on the screen.

"Mordecai? How is Jessica? Is she okay?" Tilly gripped the phone so tight she was afraid she might break it. She'd swung from being aroused in a public spot to being terrified out of her mind all in a split second. She forced herself to relax her grip on her phone.

"It's me, Tilly."

A great sense of relief filled her. Phoenix cocked his head to one side and she knew he was listening to her conversation. She didn't mind. It would save her the trouble of having to tell him everything when she was done.

Why wasn't Jessica using her own phone? Suspicion grew inside her. She didn't quite trust the serpent. "Why are you using Mordecai's phone?"

"Because I don't know where my phone is and he's sitting with me."

"What happened, Jessica? Sabrina told me a woman, a minion of Hades, burned your arm." She couldn't imagine how scared Jessica must be and wished there was something she could do to help. She badly wanted to be with her friend. Tilly was a doer, and the fact that she was doing absolutely nothing to help was eating at her.

Tilly listened to Jessica's description of the wound and her blood ran cold. "I'm not sure about this, Jessica. This is bad." She wished she could contact her granny but didn't dare. Not for anything would she bring Hades' attention to her beloved granny.

"I know." Jessica sounded almost resigned, as if she knew there was nothing to be done.

Tilly knew they were dealing with a god, but there had to be something they could do to fight him. "I'm coming over. I should be with you."

"No." Jessica grew more agitated. "Stay with Phoenix. Hades may be after you too. No sense in all of us being in one space and making it easier for him." As much as Tilly wanted to be with her friend, she knew Jessica was right. Still, it chapped her to have to stay away when Jessica needed her the most.

"What does the Lady say?" Tilly wondered if Stavros had found her or if any of the others had been able to contact her.

"Just a second and I'll ask Mordecai." She heard Jessica and Mordecai talking in the background. Then her friend was on the line once again. "They still can't reach her. Hades is doing something to block their communication."

"Shit." Tilly echoed all their sentiments.

"I'll be okay," Jessica told her, even though Tilly could tell she didn't really believe it. "Maybe you should leave town or something."

"I'm not sure that would make a difference." Tilly didn't want to leave her home and her friends. It felt cowardly. Like she was running away.

"But you can't know that. It might be safer for you to go away. Just until this blows over."

"What if it never does?" Tilly asked her friend. "What if it only ends when we're both dead?"

"We'll figure something out." Jessica said. "In the meantime, stay safe."

"I will. If I think of anything, I'll call you." Tilly paused and took a breath. "Love you, Jessica."

"I love you too, Tilly."

Jessica closed her phone and tucked it away. Phoenix took her hand once again and squeezed it tight. "I'm sorry."

Tears threatened, but Tilly willed them away. She wouldn't cry. Tears changed nothing. She needed to think. Maybe there was some way they could fight Hades and his death curse.

The waitress arrived at their table with her tray laden down with dishes. She quickly placed their meals in front of them, peeking at Phoenix as she did so. Tilly was watching closely so she caught when the waitress slipped a folded napkin under one of Phoenix's plates. Tilly held her temper and waited until the waitress left.

"Check the napkin under your fried catfish."

Phoenix already had fork and knife in hand so he set them down and reached for the napkin. He pulled it out from beneath the plate and unfolded it. Tilly could see a phone number written in red ink. No, that wasn't ink. It was lipstick.

Phoenix frowned. "What is this?"

"Her phone number." Honestly, the man might be an ancient immortal warrior who could turn into a mythical bird, but when it came to modern women, he was clueless.

"But why?" His reaction made her shake her head, but a smile twitched at her lips. Okay, so it wasn't his fault he was gorgeous and attracted female attention. She'd just have to get used to it.

Wait. Back up the truck. She didn't have to get used to anything. They weren't together. Not really. Sure, they'd had sex, but that was all. It wasn't like they were in a relationship.

"So you can call her." She said each word slowly for emphasis.

"But why would I wish to call her? I don't know her."

Tilly grabbed a spoon and dug into her gumbo. "Because she's hoping to have sex with you." She was learning it was best to be blunt when dealing with Phoenix.

His eyes heated to a molten green and her stomach sank. She should have known. He was no different than any other guy.

But Phoenix's gaze slowly meandered down her body, leaving Tilly feeling as though he was stripping her naked. "Why would I want to have sex with her when I have you?" The sensual purr in his voice made her clench her thighs together. Her panties just moved beyond damp to downright wet.

And the devil knew it. Phoenix inhaled deeply and his smile deepened. "You smell delicious."

"It's the food." No way was she playing this game with him, not in public.

He picked up his knife and fork again. "It's not the food, sweet Tilly." Thankfully, he began to eat, keeping her from totally disgracing herself. She was so aroused right now all she wanted to do was go around the table and sit on his lap, preferably with his jeans open and her skirt up. They wouldn't even have to remove any clothing to fuck.

The man was making her crazy. She understood that it was partially a defense mechanism to keep from thinking about the horrible situation with Jessica. The other part of her understood it was because Phoenix pushed all her buttons like no other man ever had. Both situations were incredibly dangerous.

The rest of the meal passed in relative silence, both of them lost in thought. All around them, people ate, children laughed and adults talked, but it felt almost as though they were alone in their own world. Tilly finished eating before Phoenix did, but it didn't take him long to devour the enormous amount of food in front of him.

"Guess you need a lot of fuel." She'd never thought about it, but it must use an enormous amount of energy when he shifted. Plus, he was a big guy to begin with.

He nodded and wiped his mouth with his napkin. He might be a warrior, but he had good table manners. "I naturally burn a lot of calories, and I want to be at full strength."

She wanted him at full strength too. No, scratch that. No more thoughts of sex. It all had to be about survival and finding a way to save Jessica. "We should go." Tilly grabbed her purse and stood. "We can pay at the counter."

Phoenix was instantly beside her. "I've got it," he told her. He reached into his pocket, drew out a wad of cash and peeled off several large bills. When they reached the counter, their waitress was already there. Gail smiled at Phoenix but all he did was hand her the money and tell her to keep the change.

Tilly didn't want to feel happy when the other woman's face fell, but she couldn't help herself. If that made her petty then so be it. The waitress shouldn't have hit on another woman's man, especially not with her sitting right beside him. It was tacky.

The air outside was stifling and it was like hitting a wall of heat when they exited the restaurant. Night had fallen and the moon was a sliver of light in the sky.

"Where are we going?" Phoenix asked her. "I assume you have a destination in mind."

Tilly nodded and began to walk toward her car. She looked around, unaccountably nervous.

"We're alone," he assured her.

"How can you be sure?" she asked. She unlocked the door, but he reached around her and opened it before she could. She slid into the driver's seat. He stood there, one hand on the door, the other on top of the car.

"Because I'd feel him." He closed the door and went around and climbed in on the passenger side, buckling up before she told him to. "Now where are we going?"

"We're going to the place I grew up."

Phoenix shook his head. "That isn't safe."

"It is," she assured him. "I haven't been back there in twenty years." She started the engine, put the car in gear and exited the parking lot. "Trust me. It's the last place anyone would ever think to look for me."

She could tell Phoenix had a million questions he wanted answered, but he held his tongue. She was grateful. There was enough to worry about without mentally traveling back to her dysfunctional childhood. Her hands tightened around the steering wheel. Before this was over, she was sorely afraid she'd have to deal with all those memories.

"It's less than an hour away. It won't take us long to get there," she assured him.

"However long it takes, I'm with you," he told her. She knew he meant more than the drive. He'd be beside her until the threat was over. She should be grateful, and she was. But more than that, she wondered what would happen after the threat was eliminated.

Hades reclined on his throne and watched the image of Mordecai and Jessica in the mirror with glee. This was even better than he'd hoped for. He knew the serpent cared for the human, but he'd had no idea just how much. It made his victory all the sweeter. It was only a matter of hours now before Jessica succumbed to his curse and he would be able to claim her soul. He planned on spending eternity taunting Mordecai with what he was doing to the woman deep in the bowels of Hell.

It really was delicious.

His entire body hummed with the power that he'd stolen from a dozen of his demons. It was nothing compared to his usual power, but it was better than feeling totally helpless as he had when the Lady of the Beasts had stripped him of his. He was using quite a lot of it to hinder communication between the Lady and her warriors, not to mention the amount of energy it had taken for him to create the death mark. It would soon be time for him to refuel.

He'd enjoyed walking through the ranks of his demons and picking some at random to kill. He had to take his fun where he could get it. It would be quite some time before he dared personally step into the human realm. Maybe decades or longer. His brothers were watching his every move. He could feel their spying eyes on him from time to time, and he played weak and pathetic whenever he sensed them.

They would lose interest over time. All he had to do was wait and slowly regain his power.

The picture in the mirror winked out the moment he sensed the presence of another god outside his door. He waved his hand at the entrance and it opened. He half expected it to be one of his brothers or at least one of their flunkies.

The sweet scent of wildflowers preceded her into the room. Persephone paused in the doorway, put her hands on her hips and glared at him. "What are you up to, Hades?"

His ex-wife strolled into the room like she owned it. He frowned when he realized how true those words were. She'd picked out almost all the furnishings, and he hadn't changed a thing after she'd left him.

"What are you doing here, Persephone?" He hadn't seen her since she'd appeared in his prison cell in Olympus telling him he was free. She was wearing tight jeans and a skimpy tank top. Both garments clung lovingly to her curves. He gripped the arms of his throne, not immune to her charms. He'd wanted her the first time he'd seen her. He wanted her still.

"Is that any way to greet a guest?" Hips swaying, she walked over to the sideboard and poured herself a glass of his finest whiskey. She lifted it to her ruby lips, sipped and made a face as she swallowed. Persephone had always preferred wine to hard liquor. He had several bottles of her favorite in the cabinet, but he didn't tell her that.

"How can you drink this stuff?" she asked.

"How can you have so little appreciation for the finer things in life?" he retorted.

She set the glass down and inclined her head. "Touché." He wanted to take back his harsh words. Persephone was the only person he'd ever met who made him want to be a better man. The feeling was uncomfortable to say the least.

He stood and walked toward her. She was much shorter than him and he'd always felt protective around her even though she was a powerful goddess in her own right. He cupped her chin in his hand. "I repeat, my love, why are you here?"

She shrugged but didn't pull away from him. The sweet scent of wildflowers clung to her milky-white skin. She was flawless. Without comparison. And she'd once been his.

"I'm just keeping an eye on you." She sighed and suddenly looked tired. "I don't want you to do anything foolish. It took a lot of convincing to get Zeus to release you from prison. You've already been stripped of most of your power by the Lady of the Beasts and I don't want to see you imprisoned in Hell for eternity. You like to come and go too much. You wouldn't be able to wheel and deal and it would drive you mad."

She knew him too well. He forced himself to release her and waved a hand around the room. "As you can see, I'm not doing anything more than relaxing in my home." She shook her head and her long black hair moved like a curtain around her. He liked the color on her but preferred her as a blonde.

"I wish I could trust you, Hades. I really do. But I can't."

They truly were opposites. He was at home in designer suits and lived for the pursuit of power. She, on the other hand, was the most honest of all the gods and goddesses he knew and was at home in casual clothing. Although she was truly a goddess when she dressed up in high heels and a designer gown. He hadn't seen her that way in decades.

He shrugged aside the sensation of loss that welled up within him. Gods and goddesses came together and split apart. It was the nature of being immortal. He was rubbing the center of his chest before he could stop himself and immediately dropped his hand.

"If you need someone to talk to…" She let her offer trail off.

"I'd like to do more than talk," he shot back, giving her a suggestive leer.

Once upon a time, she would have laughed at his sexual taunt and run into his arms. This time, she turned away and walked toward the door. He almost called her back.

"Your pursuit of power will be your downfall if you're not careful," she predicted.

She'd never understood that part of him. "Don't you worry about me," he told her.

Persephone paused in the doorway. "But I do. I can't seem to help myself." Then she was gone. Her name echoed against the walls and he realized he'd been the one to call it.

He shook himself and turned back to his throne. He had things to do and plans to make.

Chapter Five

Tilly turned the car off the main road and drove down an overgrown dirt path. Phoenix had been quiet the entire drive, but it wasn't an uncomfortable silence. It was more that both of them were locked in their own worlds. Each lost in thought.

"It's just up ahead." Her stomach was churning at the thought of being here again. Her daddy had lived here on and off over the years. He'd passed on almost a year ago and, in a surprising move, had left it to her. She'd thought about selling it but had put off making that decision. She was grateful to have it right now. Although she had no idea just what kind of shape it was in.

The trees leaned over the road, making it impossible for more than one vehicle to pass at a time. Not that she expected to meet anyone out here. Although it was possible squatters had moved in. After all, other than Tilly paying someone to check on the property every few months, the place was deserted.

She pulled into the small clearing that was almost totally overgrown and stopped the car. The headlights broke through the gloom and spotlighted the house she'd grown up in. It seemed smaller than she remembered. The white paint was long faded to gray. It looked depressing and squalid.

"You okay?" Phoenix asked her.

She shook off her bad thoughts and nodded. "I'm fine." Not giving herself time to think, she opened the door and climbed out. "Watch for snakes," she warned him. There could be snakes of both the animal and human variety. This really wasn't a good move, especially at night. "Maybe we should go somewhere else."

Phoenix came to stand alongside her. "No. This place is quiet and out of the way."

She tried to see it from his perspective. Huge cypress trees ringed the property, their limbs weighed down with Spanish moss. Tall grass grew up where once a small lawn stood. Her mother had grown flowers. It had been a pretty place once.

Tilly breathed in the heavy air. As many years as she'd lived away from here, it still smelled like home. Around them, the night was alive with sound. Insects buzzed, grasshoppers chirped and the bullfrogs sang their nocturnal song. Something flew overhead, probably an owl or a bat.

"We should go inside." Standing outside wasn't going to make the place look any better.

Phoenix took her hand and led her through the grass. The steps were weathered but held as they stepped up. She reached into her purse and drew out a set of keys. She pushed the right one into the lock and turned. The metal tumble of the latch being opened seemed unusually loud. She stood there, not able to make herself turn the handle.

As if sensing her hesitation, he did it for her. Phoenix turned the doorknob and shoved the door wide. It creaked in loud complaint.

"There's a light switch on your left." She'd kept the utilities hooked up just in case she decided to rent the place, although she never had.

Phoenix found the switch and flicked it. A dim bulb illuminated the room. Tilly was expecting the worst and was surprised that the place wasn't all that bad. She walked forward and sniffed the air. It wasn't musty. If anything, she caught the scent of lemon cleaner. "Someone's been here."

She started to move forward, but he caught her arm. "Let me look." He didn't wait for her to answer and prowled deeper into the house. Not that there was much to see beyond two small bedrooms, a bathroom and the open kitchen/living room area. She wasn't willing to be left behind, so she followed him.

He glanced over his shoulder and frowned. She stared back until he sighed and looked away. The rooms were clean and vacant of anyone else. Tilly did her best not to look at the single bed in the smallest room—her childhood room. The only other piece of furniture in the space was a chest of drawers that had seen better days. The master bedroom was just as spartan. If someone had been staying here recently, there was no sign of habitation.

They walked back to the kitchen area, and she opened the kitchen cupboards and peered inside. Several cans of beans were tucked in the back of one of them. Beyond that, there were some mismatched dishes and a few pots.

"I wonder who's been here?" Whoever it was, she couldn't fault them. They'd obviously cared for the place while they'd stayed here.

"No ideas?" he asked her.

She shrugged. "It's not Granny or one of her friends. She hated my father."

"What about your mother?"

Tilly's chest ached whenever she thought about her mama. "No. She remarried years ago and lives in Georgia."

"What about your father's family?"

That was something Tilly hadn't considered. "I wouldn't be surprised if some of them had a key. I never bothered to change the locks." She set her purse on the kitchen table and tried to shake off the ghosts of the past that lurked around her. Thankfully, the furniture was different from what had been here during her childhood. Sometime over the years, her daddy had bought new, probably new from the thrift store. He'd never had much money.

"I'll go and get our things." Phoenix left her alone in the house.

Tilly found herself drawn to the woodstove in the corner of the living room. It was the only heating source for the entire place. Tilly remembered many fires crackling in the colder months of winter and cooking there sometimes when the power went out. She wrapped her arms around herself, cold in spite of the summer heat.

Memories chilled her to the bone.

Phoenix returned and closed the door behind him. He set her bag on the faded brown sofa. One look at her face and he strode over to her, wrapped his arms around her and pulled her close. "What is it, Tilly? Why does this place hurt you so much?"

He was right. It did hurt her even after all these years. "I can still hear the echoes of her screams." The words popped out of her mouth. Outside of her Granny, Tilly had never spoken of this time to another living person.

Phoenix tightened his grip. "Tell me."

She didn't think to deny him. Maybe it was having him wrapped around her, a buffer from the past. Maybe being back here triggered memories she could no longer keep buried. Whatever the reason, she found herself telling him everything.

"There were always more tears than laughter in this house. I think any laughter at all made the rest of it worse." As a child, she'd learned early when to avoid her daddy.

Phoenix rubbed his hand up and down her spine, offering silent comfort. His heart was a low and steady beat against her ear. She clutched at his shirt to anchor herself to the here and now.

"Daddy drank more than he worked." She sighed, remembering how hard her mama had tried to make things work. "We ate a lot of rice and beans. Mama found jobs where she could, but that made Daddy angry too." Tilly remembered many fights between her parents over her mama working. Her daddy couldn't keep a job, but he hated when mama worked. Said it made him feel like less of a man.

"I'm sorry." Phoenix rocked her slowly from side-to-side.

"It is what it is."

"He hit her, didn't he?"

Tilly flinched at his question but nodded.

"And you too." This time it wasn't a question. She could feel the tension thrumming through Phoenix's big body. Strange that he was so much bigger than her daddy but she didn't fear him.

"Mama left him when I was still a kid. Granny Ledet took us in and scared Daddy off when he came looking." Tilly leaned back and offered him a genuine smile. "Granny terrified him into leaving us alone."

"I'm glad you had her." Phoenix's eyes were darker than usual, filled with concern.

"Me too." She didn't want to think about the past any longer. The present was scary enough without dredging up old memories long dead. Tilly went up on her toes and kissed Phoenix. "Make me forget." She wanted to feel something good and knew he could give that to her.

Phoenix groaned and covered her mouth with his. Tilly focused on the here and now, setting the past free.

No matter how many years he lived, Phoenix could not understand a man who would hurt his wife and child. A man's job was to protect those under his care. He knew that alcoholism was a disease, but that did not excuse abuse. Especially to a child.

Phoenix found it hard to picture the vibrant, strong woman in his arms as frightened and bruised, but knew it was that past that had forged her into the woman she was today. He wanted to love her hard and well, to make her feel so loved that the past would never have a hold on her again. Impossible? Maybe. But he was up for the challenge.

He lifted her off her feet and carried her down the short hallway to the bedrooms, stopping when she stiffened in his arms.

"I don't want to go in there." Her voice trembled, so unlike the courageous woman he'd come to know. But everyone had a weakness. His was the woman in his arms.

"All right." He turned and pressed her back against the wall. "We don't have to go anywhere you don't want to."

She twined her legs around him, shoving up her skirt in the process. A sense of desperation seeped from the very pores of her body. When she leaned in to kiss him again, he did something he thought he'd never do. He stopped her.

"Maybe we shouldn't do this." If his cock could speak, it would be swearing at him. As it was, his phoenix was not pleased with him. The creature flapped and roared in displeasure.

Tilly froze. Although she was still in his arms, he could feel her move away from him emotionally. "Put me down."

He tightened his hold on her before doing as she asked. "No. It's not what you think. I want you." He wanted her more than he did his next breath. "I just don't want to take advantage of you."

And that was entirely the wrong thing to say. He knew it the moment her eyes narrowed and her lips tightened.

"You think I'm so weak I don't know my own mind?"

He shook his head. "Truthfully, you're the strongest woman I know."

Now she looked confused. "Then I don't understand."

"Tilly." He cupped her face in his hands and rubbed his thumbs over her soft skin. "You mean a lot to me. I don't want to ever do anything to hurt you."

Her smile was slow in coming, but it was genuine. "Then love me."

He swallowed back the words *I do,* instinctively knowing it was not what she'd meant. She wanted the physical act without the emotion behind it. He wasn't capable of that. Not with her.

She leaned closer and rubbed her breasts against his chest. Even though they were both wearing clothing, it was like pouring gasoline on a spark. He exploded.

Phoenix captured her mouth, claiming it. He used his tongue and lips to taste and touch and tease. He groaned when she dug her fingernails into his shoulders. Yes, that's what he wanted. Tilly, wild and free. His.

Clothing, they were both wearing way too much. He had to stop kissing her in order to get her top off. And he would. Any minute now. But her lips were so sweet and she opened so freely to his touch, he couldn't make himself pull away.

Her tongue challenged his for dominance. He refused to fight her for it and instead enticed her to play. Tilly made a soft sound deep in her throat and capitulated. Phoenix wanted to throw back his head and roar in triumph.

But as much as he loved kissing her, he needed more. "Clothing," he muttered as he left a long string of kisses down her determined jawline.

Tilly tugged on his shirt, dragging it over his torso until he had no choice but to release her long enough to yank the garment over his head. She was wearing another one of those sexy tank tops she favored in the warm weather. This one was white with yellow flowers embroidered along the front. He traced several of the tiny blossoms before sliding the fabric over her breasts and off. The bra she wore was a deep mocha with lacy trim. As pretty as it looked on her, she'd look even better without it.

Phoenix reached behind and undid the hooks. He slid his hands around to the front and eased the straps down her arms. It was like unwrapping the most wonderful present. "Perfect."

She made a humming sound and reached for him again, but he stopped her. He lifted her until her breasts were level with his mouth. Both nipples were taut buds, high and proud.

He captured one between his lips and sucked.

Tilly was burning up. It was the combination of this place and the memories it carried, coupled with the raw need she felt for Phoenix. He'd been willing to walk away from her after she'd offered herself for him. She'd been furious with him and herself. She was not weak. But he'd deflected her anger with his easy compliment. He thought she was strong.

Well, she wasn't feeling strong at the moment. If he hadn't been holding her upright, she'd be in a melted puddle at his feet. Whenever he touched her, it felt as though her skin was on fire in the most delicious way. She yearned for him.

There was something about Phoenix that pushed everything else aside until there was only room for him. The very idea was terrifying to a woman like her, a woman afraid of losing her sense of self to a man.

But she was not her mother, and he was not her father.

The notion popped into her head but was gone a second later when he took her nipple into his mouth again and sucked. Sensual tingles raced from her breast to between her legs with each pull he took. And when he flicked his tongue over the tip, her pussy clenched in response.

He turned and carried her back the way they'd come as though she weighed nothing. It was a complete turn-on. Something cool hit her back. She blinked and realized she was staring at the ceiling. He'd laid her on the kitchen table with her legs hanging over the edge. He loomed over her like some avenging god.

No, not a god. A warrior. Her warrior.

She ignored the possessiveness she felt and reached for him. She planted her hands on his firm chest and slid her palms over warm flesh. His eyes seemed to flame from within, something they only did when they were making love. His skin shone with a thin layer of perspiration. The air was thick around them. The tiny house didn't boast air conditioning.

He moved closer to her, spreading her thighs wide with his hips. The motion pushed her skirt upward and it pooled around her waist. It also pressed his cock firmly against her mound. His shaft was thick and hard. Deep inside, her pussy began to throb. She reached out and dug her fingers into his jean-clad ass, pulling him closer. He flexed his hips, rubbing his erection against the damp crotch of her panties.

Tilly groaned and gasped. "More."

Phoenix swore and tore at the button and then carefully lowered the zipper. His cock jerked out, ready and more than willing. He dragged her panties down her legs and tossed them aside. She moaned when he pressed the thick head to her opening and pushed. He stretched and filled her. The rough brush of denim caressed her bare thighs.

Tilly planted her feet on the edge of the table and pushed upward. "*Yes,*" she hissed when he was finally all the way in. Each pulse of his cock drove her closer to coming. Her pussy rhythmically clutched his shaft.

"Hold on to me." His expression was filled with determination, but also with an overwhelming need she not only understood but also possessed. She wrapped her hands around his biceps as far as they could go, which wasn't very. Like the rest of him, his arms were massive.

He began to fuck her hard and fast. There was no buildup, no preliminaries. Just wild animal need. And she was with him every step of the way. She pushed her hips up to meet each inward stroke, wanting him as hard and as deep as she could get him.

The air around them began to crackle and sizzle. Actual flames licked at his skin. Fascinated, Tilly reached out to touch one. It tingled but didn't burn her.

"Tilly." He called her name and his entire body tensed, every muscle gathering for one final push. He leaned down, gathered her close and hammered into her. Each stroke hit exactly the right spot.

She screamed his name. Her entire body spasmed, her pussy closing hard around his cock. He drove into her again and again. His shaft jerked and his release flooded into her, setting off another round of spasms within her.

Still, he didn't stop. He kept going until both of them were dripping with sweat and totally exhausted.

"Enough," she managed to whisper. It was all she had energy for. Her body was totally drained, yet a sense of satisfaction, of completion filled her.

He lifted her, still hard and buried deep in her core. "Ah, Tilly. It will never be enough."

Chapter Six

Phoenix lay on the bed beside Tilly and watched her sleep. It wasn't very comfortable with both of them lying on their sides and a good portion of his body hanging off the side of the bed. Still, there wasn't another place in the world he'd rather be. No king-sized deluxe mattress could be more inviting then sharing this ancient, lumpy twin-sized one with Tilly.

They'd found sheets and a blanket in the closet and, surprisingly, they weren't very musty at all. He'd taken them outside and shaken them out just in case a spider or two had decided to take up residence. He'd slept in worse places. And having Tilly next to him all night made the bed just about perfect.

The sun had risen and was shining in the window of her childhood bedroom. It was morning, but they'd been up until late. Tilly was worried about her friend. They both were. But there was nothing they could do to help Jessica. That was the most difficult thing for a woman like Tilly to accept. He knew there was nothing she wouldn't do to save her friend.

He trailed his fingers over Tilly's bare shoulder. They'd taken a shower last night after they'd made love. The bathroom was cramped and the water barely a cold trickle, but he'd taken the time to soap her strong, slender arms, her shapely legs and every part in between. They'd heated the water with the sexual passion simmering between them.

His cock, which had already been awake before him, was hard and ready to perform yet again. This woman would always tempt him, would always hold his interest. She fascinated him with her quick mind and sharp wit. With her tough outer shell and the soft woman who lay beneath it.

Tilly murmured and shifted on the bed. Her elbow hit the wall behind her and she frowned. He ran his hand over her arm, rubbing the sting away. Her eyelids fluttered open and she stared at him. Then she smiled. It lit her entire face from the inside.

"Good morning." He leaned down and pressed a kiss against her forehead. Then he rubbed his nose against hers.

The sheet rustled as she pushed herself up in a seated position. "What time is it?"

"Just after ten." Like the rest of the warriors, he was always aware of what time of day it was.

"That's late." She scrubbed her hands over her face and shoved her hair out of her way. She'd taken it down last night when they'd showered and it hung down her back like a thick curtain.

"What time do you usually get up?" There was no detail he didn't want to know about her, the big and the small.

"Butt crack of dawn." She gave him a shove. "You gotta move. I need to go to the bathroom."

Phoenix swung around and rose from the bed, not the least bit shy about the fact he wasn't wearing any clothes. He stretched his arms over his head but had to bend them to keep from hitting the ceiling. A bone in his neck cracked, realigning itself after the uncomfortable night in the cramped bed.

He turned to see Tilly's eyes partially glazed over as she stared at his ass. He smiled. "Like what you see?"

She pushed off the bed. "It's too early for me to spar with you. I need coffee." He caught her as she tried to go by him, wrapped his arms around her from behind and rocked her in his arms.

"You do like what you see," he teased.

"You know you're fine." He heard the smile in her voice and laughed. He released her and patted her on the behind. She whirled around and frowned at him.

He laughed again, feeling better this morning than he had in years. She shook her head and turned away, but not before he caught the smile tugging at her lips. "I'll put on coffee," he promised.

"I'll be forever grateful." She trudged into the bathroom and shut the door, closing him out. The gesture was symbolic. Tilly was rebuilding her walls again. And he'd spend the day knocking them down. He was looking forward to it.

He held his arms out by his side and manifested a pair of jeans. Now that he had his full power back it was easy to do such things. Usually, he did things the human way, especially around others. But sometimes he wanted to flex his power, and there was no one around to see him. He glanced at the bed, and in the blink of an eye it was remade, the top blanket smooth. Leaning down, he picked up Tilly's discarded clothing and set them on the bed. The room was as good as he could make it.

Barefoot, he padded to the kitchen and reached for the coffeepot.

Tilly stared at herself in the mirror. Her eyes were a little bloodshot and her hair looked like a rat's nest, but other than that, she looked the same. There was no way for anyone looking at her to know she was in deep trouble.

And trouble had a name—Phoenix.

It was bad enough that Hades was probably after her. Adding a serious threat to her heart on top of it was more than she could handle. "What have you done?" she muttered to her reflection.

She'd had the best sex of her life, for one thing. Her body was still humming with satisfaction. And just seeing Phoenix's naked butt had set her motor revving yet again. For a woman who'd always prided herself on control, it was a sobering thought.

"Enough." She had to worry about Jessica and her own safety. There was no room for a relationship. Tilly snorted. How did one have a relationship with an immortal warrior? Her friend Sabrina managed, but she was immortal now too.

Tilly grabbed her comb and attacked her hair. When the tangles were finally dealt with, she braided the thick mass. A shower. She needed a shower.

Even though they'd had one before bed, last night had been warm. And sharing a tiny bed with a big man generated a lot of body heat.

She turned on the water and stepped beneath the stingy spray. It didn't take her long to wash away the sweat. If only she could get rid of the rest of her problems so easily. When she was done, she dried off, wrapped the towel around her and hurried back to the bedroom. She could hear Phoenix moving around the kitchen and smell coffee in the air. Wonderful, life-giving coffee.

When she entered the room, she was surprised to find the bed made and her clothing neatly piled on the end. She grabbed her overnight bag off the floor and set it on the bed. It didn't take her long to dig out underwear, a pair of cut-off jeans and a tank top. Once she was dressed, she folded her dirty clothes and tucked them into a pocket in her bag. Then she stuffed her bare feet into a pair of red canvas sneakers and left her childhood bedroom behind.

Phoenix was leaning against the kitchen counter staring out the window when she joined him. He held a coffee mug in his large hand, resting it against his stomach. He was wearing a pair of jeans and nothing else. The jeans were zipped but not buttoned. Sex on a stick. That's what he was with his washboard abs and broad shoulders. Tilly had a weakness for men in nothing more than a well-fitting pair of jeans, and Phoenix's jeans fit him like a second skin.

She started to sweat. Then he turned her way and smiled and she thought her body might spontaneously combust. "Coffee?" he asked. She managed to nod.

He set down his own cup and handed her a second one that was sitting by the coffeepot. Their fingers grazed when he handed it to her. Ribbons of pleasure shot up her arm and she frowned. Was it her imagination or was she growing more sensitive to his touch?

"Have you talked to Mordecai?" Tilly wanted news.

Phoenix shook his head. "I figured they'd call us if they had news."

She took a sip of her coffee and sighed as it seeped into her veins. It was just the way she liked it, not too strong and not too weak with two sugars. Damn, the man even made good coffee. "I'm not waiting."

Tilly found her purse and dug out her phone with one hand, not willing to relinquish her coffee. She had another swallow as she called Jessica's number. Nothing. The call wasn't going through. She tried Sabrina's number and the same thing happened. Worried, she set down her mug and stared at her phone. "I can't get through."

Phoenix frowned and closed his eyes. "I can't mentally reach either Arand or Mordecai." He opened his eyes and they were dark with concern. "Hades must be blocking us the same way he's jamming communication with the Lady."

"That can't be good." Anything that had to do with Hades was bad as far as she was concerned.

"It's not, but there isn't anything we can do about it." His calm answer infuriated her.

"We can go back." She tossed the useless phone back in her purse. "I think we should go back." Tilly hated being cut off from her friends. She also hated being here where the memories threatened to choke her. "After all, we survived the first battle with Hades because we were all together."

Phoenix closed the distance between them and took her into his arms, but she wasn't in the mood to be placated. "Let go of me." She shoved at him and was surprised when he actually let her go. Perversely, now that he wasn't holding her, she wanted him to. He had her totally confused.

"We need to stay here."

She opened her mouth to blast him again but paused when she noticed the tension thrumming through him and how his hands were fisted. He was just as frustrated as she was. Tilly released a huge sigh, totally deflated. She knew he was right, but that didn't make it any easier.

"I can't just stay cooped up in here all day." Coming here had been a mistake. She thought she'd moved beyond the hurts of her childhood, but she was wrong. The past was more vibrant here, more alive. Every room had dark memories that haunted her. She'd go mad if she had to stay inside this house much longer. The echoes from the past were too loud and painful.

"Let's go out back and sit on the deck," he suggested.

It was better than nothing. She grabbed her mug and detoured by the half-full coffeepot to get a refill first. The temperature might already be creeping up, but she needed caffeine, and they didn't have the supplies to make an iced coffee. Hot would have to do. In fact, they didn't have much in the way of supplies at all. Some fresh fruit, cheese and a loaf of bread. Enough for breakfast and lunch, but beyond that they'd have to venture out. Of course, there were those cans of beans in the cupboard if they got desperate.

Phoenix held the back door open for her. She had a feeling he'd wait forever if necessary. Tilly stepped out onto the porch and breathed in the thick, warm air. Something inside her settled and she perched on the porch rail. "There used to be chairs out here." She'd forgotten that.

"It's a nice place to sit and think." He caught the eave of the porch roof and leaned forward, staring out into the tangle of trees and vegetation.

She tried not to notice how freaking hot he looked, but it was a losing battle. "It used to be nicer. Not so overgrown." There, she was making conversation like any normal person. Not scintillating conversation, but it was better than sitting there with her tongue hanging out watching him.

"It's beautiful in a wild way." He turned to her. "Much like you."

Tilly set her mug down on the porch. Her hand was trembling too much and she was afraid she might spill it. "What do you mean, like me?"

"Ah, Tilly." He prowled toward her and cupped her chin in the curve of his hand. "You're so cautious and watchful, like a wild doe being stalked by a hunter." He traced the curve of her bottom lip with his thumb, and she had to fight the urge to touch it with her tongue. "So tough, but so fragile on the inside."

She pulled away from him. "I'm not fragile," she insisted. She'd worked hard not to be weak.

"Don't you know we're all fragile, Tilly? All of us have a soft core. If we didn't, we'd be nothing more than monsters."

His words made her chest ache and she was suddenly fighting back tears. "I don't want to be weak."

He went down on his knees before her and clasped her hands in his much larger ones. "You could never be weak. In many ways, you're too strong. You find it hard to let others help you even though you're the first one to offer help. It doesn't make you weak to need someone else, Tilly." He brought her fingers to his lips and kissed each one.

This wasn't sexual. Wasn't about getting her into bed. No, this was something totally different. She felt—cherished. That was the right word. No one had ever made her feel this way before.

She wasn't sure how she felt about this powerful warrior who was on his knees before her. All she knew was that she was in over her head. He touched parts of her she'd thought no longer existed.

"Did you ever have happy times here?" he asked her. He lithely came to his feet and stood beside her.

Although her first instinct was total denial, she forced herself to stop and think about it. "Yes. The early years were good, when Daddy was working regularly and not drinking so much. I remember Mama singing. She used to sing a lot." Tilly hadn't heard her mama sing in years. She had the sudden urge to call her and ask if she still sang.

"After she left him, I pulled away from her just like I did from him." It was a sobering realization to understand she was as much at fault for the estrangement between her and her mama as her mama was.

"You were a child and you were hurt." Such simple words, but they held a profound truth.

"Yes. I pulled away from everyone." She wrapped her arms around her waist and hugged herself.

"Even your granny?" he asked.

Tilly smiled. "Granny is a force of nature. You kinda get caught in her wake and pulled in whether you want to or not."

Phoenix threw back his head and laughed. "I think I'd like your granny."

"She'd sure like you." Tilly ran her gaze up and down his manly form. "She likes the good-looking ones."

Phoenix grinned and it made him seem not quite so hard. He'd never look young. There was too much ancient knowledge in his eyes and a sense of timelessness surrounding him. It was ridiculous how much she liked making him smile.

"What are we going to do?" Tilly had a sense of time running out.

"Whatever we have to," he told her. There was a set to his shoulders, a stubborn tilt to his head that told her he meant every word. He'd do whatever it took to save her.

Everything inside her screamed in protest at the thought of him putting himself in danger. They'd been friends and then lovers, but now they were something more.

Tilly was at a loss at how to fight the intense feelings he stirred in her. And she wasn't sure she wanted to any longer.

Hades grabbed another demon by the throat and drained the creature's life force from it. The power was pitiful compared to what he usually wielded, but it was better than nothing. Even weak, he was more powerful than all the demons in his domain. He had to be or they'd run rampant, spilling out into every other dimension.

He reached for another one. It tried to fight him, but Hades simply sent a spike of power shooting through the pitiful creature and cut off its heartbeat. He tossed the body aside, disgusted that he hadn't been able to gain any energy from the demon at all.

Hades threw back his head and roared his displeasure. Every demon shuddered and the walls of Hell shook with his anger. Mordecai had escaped Hades' vengeance. Not only was the immortal serpent beyond his reach, but now so was the woman he loved. Jessica Miller was now a part of Mordecai, the two of them one.

It was sickening how these immortal warriors gave up part of their power to a mere human. And yet they keep doing it. "Why?" he muttered.

"If you could understand that we might still be together." He whirled around and scowled at his ex-wife.

"I'm in no mood for you today, Persephone." He would have blasted any other god or goddess who dared to enter his domain uninvited. Maybe not Zeus or Poseidon. His brothers were as powerful as him. Or as powerful as he'd been. He hated being weak. Would not stand for it.

He grabbed another demon and killed the creature in front of her, draining its power. The buzz of energy flooded him. It was better than a shot of pure caffeine and made him horny. He ran his gaze over Persephone. There had never been and would never be a woman finer than she.

"Want to go to my room and talk about it?" He sauntered toward her and noticed the slight inhalation of breath. The pulse in her neck fluttered wildly. She was as affected by him as he was by her. He was glad he wasn't wearing one of his customary hand-tailored suits and was clad only in leather pants and boots, his chest bare. She'd always preferred the more barbaric side of him to the cultured businessman.

Hades trailed his fingers over the slender column of her neck and smiled when she shivered.

"Damn you, Hades." She closed her eyes and momentarily leaned into his touch.

He smiled at her. "Don't you know? I'm already damned."

She took a step back and turned from him. "I can't do this with you. Not again. You value vengeance and power more than you do me. I know that." She glanced over her shoulder and her smile was filled with sadness. "Call me if you ever decide I'm worth more." With that, she disappeared.

The pain in his chest caught Hades off-guard. He frowned and leaned against the wall. He hated weakness. And Persephone was definitely a big one of his. He took a deep breath and crooked his finger at the closest demon. With a sense of its own doom, the creature trudged toward him.

He needed to recharge. Now that Jessica was out of reach, it was time to look for Tilly Ledet.

Chapter Seven

Tilly wandered around the overgrown yard the next morning, careful to watch for snakes and other critters. Phoenix was right beside her, a silent sentry. She couldn't believe they'd been here a second night. Every hour they waited for news felt like an eternity. The only break they'd had was when they'd driven to a local store for a few groceries yesterday afternoon.

Both of them were growing tenser as time passed. She'd lain awake for hours last night with Phoenix's arms wrapped around her. Not even his lovemaking could drive away her fears for long. She'd already decided she was heading home this afternoon no matter what. Not knowing what was going on with Jessica was killing her.

She just hadn't told Phoenix her plans yet.

She hated not being able to reach her friends and worried about Jessica. Would Mordecai and the others be able to find a way to thwart the angry god? It had taken the Lady of the Beasts and her warriors five thousand years to outsmart Hades. It didn't look good for Jessica or herself.

"What was it like to be held captive in your animal form all those years?" She'd never asked him before, not wanting to bring up bad memories for him. But they'd dug through her past, and he knew things about her very few others did. She wanted to know more about him.

It would also serve to take her mind off her own problems.

Phoenix stopped and tipped his head back toward the sun. The powerful rays seemed to soak into his tanned skin. His red-and-gold hair shone like a halo around his head. "I would not wish it on my worst enemy." The quiet way he spoke gave his words more punch than if he'd yelled them.

Tilly reached out and took his hand. It was warm and strong. "You don't have to talk about it if it hurts you." That was the last thing she wanted.

He closed his fingers around hers and squeezed. "I don't mind." He led her back to the porch and they sat on the step. "Time passed differently during those years. A hundred years might pass in the blink of an eye and a single day might feel an eternity."

Tilly leaned against him, offering her silent comfort. He rested his forearms on his knees and clasped his hands together. "We could communicate in the most rudimentary way. Mostly in images or a single thought. But even that became more difficult as the years passed and we fell into despair."

"I can't imagine being that alone." Because even if they were in close proximity, the warriors might as well have been miles apart. "Never able to talk to anyone, to move." Tilly shivered. "I'd have gone mad."

She wished she could call back the words as soon as she'd spoken them. But Phoenix took no offense. "At times it felt as though I might," he conceded. "But there was always hope. And learning. We were able to absorb all the learning of the world from those around us." He peered up at the sun, not needing to squint even though it was incredibly bright. "The world is an astounding place, and humans even more so."

Tilly asked the question that had been bothering her since she'd met Phoenix. "What happened to the woman who freed you?"

Phoenix sighed and rubbed a hand over his face. "I was able to save her. It took all the strength I had to get her away from Hades. I could only do it because I was touching her. Otherwise, she would have burned to a crisp when I shifted to my animal form." He offered her a sad smile. "Because I'd gone up in flames, Hades assumed she was dead and never bothered to look for her. Once twenty-four hours had passed, she was safe from Hades' wrath and no longer a part of the curse."

"Wow." Tilly couldn't imagine how scary that must have been for the woman.

"I wasn't able to rejuvenate my form for many years. It took a long time for the phoenix to be reborn. I checked on her once I was back in this realm and learned she'd married, had children and was living a good life."

Tilly let the subject drop. She could see it upset him to talk about it. "Could you communicate with your phoenix during your captivity?" From what she'd gathered from her friends, the warrior and the animal were interconnected, two sides of a whole.

"Yes. I could still feel him at first, but that dimmed over time. Not being able to shift forms was hard on me."

"Do you want to shift now?" Tilly had glimpsed his animal side once before, during the last battle between Hades and the warriors, and she was more fascinated than afraid. She hadn't been able to have a really good look at him at the time. An oversight she wanted to correct. "I don't mind if you want to stretch a little."

He looked at her and she could see the longing in his eyes.

"It's not as easy on you as it is on the others, is it?" It couldn't be. He couldn't just become a wolf and run around the woods, or turn into a lion and stalk across the planes of Africa.

"No, it's not. It was easier when the world was less populated. But there are still vast untamed places where I can fly."

Tilly scuffed the toe of her sneaker against the wooden step. The paint was peeling, but it wasn't too bad. She really needed to sell the place or fix it up. "You can't fly here, but feel free to shift whenever you want to." She really wanted to see the mythical phoenix again.

"Are you sure?"

"Go ahead. I don't mind." That was an understatement. His tattoo was beautiful in a primal, dangerous way. The creature itself was even more so.

Phoenix brushed his hand over the crown of her head and then stood. "Don't be afraid. I'm told it can be rather dramatic when I shift."

Butterflies flapped around in her stomach as he strode to the center of the yard. Phoenix kept his eyes locked with hers as he spread his arms wide. Then he burst into flames.

Tilly jumped to her feet and stared in horror. No one could survive in the center of such a blaze.

But he had. The fire seemed to be pulled inward until it shimmered around the creature. In his place stood a proud seven-foot-tall bird. The tattoo hadn't done the creature justice. Heat rolled off him in waves as the phoenix raised his head and displayed a powerful beak that could easily crack bone. The bird flapped his wings, showing her his massive wingspan. The feathers were reddish in color and tipped in gold flame. His entire body was on fire, yet unharmed.

He was incredible.

"Wow." Tilly was at a loss for words. There was no way to describe the sheer magnificence and power of the animal. The flames traveled from his wings and spread across the grass in a wildfire. Tilly gasped and pointed.

The phoenix raised his wings and slammed them downward. The flames were immediately extinguished and a wall of heat crashed into Tilly, driving her back several steps. She threw up her arms to protect her face, but she needn't have bothered. While the heat was intense, it didn't burn her.

The creature made a raucous sound and she slowly lowered her arms. He hopped forward, propelling himself on powerful feet tipped with razor-sharp talons. Fire no longer covered him, but he was no less glorious. His reddish wings shone like a flame in the brilliant sun.

He reached out one wing and stroked the very tip over her face. It was so soft and gentle. When she stared up into the bird's eyes she could see her Phoenix in the green depths.

"That's pretty impressive."

He tilted his head back and preened at her praise. His reaction made her smile.

"Yeah. Yeah. You're handsome and you know it."

He flapped one giant wing again and playfully nudged her to one side. She grinned and righted herself. "I wish you could fly." She could only imagine how spectacular it would be to watch the giant flaming bird soar across the blue skies. Or, even better, a night sky.

She sensed his sadness and patted his chest in reassurance. "As soon as this is over you can go to one of those empty spaces you talked about and fly as long as you want."

His form began to shimmer. She sensed he was shifting back to his human form when he suddenly stopped. He shrieked. The sound was so loud it hurt. Tilly slapped her hands over her ears, stunned by the sudden change in his demeanor.

She saw it then, the swirling circling dark mass off to the left. She'd seen a portal once before and nothing good had come out of it. And the only person she knew who could create one was Hades.

Hades settled into his favorite chair with a drink in his hand and stared into his special mirror, the one that gave him a view into other worlds. He disliked the fact that it was good only for one hour per day, but beggars couldn't be choosers. And right now, it was his only doorway to the earthly realm.

He'd changed from his leather pants and was once again impeccably dressed in one of his custom three-piece suits with a hand-stitched linen shirt and Italian leather shoes. He was once again in control of his life and his kingdom. His demons trembled in fear whenever he was about, which was quite lovely and as it should be. All manner of succubi and other female demons were ready and eager to fulfill any sexual whim he might have. Too bad he didn't want any of them.

The soft scent of wildflowers still teased his nostrils and he cursed Persephone. She'd make him weak if he allowed it. He tapped his fingers on the arm of the thick wooden chair. It was time for his revenge.

As he watched, the portal grew larger. It infuriated him that such a simple think took so much effort. He couldn't hold the gateway between here and Earth open for long. But long enough to send through a handful of his demons—enough to distract Phoenix while one of them disposed of Tilly Ledet. It wasn't quite as delicious as his plans for Jessica and Mordecai had been, but it was better than nothing.

He brought the crystal glass to his lips and sipped the finest whiskey available in the world. It went down smooth and warmed his belly.

He had everything he wanted. Well, almost everything. Revenge was foremost on his agenda. Once that was done, he'd go about the business of regaining his power and running his empire. If Zeus and the others thought they could hold him back, they were sorely mistaken.

The sweet scent of wildflowers teased his nostrils again and he inhaled deeply. When he realized what he was doing, he swore and waved his hand in the air, replacing the lingering scent of perfume with the smell of sulfur. He didn't miss his ex-wife. Not at all. Revenge was everything he needed.

He peered back into the mirror, relaxed and prepared to enjoy the show.

Phoenix had been enjoying Tilly's reaction to his animal form. In the past, most people had been afraid of him. But not Tilly. If anything, she seemed enthralled. He freely admitted it made him feel good, and he found himself wanting to show off for her. He wished he could take to the skies and show her just how powerful he was. On the ground, he was a good fighter. In the air, he was unbeatable.

He missed flying, racing with the wind, losing himself in the silence of the sky. But being with Tilly was just as exhilarating. The way her eyes darkened and her scent changed when she looked at him made his cock swell. His keen eyesight noted the way her nipples pebbled against her top and how she unconsciously leaned toward him.

He wanted her again.

He'd just started to shift back to his human form when he felt a disturbance in the energy field around him. He cried his displeasure, whirled around to face the threat and came face-to-face with a portal. The black hole swirled, getting larger with each rotation.

Hades. Phoenix had seen this particular kind of portal many times in the past and it never boded well. He stepped in front of Tilly to protect her.

"Run!" His voice was more animal than man, but he managed to communicate the warning. He would protect Tilly. Keep her safe.

He whipped his wings high into the air and they ignited, burning hot and bright. If they thought to take Tilly from him, they were in for a surprise. Hell might be hot, but it was nothing compared to the flames of the phoenix.

The first demon stepped out and Phoenix slammed his wings together in front of him. He redirected his power, shooting fire straight at the opening of the portal. The demon caught fire and began to scream. Phoenix smiled and fried the next demon behind the unfortunate creature.

The remaining demons rushed out in a flurry, some going low and others jumping high. So many demons at once, it was impossible for him to get all of them. But that didn't stop him from trying. He whipped his wings wide and sent his deadly flames into the heart of the portal, burning it from the inside out. Hades' fires were dark while the phoenix's burned brighter than the sun. He was at full power while the god wasn't.

The two opposing forces slammed together, louder than a clap of thunder. The dark struggled, but the light overtook it and the portal winked out of existence. Now all Phoenix had to do was kill the remaining demons. Hades wasn't here himself. Phoenix was hopeful that meant the god wasn't powerful enough to enter this realm.

"You can't escape me." His voice was low and guttural. Angry. The demons couldn't attack him because the warriors had broken the original curse. Phoenix was safe from Hades and all his minions. But the same couldn't be said for them. Phoenix was under no restrictions.

Relishing the coming fight, he smiled. He'd send all Hades' demons back to Hell.

Then he heard Tilly scream.

He whirled around and gave a raucous cry of pain. Another portal had opened behind him and a demon now held Tilly in its grasp. She was doing her best to fight it but was no match for the hulking creature. The demon stood almost as tall as Phoenix did in his bird form. The demon's skin was leathery and two horns protruded from the sides of its head.

Phoenix immediately sent a bolt of his power into the heart of the portal, collapsing it.

The smell of death was behind him. Phoenix spun back to face the remaining demons. He'd almost forgotten them in his fear for Tilly. He shot fire at the remaining half-dozen demons and set them all aflame. They burned brightly and were quickly consumed. Their screams of agony filled the clearing. The smell of charred flesh stung his nostrils.

Satisfied they were no longer a threat, Phoenix shifted back to his human form and turned to face Tilly and her captor. "Release her," he demanded.

The demon smiled. "I don't think so. My master will open another portal and I'll take her to Hell." The creature licked the side of Tilly's face. She elbowed the creature in the solar plexus, but the demon didn't even seem to notice.

He took a step toward them but stopped when the demon tightened its hold on Tilly's neck. "Come any closer and I'll snap it. My master wants her alive. If that's not possible, dead is just as good."

Phoenix swore and glanced at Tilly. She was angry, but he could also see fear in her dark brown eyes.

As if on cue, another portal began to open. The black swirling mass swallowed the light around it. If the demon got Tilly into the portal, she'd be lost to him forever.

"Do you trust me?" he asked her.

She tried to nod but couldn't move her neck. "Yes," she gasped before the demon tightened its hold.

Phoenix took a deep breath. What he was about to try was incredibly dangerous. He didn't even know if it was possible. But better Tilly die with him if he failed than end up in Hades' clutches.

She is ours and we are hers, he told the Phoenix. The great bird roared his agreement.

He spread his arms wide and jumped toward them. The demon yelled as Phoenix ignited, shifting once again to his bird form in midair. Flames shot out from his body, consuming Tilly and the demon in a fiery cocoon. Phoenix yanked Tilly away from the demon and cradled her into his arms. Because he hadn't been holding her when he'd shifted, she hadn't been protected. Using his powerful wing, he knocked the flaming demon into the swirling portal. The black mass closed in on itself, collapsing into nothingness.

Throughout it all, Tilly never made a sound. Was she burned? Was she even still alive?

Phoenix knew he only had one chance to save her. He opened his heart and began to pour his healing life force into her even as he smothered the flames that engulfed her. If she was a part of him, the fire would not burn her and whatever damage had been done would heal.

At least he prayed that's what would happen. It was his only hope.

He shifted back to his human form and held her close to his chest. White light surrounded them. Color quickly bled through the white until they were in the center of a circular rainbow.

"Tilly." He whispered her name, afraid to look at her, afraid he would see nothing but charred, burned flesh. If she died, he did not want to live. Tilly was his heart. His very soul.

The lightest touch on his chest jolted him and he jerked his gaze down to hers. Tilly's skin was unblemished and her brown eyes were filled with awe. "You saved me."

"I had to," he told her honestly. "I love you."

Shocked by what he'd just said and the fact she hadn't died, all she could do was stare up at him in wonder. Every nerve ending in Tilly's body was alive, flooded with life-giving energy. Light containing every color of a rainbow and more danced over her skin and penetrated every pore of her body. She was also totally naked, her clothing having been completely consumed by the phoenix's flame. "What have you done?" she managed to ask. She felt the same but different. Better.

"What I had to." He swooped down and captured her mouth with his. The kiss was hot and forceful. Their tongues tangled and she moaned when he lifted her right off her feet. She clutched at his powerful shoulders. She tasted his relief and his desperation.

He left her lips and dotted her face with kisses. "I shared my life force with you. I had to. The fire was burning your body and I had to save you. I thought my immortal energy would heal any of the damage from the blaze."

He released her and ran his green-eyed gaze over her from head to toe. "You're really all right?"

Tilly nodded. Other than being a little lightheaded, she felt great. "The fire," she began.

He nodded. "I didn't have any other choice." There was pure torment in his eyes. "If the demon had gotten you into the portal, you would have been lost forever. Hades would have had you."

Phoenix fell to his knees in front of her. "Forgive me."

Tilly stared down at the proud warrior before her. She caught his beloved face in her hands and lifted until he was looking at her. "The fire didn't burn me." She gave a small laugh. "My clothing might not have made it, but I'm fine." It was the most amazing thing. The flames had surrounded her like a protective barrier between her and the demon. A living creature, the fire had pushed the demon away from her.

"Truly?" He covered her hands with his. "You're not just saying that?"

She shook her head. "No. It surrounded me. Protected me."

He released a huge sigh. "I'd hoped, but I didn't know it was possible. Not without me holding you."

"How?" The fire should have burned her to a crisp.

"You are ours." His simple words coupled with his declaration of love made her weak. She trembled and her legs shook. Phoenix surged to his feet, caught her before she fell and lifted her into his arms. "You're immortal now."

He walked up the porch steps and went inside the house while she tried to wrap her head around that idea. He carried her into the bedroom but didn't release her. Instead, he sat on the bed with her still clasped tight in his arms. He yanked the blanket from the bed and tugged it over her.

"You are safe for all time now. You are part of me so Hades can no longer harm you. The original curse stated that he cannot harm us now that we are free. Since you are now a part of me, you are now off-limits to him."

"Oh my God. You're right." Tilly's mind was racing. "We need to call Mordecai. That's how he can save Jessica." She threw her arms around his neck and kissed him on the lips. "You're brilliant." It was such a simple idea, but it was the right one. "Where's my phone?"

Phoenix reached out his hand and her purse glided in through the open bedroom door. "Wow, that's cool." Tilly held out her hand but nothing happened. She dropped it back down by her side. "That's not fair."

Phoenix chuckled. "You are immortal, but you do not have my powers."

She shrugged. "I'm not complaining." She dug out her phone and quickly placed the call. "It's ringing." Tilly was profoundly relieved when it was answered. "Jessica? Are you okay?

"I'm fine. I'm immortal." Jessica laughed. "How cool is that? But how are you? Is everything okay? We haven't been able to get hold of you."

"Hades was blocking communication. We couldn't contact you either. I'm doing great. I'll tell you all about it when I get back."

"Tomorrow," Phoenix prompted. He settled back against the headboard and stretched his long legs out on the mattress. She was still ensconced on his lap.

"We'll be home later this afternoon," she assured Jessica.

"You're sure you're all right?" her friend asked. "Is it safe to stay there? Have you seen Hades?"

Tilly smiled at Phoenix while she answered her friend. "We're safe and I'm feeling wonderful. I'll probably be around for a long time."

Jessica squealed. "You're immortal too?"

Tilly heard Mordecai's voice in the background but was finished talking. Now that she knew her friend was okay, she and Phoenix had a lot to discuss. "I'll call you later. Gotta go." Tilly ended the call and tossed her cell phone into her purse.

She took a deep breath and asked the big question. "What's next?"

Hades couldn't believe it. Once again, he'd been defeated by one of the warriors. "I don't understand," he muttered. Almost a dozen demons burned to a crisp. Not to mention the demons he'd had to kill to get enough power to open three separate portals.

The vision in the mirror winked out, his hour for the day spent. Alone in his cavernous room, he brooded. He didn't notice the priceless art on the walls, the antique rug on the floor. The liquor in his glass might as well have been water, for he did not taste it when he absently took a sip.

The phoenix had shared his power, his immortality with the woman just as all the other warriors had done. "They threaten their own lives, their own existence. And for what?"

"For love."

Hades came to his feet and roared his fury. "Love." He shook his head and strode toward his wayward ex-wife where she materialized from out of the shadows. "She'll run from Phoenix the first chance she gets. Then where will he be?" He caught her by the shoulders and yanked her toward him. Persephone didn't resist him. He hated the look of pity in her gaze and shook her.

"Perhaps," she answered, her voice calm and composed. "But perhaps not. Only time will tell."

He thrust her aside. "Everyone leaves. It is the way of things."

"No, Hades." She put her hand on his arm but he shrugged it aside. "Not everyone."

"You did." He sounded more like a petulant child than a god and hated himself for it. More than that, he hated her. She'd done this to him. "Be gone from my sight."

She inclined her head. "As you wish. But remember, you're the one who drove me away." With that parting barb, she was gone.

He stared at the empty space for long moments and then shook himself. "There's only one warrior left who isn't attached to a woman. Surely there must be someone or something the jaguar cares about." If there was, he'd find out. And this time he wouldn't fail.

Chapter Eight

Phoenix knew he should get off the bed and let Tilly rest. In spite of how she felt, her body had been through an ordeal. He tried not to notice how the blanket had dropped in the front, exposing the curve of her breasts, but it was impossible. Tilly was a part of him now. He could sense her in his heart and soul.

"What's next?" he repeated her words back to her. "Whatever you want." He trailed his fingers down her bare arm, fascinated by the goose bumps that rose on her skin.

Tilly licked her lips and twined her arms around his neck. Her lips were silky soft against his. "I really think we should celebrate. Don't you?"

He caught her braid in his hand and gently tugged her head back. "I believe you are right." He didn't just kiss her then, he consumed her. She was as necessary to him as air. More.

And he didn't know if he was going to be able to keep her.

He knew Tilly feared being in a relationship. Feared having her life revolve around a man. Could he let her go?

He honestly didn't know. He did know he'd do whatever it took to make her happy.

Their tongues playfully battled until both of them were panting for breath. She tasted like hope. Like the promise of tomorrow. And he wanted more.

He tried to ease her off his lap but she wasn't going. Tilly straddled him and the sheet fell away. He tugged it aside, wanting nothing between them. She stared into his eyes and he lost himself in her chocolate gaze.

"Touch me," she ordered him, and he was more than happy to comply. Her skin was warm and inviting. Phoenix ran his fingers between her breasts, loving the way she sucked in her breath. Her nipples were taut little buds, begging for his touch.

He wrapped his hands around her hips and skimmed upward, following her enticing curves. The muscles in her belly jerked and she made a little sound of pleasure. His cock began to throb. He willed his pants away, needing to feel her naked skin against his.

She made another humming sound deep in her throat as she reached for him. He groaned when she wrapped her fingers around his shaft. "Is all this for me?" She batted her thick eyelashes at him.

He knew she was teasing, but he was totally serious. "All for you. Only for you." She was it for him. He knew it just as he knew the sun would rise tomorrow. There would never be another for him.

He cupped her breasts and ran his thumbs over her puckered nipples. He was fascinated by the difference in their skin tone. She was strong but delicate. He was big and muscular. That she would trust him like this gave him hope they might have a future.

He groaned and gritted his teeth against the ecstasy that poured through him at her touch. She stroked his cock from base to tip and back again, her touch firm and sure. His balls tightened to the point of pain.

"I want you, Tilly. Now." His voice was lower, more guttural, but it couldn't be helped. She pushed him to the edge.

"Not yet." She shimmied backward on the mattress until she was perched around his knees. Then she leaned forward and lapped at the head of his shaft.

Phoenix hissed as he sucked in a breath. She blew on the damp head of his cock and then dragged her tongue over the slit. Her mouth was pure heaven, the heat surrounding him as she took him in. "Tilly." That was all he could say. Words were beyond him as she sucked his dick.

He didn't want it to end this way. He caught her shoulders and eased her away. She looked at him with a question in her eyes.

"It's too much," he told her.

Phoenix rolled, careful not to take them both off the narrow bed, until she was beneath him. He kissed his way down her body until he was lying between her spread legs. The bed was short and most of him was hanging off the end. But the discomfort was worth the prize. He shoved her thighs apart and breathed in her sweet, musky scent. His entire body quivered and he licked his lips in anticipation.

He swept his tongue over her slick labia, tracing the folds like a road map, not missing a single curve or line. She moaned and arched into his touch. A sense of pride filled him when he scented more of her arousal on the air.

He found her clit and teased the tiny bud with the tip of his tongue. He loved the forceful way she reacted to his touch. She gripped his hair hard and tugged him closer. He blew on her heated flesh. Then he wrapped his lips around the nub and sucked. Tilly gasped, dug her heels into the mattress and lifted her hips, trying to get closer.

"*Yes,*" she moaned, undulating beneath him.

The sound of her pleasure, the tantalizing smell of her arousal, the feel of her fingers clutching him all pushed him to the edge. She was close now. He could tell by the franticness of her movements and the volume of her moans.

He moved, lifting her off the bed so he could lie down with her over him. Once again, he cursed her tiny bed and dreamed of a day they could try out his king-sized one. He settled her on his upper thighs and steadied her. This had to be her decision. "Take me," he told her. *Claim me*, his heart cried.

If she didn't, he knew he'd have to set her free, no matter that it would break his heart and shred his soul. He only prayed he would be strong enough to do what was right, to give Tilly what she needed.

Tilly knew she'd never been this aroused before. It went beyond the physical. It felt spiritual, emotional. What she needed wasn't just Phoenix's body, but all parts of the man himself—mind, body and soul. A light sheen of sweat covered her skin and her pussy ached for him to fill her. She was so close to coming.

Why had he stopped?

Even though she knew he could move incredibly fast for a big man, it always surprised her. He was lying under her but he wasn't the least bit relaxed.

Every muscle in his large body was delineated. She could sense the tension rising from him in waves and knew not all of it was because he was sexually aroused.

He'd told her he loved her and she hadn't said a word in response. Tilly was totally conflicted about her feelings for Phoenix. He meant more to her than any other man ever had or would. He'd saved her life and given her immortality. But did that mean she loved him?

She wasn't sure she understood what romantic love really was. She hadn't had a good example growing up, and books and movies didn't exactly always provide a realistic view.

What she did know for certain was she wanted him. She flattened her palms on his massive chest and traced the hard bands of his muscles. A thin mat of reddish-gold hair tickled her fingers. His chest hair thinned as it moved lower.

She followed the line of hair downward until it hit his groin. His cock was hard and throbbing. The veins pulsed with each heartbeat. The bulbous head was thick and deep red in color. She knew he'd fit inside her, had done so before, but Tilly also knew he'd fill her pussy to the max, stretching her in the most delicious way.

"Tilly." He said her name with such emotion it made her shiver. "Take me," he told her again.

Her pussy was throbbing with need. She'd figure everything else out later. Right now, she wanted to feel Phoenix inside her.

She took his cock in her hand and shifted until she was able to notch the head against her opening. He arched upward and he slid in several inches before he stopped. His gaze was blazing with sexual passion, but he waited for her to complete their joining.

Tilly sat down hard, driving his shaft deep. She gasped and bit her bottom lip to keep from crying out as his broad shaft filled her, hitting all the sweet spots as he tunneled deep. Her pussy throbbed around his pulsing cock. He cupped her breasts and teased her tender nipples.

"Fuck me. Take me." His raw words pushed something deep within her. She'd take him all right. She'd take both of them over the edge into oblivion.

She began to move, rising up until only the crown of his cock was still inside. Then she sat back down, driving him deep. She did this over and over, needing him harder and deeper with each thrust.

Phoenix lightly pinched her nipples until she was gasping and moving faster over him. She threw back her head, closed her eyes and rode him like her life depended on it. And maybe it did.

Heat surrounded them, playing over her skin like a gentle caress.

"Tilly." There was such wonder in his voice that she opened her eyes and stared at him. "Look."

She followed his gaze to her arms and gasped. Red flames danced over her skin. It didn't burn. Didn't hurt. It felt more like a caress. "That's amazing."

"You are part of the phoenix, part of me."

Tears filled her eyes, but she blinked them back. She didn't want to cry, but the emotion of the moment was almost too much. Tilly focused on the one thing she could control—the sexual tension thrumming between them.

She picked up her pace, fucking him faster. He groaned, gripped her hips and helped her, slamming his hips upward with each one of her downward strokes. She loved making love like this, where she could see him and stare into his eyes.

She also liked being in control.

But a part of her liked it when he took that control away from her. "Phoenix," she gasped, not quite sure how to ask for what she wanted. But she didn't have to. He flipped them both over and somehow he managed to stay buried deep inside her. Then he began to fuck her. He hammered into her and she wrapped her legs around his waist and clung to his shoulders.

Fire continued to tease their skin until it surrounded them. But it didn't burn them or the bed. The flames were protective.

Each time his cock filled her pussy, it stimulated sensitive nerve endings until she could no longer bear it. She cried his name as she came. Fireworks exploded behind her eyes and her pussy clamped down hard on his cock. He yelled her name and thrust again and again, filling her with hot jets of his pleasure.

When he was spent, he collapsed next to her, moving only his upper body to the side. They were still joined, his cock pulsing heavily inside her. She moaned as another spasm made her entire body tremble.

Neither of them spoke for the longest time. Tilly was content to play with Phoenix's gorgeous mane of hair, twining her fingers through the thick mass. He stroked her arm and nuzzled her neck.

This time, it was he who raised his head and asked the question, "What's next?"

Tilly shrugged. "I'm not sure. Any ideas?" It was hard to think past the moment with their bodies still joined.

Phoenix sighed and eased out of her. He was still semihard and getting harder by the second. "What do you want to happen?"

Tilly sat up, curled her legs into her chest and wrapped her arms around them. "I don't know."

Pain flashed in his eyes, but was quickly gone. "I love you, Tilly," he began. Her heart started to race and she broke out in a cold sweat. "Love isn't a trap. True caring means wanting the other person to be happy no matter what," he continued.

Phoenix rolled from the bed and stared down at her. "So I'm letting you go."

Her stomach dropped and she began to tremble. "What?" That's the last thing she expected him to say.

He raked his hands through his hair. He was magnificent, his naked body the epitome of masculine perfection. But it was his words that were squeezing her heart.

"I'll be here for you whenever you need me." He leaned down and cupped her face. "I love you, Tilly. That means I never want to control you or hurt you. You're free. Be happy." He dropped a quick kiss on her lips, turned and strode into the bathroom, leaving her there on the bed totally dumbfounded.

He shut the bathroom door behind him and she stared at the cheap wooden panel. She'd gotten what she wanted. She was free. Unencumbered. Then why did she feel as though her heart had just been ripped from her chest? She rubbed the tender spot and tried to think.

Phoenix had said he loved her, but he was letting her go. Maybe he didn't really love her and this was his way of getting out of any entanglement. Even as she thought it, she knew that was a lie.

What did she want out of life?

Tilly rocked back and forth, trying to order her thoughts. It wasn't easy when she was surrounded by the smell of sex and the dark musky scent of Phoenix.

She unclasped her legs and slowly climbed out of the bed. The water came on in the bathroom, but she ignored it and left the small bedroom and padded to the other room. Her parents' room. She placed one hand on the wall. She could almost feel the vibrations of her father's anger. See her mother cowering in fear.

Tilly leaned against the wall and took a deep breath. She raised her hands in front of her and concentrated. It took a bit of effort, but tiny flames ignited at her fingertips. Maybe she couldn't burst into flames like Phoenix could, but he was a part of her, as she was a part of him.

His possessiveness wasn't to be feared. Tilly dropped the walls that surround her heart and barricaded her soul. Behind them, she found something she'd never thought she'd find—love.

The past was just that—past. She was no longer a child. The only thing holding her back was a memory. Was she brave enough to take a chance on love, on her and Phoenix? Because she did love him. There was no point in lying to herself.

Phoenix meant more to her than any man ever had. He'd become an important part of her life so gradually. He hadn't forced his way in. He'd simply made a place for himself in her existing world.

"You're an idiot," she told herself. Phoenix was ready to walk away from her because he thought that was what she wanted. She'd come to know him well. He was an immortal warrior. He didn't play games and said exactly what he meant.

Tilly pushed away from the wall and strode toward the bathroom. She didn't bother to knock before she shoved the door open. Phoenix stood in the tiny shower, his back facing her. She knew he was aware of her. The tattoo on his back moved when he tensed.

Slowly, he turned to look at her. There was no expression on his face.

She knew she'd hurt him, but she would make that up to him. "I love you." She blurted out the words she'd never said to any man.

He slicked the water out of his face. "What did you say?" His voice was incredibly deep, the way it got when he was aroused. She glanced down at his cock. Yup, he was definitely aroused.

"I said I love you." She walked toward him, ignoring the water dripping on her and the floor. "I've never said that to another man." She took a deep breath and let it out. "I know I have issues with commitment, but I want to be with you."

"For how long?" He wasn't making this easy on her.

"For as long as we both want."

"I want forever." He reached out, wrapped his muscular arm around her and dragged her into the tiny space. He pressed her back against the wall and loomed over her.

He really was huge, but his large size always made her feel protected, not threatened. And that really said it all. She trusted Phoenix. And she loved him.

She twined her arms around his neck. "I'd like forever too." She couldn't imagine a time she wouldn't want him.

A huge smile crossed his face. He lifted her and slid his cock into her slick pussy. Because of her arousal and the water, he fit easily. She gasped and gripped his shoulders. "I think it will take me forever to be sated," he told her.

Tilly smiled and deliberately clenched her pussy muscles around his shaft. He groaned and began to work his hips, pressing in and out. "I'm willing to try if you are," she told him before she totally lost the ability to speak.

A long time later, they were curled up in bed once again. She was half lying on Phoenix. She knew the space was cramped, but he hadn't complained once. "I think I'm going to sell this place."

He tilted his head so he could see her face. "Are you sure?"

She ran her fingers over his hard jaw. "Yes. It's time. The past is over and done with. I'm looking forward to the future."

"That's good." One corner of his mouth kicked up. "And does this future include a bigger bed?"

Tilly began to laugh. "It does. Let's get dressed and drive back to the city." She walked her fingers playfully over his chest. "I bet we can find a bed or two there."

He bolted from the bed with her in his arms, making her laugh. "I take it you're in a hurry?" she asked.

He lowered her down until her feet touched the floor and then patted her bare butt. "Whatever gave you that idea?" he replied, totally deadpan.

She adored his dry sense of humor and laughed. "I have no idea. Maybe I'm mistaken." She took a step toward the bed, but he wrapped his thick arm around her and yanked her back.

"You need to get dressed. The faster the better." He nipped at her neck, sending shivers down her spine.

No, forever wouldn't be long enough for her to spend with this man. "Since you can poof into your clothing—" which wasn't really fair since she couldn't, "—you can pack up the few things we brought with us and load them in the car."

Phoenix dropped a kiss on her mouth. "Whatever my lady wishes."

She knew he meant that. He'd never try to change her or control her. "I love you." She needed to tell him again.

His gaze grew solemn and he wrapped his hands around her face. "You are my life. My everything." Then he grinned. "Life with you will always be interesting."

Tilly laughed, knowing he was right. She was strong-willed, but he was confident enough to handle anything she might throw at him.

Epilogue

Stavros sat on the fringe of the group, watching them all interact. Both Jessica and Tilly had been saved from Hades' wrath, and Mordecai and Phoenix had claimed their women. Everyone was happy.

Everyone but him.

As always, he was alone. And he'd have to stay that way. No way was he going to get involved with a woman and bring Hades' attention to her. No, he would not do something so selfish.

"Are you all right?" Phoenix sat down beside him and handed him a beer. He took the fermented beverage and drank deep. He rather enjoyed the brew. The alcohol had no effect on him, but he liked the flavor.

"I am fine." He pointed the bottle at Tilly. "Your woman looks well."

His friend gave a low rumble of pleasure and a satisfied smile filled his face. "She is perfection."

Stavros wondered what it would feel like to be that connected to another person, a woman. All the women were now a part of their mates, shared their immortality. It was a gift from the Lady of the Beasts, but one he could never avail himself of.

"Are you going in search of the Lady again?" Phoenix asked.

"Yes." Whatever Hades was doing, he was still blocking their communication with their goddess. It might be months before she'd notice unless she needed to be in contact with them for any reason. And Stavros rather thought she was giving the warriors and their women time to enjoy themselves and discover their new lives. No, the goddess would not contact them unless there was an emergency of some kind.

"Be well, my friend." Phoenix glanced toward his mate. "You will find your woman someday."

Stavros shook his head. "I cannot. For how can I get to know a woman without drawing Hades' attention to her? And if I can't get to know her, how will I discover if she is the one?" It was a dilemma he could see no way out of.

Phoenix clapped his hand on Stavros's shoulder. "Don't give up. You will know if the woman is the one." Phoenix placed his hand over his heart. "You will feel it here."

Stavros said nothing, and Phoenix left him to his thoughts. His friend was wrong. He couldn't allow himself to get close enough to any woman to discover if she was his mate. He'd seen enough death in his long life and now all he wanted was peace.

Lure of the Jaguar

Dedication

To all my wonderful readers. You're the best!

Chapter One

Stavros studied the woman as she crept through high grass. She was quieter than most of the people who crossed his path, more in tune with her surroundings. He was perched high in a cypress tree, his dense body hidden by the Spanish moss that covered the limbs. He flicked his tail lazily as the woman raised her camera, peered through the lens and took a series of pictures.

He had no idea who she was, but she'd been creeping around the bayou for several days now, and he'd taken to watching her. She was entertaining, something to break up the monotony of his days. It was easy to follow her in his animal form. As a black jaguar, he could easily climb trees and blend with the shadows.

He was careful not to get too close to her. He didn't want her to see him, not that it really mattered, he supposed. All she'd see was an elusive cat, one that wasn't supposed to exist in this part of the world. No, it was more that he couldn't allow himself to become attached to anyone. Ever.

Not with the threat from Hades looming over him. The god had shown himself a poor loser in the more than five-thousand-year-old war with the Lady of the Beasts and her seven immortal, shapeshifting warriors, of which Stavros was one. He and the others had survived a curse and a battle for their souls. Now they were safe. He was safe. But Hades was not done trying to get his revenge. The devious god had already attacked two human women that were close to the warriors.

Stavros wasn't going to give Hades the opportunity to hurt anyone else.

Thankfully, both women had been saved by his fellow warriors. Jessica Miller and Tilly Ledet had found themselves mated to Mordecai and Phoenix, respectively. That was fine for them. Stavros knew his friends had deep feelings for their mates.

But he was alone.

There was no woman waiting for him. No one he wished to share his immortality with. And that had been the price of saving the women's souls from Hades.

The woman below him straightened from her crouch, arched her back and stretched her arms over her head. She wasn't very big, maybe five-three or so, but she was all woman. The jeans she wore emphasized her generously curved hips, and the khaki-colored T-shirt she wore clung to her full breasts. The man stirred inside the jaguar, but he fought for control and held his animal form.

Her hair was black as midnight and she kept it confined in a thick braid, which hung halfway down her back. Her skin was tanned from being outside, and that made her blue eyes appear even more vivid.

In truth, he was fascinated with her. But he would never approach her. To do so would bring Hades' attention her way. Stavros had already spent way too much time observing her from afar. He made sure never to remain around her for long, spending much of his days and nights simply wandering the bayou.

As though sensing his scrutiny, she glanced up at the tree where he was perched. He froze, not moving an inch or twitching a whisker, confident that he was concealed from her view. Still, it was a reminder for him to be more cautious. She was alert in a way most hunters were, attuned to her environment. But then again, she was hunting. She simply used her camera instead of a gun to shoot her prey.

She looked away when an alligator bellowed in the distance. She nibbled on her bottom lip and, for a moment, he thought she might try to find the gator. Instead, she turned in the opposite direction. He gave a sigh of relief when he realized she was heading toward the cabin she was renting. He had no idea how much longer she would be staying in the area but hoped she would be leaving soon. It would be safer. For both of them.

He twitched his ears, listening to every sound around him, quickly sorting through and cataloging them. When he was certain he was alone, he made his way down the trunk of the tree. He landed on four paws, a silent wraith. He slipped through the tall grass, keeping low as he followed her to make sure she got home safely.

He didn't question why he did such a thing. It was as instinctual as breathing.

Antoinette Richards glanced over her shoulder but saw nothing on the path behind her. That didn't mean there wasn't something there. She'd been a wildlife photographer her entire life, starting when she got her first camera at the age of six and took a picture of the robins that ate from the family backyard birdfeeder. Since those early times, she'd progressed in her chosen career and traveled all around the world for her art.

If there was one thing she'd learned over the years, it was to trust her instincts. And right now, they were telling here there was something out there watching her.

She wondered if it was the huge panther she'd caught sight of several times over the past few days. She'd seen the tip of a tail, a flash of a body concealed in the foliage and one partial track in the dirt. Technically, the term panther wasn't even correct, even though it was used by many local people to describe cougars.

Whatever it was, it wasn't a cougar, it was big and it wasn't native to the area. She kept hoping she'd be able to catch whatever it was on film so she could finally figure out exactly what kind of cat it was.

She turned her attention back to the path before her and carefully placed her feet to do as minimal damage to the ecosystem as possible. She was respectful of the environments she worked in, knowing many of them were sensitive to any intrusion by mankind. But she did pick up her pace.

She hitched her camera bag higher on her shoulder and tried to contain her burgeoning excitement. The trip this morning had yielded her some spectacular shots. There was one of a bullfrog sitting on a log next to a colorful wildflower that was a sure winner, and another of a delicate butterfly perched on a blackened tree limb sticking out of the swamp. She'd also captured shots of several species of birds, a couple of small snakes and even a turtle. She'd have to research to find out the exact types of snake and bird, but she didn't feel they were anything rare. More indigenous to the area.

Toni swallowed her disappointment at not crossing paths with the more elusive black bear or cougar, but there was still time for her to capture their images. She had three more days here in Louisiana before she headed back to Maine, where she made her home and based her business.

The small house came into view. It wasn't much, but it was cheap and it gave her a roof over her head and a place to sleep. It also had a full bath. All in all, it was a heck of a lot better than some of the places she'd stayed in over the years. It sure beat camping out.

Toni quickened her steps, eager to see the images she'd captured on her computer screen. She made a good living selling her work to wildlife magazines, and some of her less-than-perfect shots were sold online as stock photos. But it was her art photography that was the heart and soul of her business. Those rare, elusive images that struck a chord in the hearts of people who saw them.

She hurried up the rickety steps and dug the key out of her pocket. When the door opened, she stepped inside and peered back out into the overgrown yard. The sun was almost at its peak and she squinted against the glare.

Was there something moving out there?

She raised her camera, the gesture automatic. Peering through the lens, she panned the area and studied it carefully. Nothing. Toni slowly lowered the camera and sighed. "You're imagining things." But she knew she wasn't. Whatever animal was out there didn't want to be seen. She shivered at the thought of a cougar stalking her. She wasn't sure if it was from fear or excitement or a combination of both.

There were photos waiting to be viewed and she was starving. Her stomach chose that moment to growl and remind her she'd skipped breakfast to get outside just in time to shoot dawn rising over the bayou. She'd gotten some spectacular shots of birds taking off from the water. She really should get something to eat. Even more than that, she needed to drink. She'd taken one bottle of water with her this morning, but it was long gone. It was easy to become dehydrated in the Louisiana summer heat.

"Crap." She dumped her bag, hurried to the kitchen, yanked open the refrigerator and pulled out a bottle of water. She tucked it under her arm and grabbed a granola bar from the box she'd left on the kitchen counter. Booty in hand, she hurried back out the open door and sat on the porch step.

If there was something out there, she wanted a shot of it. Black leopards were occasionally reported in the area, even though they weren't supposed to exist here. Toni had visited South America a few years ago and captured a stunning black jaguar on film. She'd blown up the image and it hung in her bedroom at home in Maine. The creature had been huge and majestic and had captured her heart with its primitive, deadly beauty.

With her camera slung around her neck, she twisted open the water and had a swallow. The cold was soothing and refreshing. She set the bottle next to her, tore open the granola bar and had a bite. It wasn't exactly tasty, but it did fill a hole.

She promised herself she'd cook something better later. Her stomach protested, having heard that promise too many times before to actually believe it. She wolfed down the bar and stuffed the wrapper in her back pocket to dispose of later.

Toni picked up her camera again and peered through the lens. Whatever was out there, she'd see it as long as she was patient. Plus, she was close enough to the house that if it were a bear or a cougar, she could get inside to safety if it became necessary. She didn't think it would. She'd learned over the years of trekking around the world that most animals would leave you alone if you stayed out of their way.

The only exception to that rule was humans. And she'd had more than her fair share of run-ins with nasty two-legged creatures, which is why she always carried a weapon. Of course, her gun was in her tote bag in her bedroom. She hadn't anticipated needing it. And she should have.

She, better than most, knew just because an area seemed isolated, didn't mean it was. Plus, the sparsely populated bayou was the perfect place to run drugs and moonshine.

Her instincts were telling her it was a four-legged creature out there. Still, it wouldn't hurt to be prepared. She slowly climbed to her feet and hurried inside to grab her weapon. And while her back was turned, she missed seeing the black jaguar melt into the surrounding woods.

Hades leaned back in his chair and studied the scene in the mirror. He absently tapped his index finger against his jaw as he contemplated what he'd just seen. This was his last chance at revenge against the Lady of the Beasts and her warriors. And damn, the jaguar was being stubborn. He'd removed himself from the city and was now living isolated in the bayou. The rest of the warriors had found and mated with human women of their choice. Hades still couldn't understand why they would share their immortality with a mere human female. His goal in life was to gain power, not give it up.

Still, there was something there. Otherwise, why would the jaguar spend so much time watching the woman? He cocked his head to one side and let the information flow into him—Antoinette Richards. That was her name.

The mirror went black and Hades bit back a curse. He hated the fact that the enchanted mirror only allowed him a single hour in a twenty-four-hour span to view any world beyond his own realm. And he was trapped in Hell at the moment, compliments of his brothers, and all because he'd sought to take over the world.

Really, Zeus and Poseidon should be impressed with his efforts. It's not as though they concerned themselves with the humans. But they didn't like the idea of him having more power than them. Damn them.

Still, Hades had options. He might not be able to leave his domain, but he had plenty of demons who could. And they were expendable. He'd killed hundreds of them since his release from his prison. Their life force gave him a minor boost of power, but it was fleeting and nothing compared to what he'd had before the Lady of the Beasts had drained him.

"Damn female," he muttered, wishing he could wrap his fingers around the slender neck of the goddess who'd bested him. It was inexcusable, especially since he'd kept her imprisoned for five-thousand years. She should have been weak, unable to escape his realm. That she'd not only beaten him but also tricked him into freeing her warriors was a sore spot that demanded restitution.

"Who are you talking about? Or should I ask?" The feminine voice sank into his pores like a caress.

He should have known she'd be around. She'd been keeping a close eye on him since she'd convinced Zeus to free him from prison. He turned his gaze toward the door and studied his ex-wife, the beautiful Persephone. Even now, his fingers itched to touch her alabaster skin. She was wearing jeans and an emerald-green blouse. He narrowed his eyes and his cock swelled when he realized she wasn't wearing a bra beneath the silky material. Beneath his gaze, her nipples pebbled.

Sexual attraction had never been their problem. Ethics, or rather his lack of them, had been.

"What are you doing here, Persephone?" He stood and adjusted the cuffs of his hand-tailored linen shirt, tugging them to just below the sleeves of his Armani suit.

She shrugged and wandered around the room. She ran her finger over the edge of a gilt frame that hung on the wall. Hades barely noticed the masterpiece by Da Vinci set in the frame. All he could see was the tip of her finger rubbing against the wood. He wanted that finger and the rest of them running over his body.

His cock jerked, reminding him of how much he still wanted her, and his temper flared. "I didn't invite you here." His voice was deep, his tone cutting.

"I didn't think I needed an invitation." She walked toward him, swaying her hips seductively.

"You're not mistress here anymore," he reminded her. It cut him to his core that she'd walked away from him, left him. His home, once his pride and joy, hadn't felt the same since.

Sadness flickered in her eyes for a moment before it disappeared, and Persephone turned away. "I'll leave you alone then."

His eyes were glued to the sway of her behind and the proud bearing of her shoulders. He almost called her back. Instead, he fisted his hands by his sides and reminded himself that she'd left him. It had been her choice.

Damn the woman. Why did she always leave him feeling inadequate? He hated that particular emotion more than any other.

She disappeared, leaving him feeling bereft. He growled, hating any sign of weakness.

Hades glanced toward the darkened mirror. He would have his revenge, and then he would grow strong again. He didn't need the warriors or the power of the Lady of the Beasts to gain control of the Earth. There was more than one way to accomplish his goal of world domination.

But first, he had to deal with the last warrior. If he could take some minor revenge against Stavros, he'd finally be able to put this episode behind him and forget the warriors and their goddess ever existed.

It couldn't happen fast enough to suit him, which is why he needed help. There were plenty of greedy, devious humans who were only too willing to do his bidding in exchange for a favor.

He put Persephone out of his mind, which was much harder to do than it should have been. He was done with her. He didn't need her. He didn't need anyone.

Hades yelled for one of his demons. The scaly creature immediately raced into the room and cowered before him. The male demon was smaller than most, but his mind was cunning. Although he would never admit it, Hades missed Mordecai, the sneaky serpent who'd infiltrated his domain in order to help his fellow warriors escape Hades' wrath. The immortal warrior had been intelligent and brutal, a combination he admired. He also hadn't had to have everything spelled out to him. Mordecai had always seemed to understand what Hades had wanted before he'd even wanted it.

Persephone had been like that too. But she'd concerned herself with seeing to his home and his happiness.

Hades began to pace, momentarily forgetting the demon standing before him. He didn't need happiness. He needed power. But more than that, he needed revenge.

He stopped and faced his demon. "This is what I want you to do."

Chapter Two

Stavros knew he really should leave the area, maybe go back to New Orleans for a while. Or he could easily transport himself to South America in the blink of an eye now that all his power had been restored. But he couldn't make himself leave her. He didn't even know the woman's name, but it didn't matter. There was something about her that drew him. Watching her work was a pleasure. She lost herself in her surroundings, heedless of her own safety, intent only on getting the picture she wanted.

Obviously, it wasn't safe to leave her on her own. Someone had to look out for her.

He stepped out onto the porch of his temporary home, thankful once again that Sabrina, the woman mated to his fellow warrior Arand, was allowing him to stay at her granny's home in the bayou. It was isolated and he could run free as both a man and a jaguar. Best of all, he was alone. As much as he'd enjoyed living in a city as vibrant as New Orleans, he craved the solitude of nature.

Naked, he stretched his arms over his head and enjoyed the pull and flex of muscles and bones. He'd lived all over the world, seen places that no human ever had, but he'd never had a home, never settled down. His fellow warriors had finally put down roots with their mates. Stavros feared he'd wander forever.

He shook off the melancholy thought and simply enjoyed the warmth of the sun and the warm breeze brushing against his bare skin. After thousands of years in captivity, Stavros found great pleasure in the simple things in life. And being able to stand outside on a beautiful summer morning and soak in the sunshine was one of them.

A tree branch rustled, and he turned to face his unseen foe. There was someone out there. He cursed himself for becoming lax. Not that he needed to worry. He could disappear in the blink of an eye if he had to, but he hated the idea of anyone disturbing this precious moment.

He raised his head and sniffed the air. He cursed again, but for an entirely different reason. He recognized the clean scent of soap tinged with a hint of lemons combined with the sweet perfume of woman. One specific woman. It was her, his mystery woman.

"Who's there? Show yourself," he commanded. He reached for his jeans that were thrown over the railing and pulled them on. "I know you're out there." He carefully pulled up the zipper over his semi-aroused dick. "Don't make me come out there." Now that she was this close, he wanted to meet her.

Toni swallowed heavily and stared at the half-naked man, grateful that he'd put on a pair of jeans. Although the way the worn denim clung to his legs and butt left nothing up to her imagination.

She fanned her hand in front of her face. She was hot and sweaty and not just due to the early morning heat. No, it was the man standing on the back porch of the tidy little house that was making her skin tingle and her clothing feel too tight.

Toni had had no idea she had a neighbor this close by. This was the first time she'd walked in this direction. She'd planned on ignoring whoever lived there if possible, but then she'd seen him standing there, wearing nothing more than the morning sunshine, and she'd been frozen in place.

The man was a god. He was tall and broad shouldered, with a thick chest and lean hips. His body was sculpted with muscle, without a hint of body fat to soften his appearance. Hair as black as midnight hung in a silky curtain to his shoulders. His features were rugged and she'd automatically brought her camera up and clicked off a few pictures. She knew she'd never show the shots to another person. These were for her personal collection.

When he spoke, his voice was a deep rumble that made her nipples pucker and her pussy clench. What was wrong with her? She never had this kind of reaction to a man. Yes, he was handsome. Okay, so he was drop-dead gorgeous. But he was still just a man.

"Don't make me come out there." There was enough of a threat in those words to make her bristle. She thought about running but had no doubt he'd catch her. Not only were his legs longer than hers, there was something about him, something primal and fierce, that told her he would find her no matter where she hid.

Taking the bull by the horns, Toni stepped out of the woods and into the small yard. She had her cell phone in her pocket and her gun tucked into the outside pocket of her camera bag. She was safe enough.

He came down the two steps until he stood in the yard, his bare feet planted on the warm ground. Hands on his hips, he studied her. And she stared right back. Up close, he was even more devastating to her senses.

And his eyes. Dear Lord, his eyes were dark, fathomless depths. She could get lost in them. There was such sorrow residing there. She found herself wondering what he'd been through in his life.

Realizing she was staring, she straightened her shoulders and introduced herself. "I'm Antoinette Richards. Toni. I'm staying at the house about a half mile that way." She pointed back the way she'd come.

The stranger took a step closer. "Toni." The way he said her name made her shiver. She bit her bottom lip to keep from moaning aloud. What was wrong with her? She'd never had such a visceral reaction to a man before.

"I'm taking pictures." She held up her camera and then wanted to groan. Of course she was taking pictures. Any idiot could see the camera hung around her neck and the bag slung over her shoulder.

"And you are?" she asked.

"Stavros." He took another step forward, his feet not making any sound. There was an alertness about him that reminded her of a wild animal. And the way he moved—so fluid and with clear intent—was so much like a wild cat, a leopard or tiger.

Get a grip, Toni. She took a deep breath, realizing she'd been holding hers for too long. She sucked in some air and dug her fingers into her camera strap to ground her.

"Nice to meet you." She was proud of the fact her voice sounded steady when her insides were jittery and her knees were like jelly. Stavros wasn't a local name, nor was his accent Cajun. She wondered where he was originally from.

"You shouldn't be here." He frowned, flattening his dark brows into a straight line. His jaw tightened and she could see the steady beat of his pulse in the vein in his neck.

Toni was struck with a sudden urge to run her tongue up that vein, to stroke her hands over his tanned skin and rub her breasts over his naked chest. And then his words sank in and she frowned.

"I didn't mean to trespass." A lot of folks who lived out here weren't friendly to strangers. She understood and respected that. But he was the one who'd asked her to come forward. She would have just gone on her way if he'd left her alone. "I'll be going."

She swung around to leave. The man might look like a god, but he had the manners of a troll. Too bad.

"Wait."

She paused and glanced over her shoulder. He was still standing in the same spot, raking his fingers through the thick mass of his hair. It looked so soft she wanted to touch it, which was really stupid. The guy obviously wanted her gone.

"What?" she asked.

He sighed. "It's not safe for you to be out here alone."

Toni studied him intently. Was he for real? When his frowned deepened, she realized he was dead serious. She found herself smiling, unable to stay irritated with him. "I'm perfectly fine. I've worked all over the world and never had any trouble."

Not quite true. There'd been that little problem with a Bedouin tribe... But she'd gotten out of that situation just fine. She was home in the United

States of America, not in some war-ravaged country. "I'm perfectly safe," she promised him.

He cursed under his breath, and while she couldn't quite hear what he said, there was no mistaking it for anything but cussing. He turned away and stalked up the stairs and into the house, leaving her standing there alone.

Toni couldn't leave if she wanted to. Her eyes were glued to the incredibly lifelike tattoo that covered his entire back until he disappeared inside. It was a black jaguar. The creature snarled at her as Stavros walked away. Wow. Whoever had inked that was a hell of an artist. And it must have taken a long time to get a tattoo that detailed done.

And every hour of his pain was worth it. The jaguar was a work of art. So lifelike she wanted to reach out and stroke it. In fact, she'd raised her hand to do just that.

Toni quickly pulled her hand back to her side and turned away. Time to go. She'd spend a few hours shooting pictures. That would calm her racing heart. Or at least she hoped it would.

A part of her wanted to stay and see if Stavros came back out, and for that very reason, she made herself leave. As the bayou swallowed her up again, she muttered under her breath. "The last thing you need in your life is a man, especially a mysterious, dangerous one." There was no denying that he was dangerous. An air of menace, like he was ready to pounce any second, surrounded him.

No, Toni was better off on her own in the woods. It was safer with the gators than with Mr. Tall, Dark and Dangerous.

Stavros swore at himself as he grabbed a T-shirt and dragged it over his head and stuffed his feet into a pair of sneakers. He really should leave her alone. After all, she was only here for a short time and would soon be gone.

Toni. He had a name for her now, and that only made his attraction to her even more pronounced. The big cat inside him had stretched and purred the moment she'd come into view. She was better close up than she'd been from a distance.

There was such innate intelligence and pride in her gaze. Was there anything sexier than a self-assured woman? Not to him. She was small in stature but seemed larger because of her self-confidence. Her hair was pulled back in her customary braid, and he wanted to unwind it and see it spilling around her shoulders and down her back.

And her curves. Dear goddess, her curves. His hands ached to shape the fullness of her breasts, the slope of her hips and the roundness of her ass. Toni was all woman.

He ignored his erection, which was throbbing incessantly behind the zipper of his jeans and prowled back toward the door. As he'd suspected, she was gone.

He should just let her go. Just close the door and forget about her.

Stavros was down the steps and across the yard in a heartbeat. He cocked his head to one side and listened. Although she was quiet, he could easily hear her creeping through the trees. He took a deep breath and followed her.

There was no reason to think Hades was watching him. After all, it had been weeks since the god had attacked Jessica and Tilly. Perhaps Hades was truly done with him and his fellow warriors.

Stavros glanced over his shoulder and sniffed the air. Nothing but trees around him and marshy ground beneath his sneakers. As always, the world was alive with the music of the bayou. Grasshoppers chirped, insects buzzed and birds sang. There was nothing here that shouldn't be here, other than Toni and himself.

Quickening his pace, he hurried after her. He realized he was smiling and a sense of anticipation hummed inside him. Stavros was hunting for the first time in years. Not to kill, but to protect.

He no longer questioned the instinct. It was simply a part of him. Just like breathing.

Toni needed his protection. It was his job to make certain nothing bad happened to her while she was here. He wanted her in his sights and picked up his pace.

He stopped when he caught a glimpse of her crouched down on the spongy moss near the edge of the swamp. She held her camera to her face and he heard the muted clicking noise as she took several pictures in quick succession. He narrowed his eyes and saw the large gator sliding through the water only a few feet away from her.

Damn the woman. Did she have any idea how dangerous that was? How fast the gator could move?

Stavros rushed forward, grabbed her around the waist and dragged her away from the water's edge. "What in the name of the goddess are you doing?" He didn't mean to roar at her, but wasn't able to stop himself. All his primal instincts were on overdrive when it came to Toni Richards.

Toni whirled on her attacker and struck out, her right fist flying. She cursed when she realized who it was and tried to pull her punch. Not that she needed to. Stavros caught her hand easily. Instead of knocking it away, he grabbed it and pulled her closer. She landed against his solid chest with a thud.

Thankfully, her camera was secured around her neck with a thick strap, and she hadn't dropped it during the altercation. The expensive piece of equipment hung down her back, undamaged.

"What in the hell are you doing?" All her emotions were bubbling close to the surface—fear, anger and arousal.

"Saving you from yourself," he shot back.

She tried to pull away from him, but Stavros only tightened his hold on her and slid one muscled arm around her back, pinning her against him. She glared at him, but he seemed unmoved by her anger.

"I didn't need saving." She thumped her fist against his chest to make her point. She didn't worry about actually hurting him. The man had muscles on his muscles.

"That's a matter of opinion." A lock of dark hair fell across his forehead and his eyes seemed to grow even darker the longer he stared down at her. He swore in a language she'd never heard before and then lowered his head and kissed her.

Toni lost all sense of place and time when his lips touched hers. They were firm and soft and teased a path across her mouth. She moaned and he slipped his tongue inside. Her entire body clenched and her insides turned molten.

She'd been kissed many times in her life, but never had she experienced anything this hot and mind-numbing. Stavros explored her mouth, taking his time as he mapped the moist, dark landscape. Then he coaxed her tongue into his mouth and sucked on it.

She went up on her toes, trying to get closer to him. She wrapped her arms around his neck and held him close as she kissed him back. Heat enveloped her. Her breasts ached and her pussy throbbed. It took every ounce of restraint she still possessed not to rub herself against him.

And there was no doubt in her mind that he wanted her as much as she did him. His cock was hard and thick and pressed firmly against her stomach. She slid one hand beneath the hem of his shirt and found smooth, hot skin. Toni inhaled deeply, drinking in his male scent, a combination of the earthy tones of the woods and hot male.

He coasted his hands down her back to her butt. He cupped the curve of her ass and pulled her more firmly against his body. When he lifted her slightly, her mound aligned with his erection.

He tore his mouth from hers. "Let's go back to your place."

His words brought her back down to earth with a heavy thud. What was she doing? It was a lot more difficult than it should have been, but she pressed her hands against his shoulders and pushed. "Let me go."

Stavros immediately released her and took a step back. She wasn't sure if she was impressed by his control or pissed off because she felt entirely out of control. She straightened her top and ignored the fact that she could still feel the heat from his hands on her behind.

"That shouldn't have happened," she told him.

He tilted his head to one side and studied her. "Yes, it should have."

The man was too cocky for his own good. "Listen, buddy, I'm not looking for a vacation fling." Too many men made the mistake of thinking because she was alone she must want or need a man.

Stavros reached out and tenderly traced the curve of her jaw. She shuddered before she got her unruly body back under control. Really, it wasn't fair. The man touched her and she lost all control, forgot the rules she lived by, the biggest of which was no men while she was on a shoot.

"Whatever this is, it's not a fling." His deep voice penetrated her skin and sank into her cells. She wanted to melt into a puddle at his feet and that just pissed her off.

She turned away and his hand fell back to his side. "Whatever it is, I don't want any part of it." There, that was decisive and assertive.

"Liar." His soft taunt made her glare at him.

"Okay." She decided to go with total honesty. "I want you, but I'm not going to do anything about it." Toni tugged her camera around to the front and reached down to pick up the camera bag she'd set aside when she was shooting the gator. She tugged the strap over her shoulder and settled the bag comfortably against her.

Work, that's what she was good at. Not relationships. Most men didn't understand her need to travel to remote places around the world. Nor did they understand her need to be around nature. She liked big cities as much as the next person, but her soul craved the wide open spaces.

She understood the animals whose images she captured more than she understood most people.

Stavros didn't seem angry with her bluntness. No, his lips twitched upward. The man seemed amused. And that just pissed her off even more.

She turned and headed back toward her cabin. The faster she got away from Mr. Tall, Dark and Dangerous, the better.

She hurried through the woods, listening hard for any sound to indicate he was following her. Disappointment struck her hard when she heard only silence. Had she wanted him to come after her?

Toni shook her head. That wasn't like her at all. She didn't play those kinds of games with men.

She glanced over her shoulder and stumbled. She would have fallen flat on her face if Stavros hadn't grabbed her by the shoulders and pulled her upright. Angry at being clumsy and ridiculously pleased to see him, she verbally attacked. "Why are you following me?"

Stavros shrugged his broad shoulders. The almost lazy motion pulled the material taut over his chest. She knew what was beneath that thin cotton T-shirt, had seen his spectacular muscles up close. The man was too distracting for her good.

"You need someone to watch over you." His voice seemed to vibrate deep in her soul.

"I don't need anyone," she shot back. She'd always been a loner. The only child of older parents, she'd spent much of her childhood playing by herself. Not that her parents hadn't loved her, but parenthood had been more demanding than they'd imagined, and they'd been happy enough to leave her to her own devices. They were currently on a trip around the world, and she occasionally got postcards from them. She talked to them on birthdays and at Christmas, but other than that, they lived separate lives.

He just cocked one eyebrow as if to question her statement.

Toni stomped away, leaving him to follow or not. She was going to work. He'd get bored soon enough when she lost herself in her photography. People always did. They didn't understand her fascination with capturing a perfect moment in time. She'd sit still for hours waiting for the image she wanted.

No, he'd lose interest and leave her alone sooner rather than later.

And, inexplicably, that made Toni sad. Not that she wanted him to stay with her. Of course she didn't. But it occurred to her that it might be nice to have some company.

Chapter Three

Stavros leaned against the trunk of a fallen tree and watched Toni work. She wasn't like most humans. There was a depth of patience within her that rivaled the greatest warrior. She'd sat unmoving for the past three hours, staring intently at the tiny clearing in front of them. A variety of birds had come and gone, and even a deer had made a brief appearance.

The only sound that came from her direction was the slight whirr of the camera as she took picture after picture. The sun was high in the sky and Stavros squinted up at it. It was early afternoon, but Toni didn't seem like she was getting ready to take a break anytime soon. Not that he minded. He was enjoying the view.

He smiled as she shifted ever so slightly to the right and leaned forward to take a shot. He looked in the direction she was aimed toward and saw the flick of a yellow tail. Stavros took a deep breath and caught the scent of the big cat. Yes, that was a cougar.

Toni was practically quivering with excitement even though her body remained still. He was glad he was with her. She could take pictures to her heart's content and not have to worry about the cougar bothering her. Not with him here.

He scowled when he imaged her out here all alone, which she would have been if he hadn't followed her. Still, he knew better than to say anything about that. He was quickly learning that Toni was very independent. He knew what it was like to be caged, and he wouldn't do that to another person.

The big cat stretched in the afternoon heat and then settled in beneath the shade of a tree on the edge of the clearing. The creature was obviously waiting for game to show while it kept itself cool in the afternoon heat.

Toni moved an inch at a time, slowly repositioning herself for a better shot. He had no idea how many she took before she settled back to wait. They passed nearly an hour that way until the cougar grew tired of waiting. The cat stood and stretched before it sauntered off.

Even though he watched the cat out of the corner of his eye, most of his attention was on Toni. Once again, she took picture after picture, stopping only when the cougar was completely out of sight.

She turned and smiled at him, and his heart stopped beating for a suspended moment in time before it began to race. Something inside him shifted and clicked into place.

No, this couldn't be happening. Not to him. Not now.

She must have sensed something was wrong, because Toni's smile slowly disappeared. "What is it? What's wrong?"

Stavros couldn't tell her. What could he say? I'm an immortal shapeshifting warrior and you're my mate. That would go over well. Not.

There was no time for her to get to know him. No way to make her understand who and what he was. And if Hades ever caught a whiff of his feelings for Toni, he'd be after her in a second.

Stavros glanced around and cursed himself for a fool. His being near was endangering her. He'd given in to his own wants and needs and disregarded her safety. He knew better.

Hades might not be here now, but there was no telling when the god might be watching. Stavros knew what he had to do.

He slowly stood, turned and walked away from Toni without a word. It was the hardest thing he'd ever done. His jaguar was growling at him, not pleased at all. The animal part of his nature wanted to go back, scoop Toni up and carry her somewhere where he could make love to her and protect her from all harm.

But that was nothing more than a fantasy. A dream that could never be.

"Stavros?" He hesitated when he heard her call out to him. Cursing himself for a fool, he turned and looked at her one more time. She was standing in the path with the sunshine spotlighting her. Her hands still gripped her camera and she was frowning at him. Her blue eyes were filled with questions he couldn't answer.

Stavros turned and walked away. Agony ripped through him. It felt as though he'd torn out his heart and left it on the path behind him.

If he thought for one second he could make her fall in love and agree to spend eternity with him before Hades discovered her, he wouldn't hesitate. But her safety was more important than anything else. And if he had to walk away to save her, that's exactly what he'd do.

The darkness swallowed him. Once again, Stavros was alone. A single tear trickled down his cheek. He ignored it and kept going.

Toni didn't understand what had just happened. Stavros had sat quietly next to her for hours. She'd felt his gaze on her as she'd worked. His quiet presence had made something cold and hard inside her crumble away.

She'd begun to trust him. To believe that he understood her in a way no one else ever had.

She rubbed her chest. Her heart ached and she had only herself to blame. She knew better than to allow anyone to get close. But it had been so easy with Stavros. There was something about him that called to her in the same way the most elusive animals on the planet did.

"Stupid," she muttered. "He's just a hot-looking guy. Nothing more." She forced herself to look away from the path between the trees that had swallowed Stavros up, taking him from her sight. She was alone. "And that's the way I like it," she reminded herself.

Her earlier pleasure over capturing the cougar was gone, and that pissed her off. This was what her entire trip had been about, and Stavros had stolen her happiness. No, even worse, she'd allowed him to take it.

"Suck it up, Toni." She looked around to make sure she had all her gear before heading back toward her cabin. She needed a shower after sweating for hours in the hot afternoon sun, and she desperately needed something to eat. Usually, she couldn't wait to see the images she'd captured, but that sense of urgency was missing as she made her way back to her rental unit.

She stopped at the edge of the clearing by the house and waited until she was certain no one was around. No matter what else was happening in her life, Toni was always safety conscious. When she was convinced she was alone, she hurried to the house, let herself in and locked the door behind her.

Toni realized she was feeling slightly spooked, like something or someone was following her. She set her bag and camera down on the kitchen table, which she'd turned into a large workspace, and peered out the window. Nothing.

She took a deep breath and slowly released it. There was nothing to worry about. She was just out of sorts because of Stavros. The man certainly blew hot and cold. One minute, he was kissing her socks off, and the next, walking away like she didn't matter at all. She was better off without him.

Toni kicked off her shoes and headed to the small bathroom to shower. It didn't take her long to wash away the day's sweat, dry off and dress in clean clothes. She didn't linger. Now that she was home, she was eager to see her pictures.

Still, she made herself a bowl of cereal before removing the memory card from her camera and sliding it into her laptop. She had several more memory cards in her camera bag but was eager to see the shots of the cougar.

Her cereal grew soggy in the bowl and the sun sank in the west as Toni went through the photos one at a time. There was one in particular that caught her attention, and she went back to it again and again.

The cougar was relaxed but alert. You could tell he was ready to explode at a moment's notice. The predator was at rest, but the hunter was poised to kill. It was primal and raised goose bumps on her arms. This was the money shot. She knew it with all her heart and soul.

Toni swallowed hard when she realized who the cougar reminded her of. Stavros. He'd reclined against the fallen tree much like the cougar had lazed in the shade. And like the mighty cat, there was a sense of alertness, of preparedness about Stavros. He was a predator, like the cougar.

"Shit." Toni pushed away from the table and began to pace, almost bumping into a chair. She blinked and glanced out the window. "When did it get dark?" Once again, she'd lost herself in her work.

She made a face at the soggy cereal. No way was she eating that. Looked like it was a sandwich once again. She had some shaved turkey and a tomato she could slice to make it a little more substantial.

Yet she didn't head toward the refrigerator. The short hairs on the back of her neck rose. Not questioning her reaction, Toni pulled on her shoes and went to her camera bag. She unzipped the side pocket and drew out her weapon. The gun was heavy in her hand, and she prayed she wouldn't have to use it.

She closed her laptop, the only source of light in the cabin, and crept over to the living room window. She stood there and waited for what seemed like forever. And just when she was beginning to think she was imagining things, she saw movement on the edge of the clearing where the yard gave way to the edge of the bayou.

Stavros. Her heart skipped a beat when she thought it might be him.

Then she saw another movement. And another.

Toni swallowed the lump in her throat. Her heart began to race. Whoever was out there, it wasn't Stavros. Maybe it was nothing, but three men skulking in the woods was never a good sign. She reached into her back pocket for her cell phone. She swore when she saw the battery was dead. She'd forgotten to charge it. Again.

Toni gripped her weapon and wished Stavros was with her. She might not know him that well, but she knew in her heart he was one of the good guys and would protect her.

But like most critical times in her life—good and bad—Toni was alone.

Stavros cocked his head to one side and listened. He was in his jaguar form, stalking through the night, trying to outrun his need to go to Toni. He chuffed and listened harder. The night was unusually quiet. The insects had gone still, the owl had stopped hooting and the opossum two-hundred yards to his right was frozen in place. They all sensed something.

A chill of fear raced down his spine.

Stavros frowned. It wasn't his fear he was feeling.

Toni.

It struck him like a lightning bolt. It wasn't his fear he was sensing, it was hers. He didn't question his instincts. The connection he'd felt with her earlier was strong. Whatever was happening at this moment, Toni was afraid. He yowled, his cry sending a flock of egrets into flight.

Stavros raced toward the house where Toni was staying, praying to the goddess that he wasn't too late. He should have been with her. In trying to be noble, he might have hurt her even more. If she died and he discovered Hades was responsible, he'd descend into Hell itself and kill the conniving god once and for all or die trying.

Toni crept into the bedroom. Her plan was to sneak out the window and hide in the bayou until those men were gone. She'd taken precious seconds to grab her memory cards and tuck them in her pocket. As much as it pained her to do so, she left her cameras and laptop behind. She could always replace her equipment. Her work, on the other hand, was irreplaceable. Her gun was tucked in the waistband of her jeans.

She pushed at the windowpane and swore when it stuck. She bent her knees and shoved with all her might. The window went up three inches, but not without making a loud creaking sound. She held her breath and waited. When there was no shout of discovery, she pushed again. The glass rose until it was about halfway open and then stopped.

It would have to be enough.

Toni threw one leg over the edge of the window and squeezed her body through the opening, thankful for once that she wasn't all that big. She crouched by the side of the house and made herself as small as possible. Then she listened.

She didn't hear anything at first. The night was quiet. Too quiet. The bayou was always alive with sound. Now it was still, the air heavy. A bead of sweat rolled down her back.

"Are you sure this is the place?"

Toni stilled at the whisper only a few feet away from her. She scrunched lower and kept her breathing shallow and light.

"That's what he said," answered another man.

He? Who was *he*? The only one she knew around here was Stavros, and he wasn't the kind of man to send someone skulking around a woman's home.

"Quiet." This voice was lower, more ominous. "We need to get her and get out."

Toni's blood ran cold. Did they mean to kidnap her or kill her?

"Why does he have such a hard-on for this photographer chick?" the first man asked.

There went the idea that this was a case of mistaken identity. As far as she knew, she was the only photographer chick in the neighborhood. The men moved off to the side of the house and Toni crept to the corner, careful where she put her feet. The last thing she wanted to do was make a sound and alert them to her presence.

"Don't know and don't care." This came from the last man, the one who seemed to be in charge. "Our job is to deliver her to him." She couldn't see any of them well, but this man was larger than the other two. "I don't want him coming after me."

Crap. Her would-be kidnappers were afraid of this mysterious man. That wasn't good. Toni had no idea who would be after her or what she'd done to gain the attention of such a dangerous person. Not that it mattered. Not now. The only thing she had to concern herself with at the moment was getting away.

If she made it to the woods, she could hide until morning and then make a run for her car. If they were still here in the morning, she could walk to the nearest gas station, which was about ten miles away. She couldn't even go to any of the neighbors for help. She had no way of knowing if one of these men was her neighbor.

Stavros popped in her head again, but she immediately dismissed him. She wouldn't go to him for help. He'd walked away from her and was virtually a stranger anyway. For all she knew, he was behind this.

Even as she thought it, she knew that was wrong. Call it instinct. Call it foolish hope. She knew Stavros wouldn't hurt her.

Not that he wasn't dangerous, because he most certainly was. But not to her.

"I'll go around back," one of the men whispered.

She had to move. Now. If he came around the corner of the house, he'd see her. Toni came up out of her crouch and began to move as quickly and quietly as she could, heading toward a lone shrub about ten feet away. It wasn't much cover, but she didn't need it for long. As soon as the men entered the house, she was out of here.

She almost made it. Would have made it if it weren't for an errant rock. She tripped and stumbled forward, barely catching herself before she fell. But the noise alerted the men.

A flashlight beam spotlighted her and she blinked against the sudden glare.

"Over here," one of the men yelled.

Toni wasn't waiting around to find out which one of them had spotted her. She took off toward the woods, praying she wouldn't run into a tree and knock herself out cold. She had her hands out in front of her as she lurched over the uneven ground.

She was almost there when a blood-curdling yowl split the night.

Toni barely managed to avoid a tree. Grabbing the trunk, she held on to the scratchy bark, trying to orient herself. She heard a low growl that sent a shiver down her spine. It was a big cat, maybe even the cougar she'd seen earlier. And it was close.

Then she heard a man scream.

Stavros raced through the night at top speed. With his preternatural vision, he could see everything around him just as easily as he could in the daylight. He jumped over a fallen log without hesitation. He could smell the men now. Their bodies reeked of sweat and alcohol.

There was no doubt in his mind that Hades had sent them, but maybe he was wrong. Maybe they were drug dealers or running moonshine.

Whoever they were, they'd made the mistake of coming after his woman. Because whether she knew it or not, Toni was his.

His fear abated slightly when he caught a whiff of Toni's sweet scent. Even though it was overlaid with the stench of fear, there was no mistaking it was her.

She was outside the cabin, hiding among the trees.

He'd find her as soon as he dealt with these men. He growled and let it build into a fierce yowl.

One of the men screamed. Another whirled in a circle, and Stavros could see the gun in his hand. His anger turned cold inside him. These men had come to hurt Toni. He couldn't allow that.

"What is it?" one man asked.

"Cougar," the one with the gun replied.

"That doesn't sound like a cougar," the third man added. "I ain't stayin'". With that, the man started to run. The man with the gun calmly turned and shot his companion in the leg. The man fell to the ground and the scent of blood filled the air.

The man yelled and grabbed his leg. "I'm shot. Why the hell did you do that, Roy? Goddamn, that hurts. I'm bleeding like a stuck pig."

"It's only a flesh wound," Roy replied, seemingly unconcerned. "And we can't leave. Not without the woman."

"You didn't have to shoot me."

"Shut up, Paul. I could have killed you. You'll be fine."

"The blood will attract the cat," Paul protested.

"That's the idea," Roy replied. "When it shows itself, I'll kill it. Then we'll go get the girl."

Stavros watched as the unnamed man went to Paul, stripped off his shirt and wrapped it around the wound. They thought they were the hunters.

They were mistaken.

They were now the prey.

Chapter Four

Toni shivered in spite of the heat. It was a hot Louisiana summer night, but she was chilled to the bone. Her thin cotton T-shirt stuck to her skin with sweat. She wrapped her arms around herself, desperate for some warmth.

The man with the gun had shot one of his companions. And if he'd shoot his buddy, he'd have no problems killing her. She had to get out of here. But she didn't know where to go. Here there were three men, at least one of which had a gun. And out there in the bayou were poisonous snakes, gators and a very large predator.

At this point, Toni figured she'd be safer with the cougar, gators and snakes.

The air behind her stirred and, before she could move, a hand was slapped over her mouth. She threw her head back against her attacker to try to throw him off while she brought her gun around. The safety was still on and she flicked it off with her thumb. She'd never shot an actual person before—paper targets didn't count—but she knew she could do it if it meant her survival. She didn't even get close before her hand was captured in an iron grip.

"*Shh*. You're safe. It's me." His voice was little more than a toneless whisper.

His voice broke through her terror. Stavros. Somehow he was here with her. All the fight went out of her and she sagged against him like a balloon being deflated. He slowly released her hand but kept his palm over her mouth. After another second, he lowered that hand as well.

"What are you doing here?" she demanded. She kept her voice pitched low so the men wouldn't hear her. Toni tried to turn around and face him, but he grabbed her shoulders and applied just enough pressure so she couldn't move.

He pushed her down until she was crouched by the base of the tree. "Stay here," he ordered, not bothering to answer her question.

She bristled at the command, but before she could tell him she had no intention of staying anywhere he put her, he was gone. She blinked, unable to believe a man as large as Stavros could disappear so easily, blend so quickly with the surrounding night.

The darkness had thickened in the last while, the slice of moon cloaked by the clouds. She swallowed hard and peered through the trees. Where was Stavros? What was he doing?

He was crazy to take on those men by himself. They needed to call the local police.

She shifted her weight and realized she was no longer shivering. Nor did she feel quite so afraid. Not with Stavros here. She wasn't sure how she felt about that. She'd never depended on a man before. But these were extenuating circumstances.

Her legs cramped and she moved, shifting her position for a better view of the yard. The three men were still there. One was lying on the ground with another one next to him. The third man, the one with the gun, turned slowly from side-to-side, watching the woods.

It occurred to her this would be a good time to run. With the men worried about the cougar, they wouldn't be looking for her for the next while.

Stavros, the idiot, was out there with the wild cat and the gunmen. She didn't even know if he had a weapon or any way to defend himself. No way could she leave him. Her hand tightened around her weapon and she forced herself to relax her grip.

No, she couldn't leave Stavros. They were in this together.

She hunkered down to watch the small clearing, all the while cursing men in general and Stavros in particular.

Stavros was back in his jaguar form, sliding through the underbrush. The scent of blood filled his nostrils and he twitched his whiskers. The injured man might die from his wounds if they didn't get the bleeding stopped soon. Not that he cared. They'd come to hurt Toni.

"Do you see him, Roy?" Paul asked. He was sweating profusely now and blood continued to seep from his wound.

"No. Now shut up and let me listen." He swung his flashlight from side-to-side, sending its beam over the surrounding woods. Roy was nervous. Stavros could smell it. He had to take this man down first. He was the deadliest of the bunch, the most unpredictable.

Stavros launched himself from the shadows and leapt toward Roy, easily clearing twenty feet in one leap. He swiped at the gunman with his long, lethal claws. The gun in Roy's hand jerked and his shots went wide.

Roy screamed, but the terrified yell was quickly cut off when Stavros sliced through his jugular without a moment's remorse. Blood spurted from the wound and Roy fell to his knees and then backward, hitting the ground hard. The gun and flashlight dropped beside him. The flashlight rolled a couple of inches before stopping. The light created a pool of light around Roy, spotlighting his dead body.

The other two men yelled in terror as Stavros disappeared into the shadows and blended once again with the night. "What the hell was that?" Paul screamed.

The other man was crossing himself and praying. "That ain't no cougar. That thing was huge." He stumbled to his feet and backed away.

"Don't leave me here, Billy," Paul implored. "Help me." His friend ignored him and ran, leaving Paul to his fate.

Stavros circled around and caught the fleeing Billy as he abandoned his friend. The man pissed his pants when he caught his first glimpse of the massive jaguar. Stavros wrinkled his nose at the pungent smell. The man held his hands out in front of him as though he could ward off Stavros, but nothing could save him from the jaguar's wrath. Stavros raked his deadly claws across Billy's throat. The wounded man clutched his shredded neck and fell to the ground, gurgling out his last breaths.

Stavros turned his back on Billy and silently padded back to Paul, who was valiantly trying to pull himself toward Roy's body. Paul caught a glimpse of Stavros and whimpered as he dragged himself closer to the abandoned gun. Stavros beat him to the weapon and shoved it aside with one large paw. The illumination from the flashlight allowed the other man to see him perfectly.

He hunkered down next to Paul and stared at him, deliberately intimidating the man. He had questions and he wanted answers. He also didn't want to waste time with a lengthy interrogation.

Paul whimpered and Stavros began to shift, intentionally keeping the process slow to add to the man's terror. Paul was crying and calling out to his deity for help by the time Stavros was a man once again. Stavros could have warned him to save his breath. He suspected that Paul and his buddies had aligned themselves with a dark god who would never let them go.

They'd sealed their own fate.

"Who are you?" Paul asked. "What are you?" Tears ran down his face and snot ran from his nose.

"Who sent you?" Stavros asked. "And don't lie to me." He tapped the side of his nose. "I can smell a lie."

Toni was hyperventilating. She only realized that startling fact when her vision started to dim. That was no cougar in the clearing behind the house. The cat was enormous. Too huge to be real. Yet it was very real. And its coat was black.

Jaguar.

She'd caught a glimpse when the moon had momentarily peeked out from behind the clouds, and another when the large cat settled in front of the light from Roy's flashlight.

Impossible. Jaguars didn't exist in this part of the world. And, as far as she knew, there were none as gigantic as this one.

The animal made quick work of two of the men. Toni cringed, feeling pity in spite of the fact these men had come to harm her. Dying at the hands, or rather the claws, of a big cat was a hard way to go.

The animal prowled closer to the injured man, hunkering down in front of him. Toni was surprised the beast didn't just attack, especially because of the bloody wound on the man's leg.

Toni blinked when the animal began to change. She rubbed her eyes with her free hand, unable to believe what she was seeing. There was no longer a large cat in the clearing, but a man. And not just any man. Stavros.

And he was stark naked.

She swallowed hard. Okay, she'd either just gone on a bad drug trip—and she'd never done drugs in her life—or she was hallucinating. There was no other explanation for a giant jaguar to become a man.

Then she remembered the jaguar tattoo she'd seen on Stavros' back. That had to be it. Her mind was obviously manufacturing the connection. Toni pinched her arm and frowned when it hurt.

She was awake. Stavros was still in the clearing with the injured man. And he was still naked.

Had it been Stavros all along? Had she created the jaguar to protect her out of her imagination? Toni was too scared and confused to make sense of any of this.

"Who sent you?" Stavros asked. "And don't lie to me. I can smell a lie." It was his tone more than his words that sent a shiver down Toni's spine. Slowly, she came to her feet. The muscles in her legs protested after being in an uncomfortable position for so long. She inched closer to the men, unable to take her eyes away from the macabre scene unfolding before her. She kept her gaze averted from Roy's dead body.

"A guy. I don't know who he is," Paul hurriedly added. "Honest. He asks us to do stuff for him from time to time."

"And what do you get in return?" Stavros asked. His tone was calm, but Toni heard the underlying fury.

Paul shrugged and rubbed his hand across his face. He was trying to act tough, but even Toni could tell he was scared. His hands were noticeably shaking. "Money."

"Money." Stavros chuffed and it sounded exactly like a big cat.

Toni's chest was rapidly heaving and she forced herself to breathe in through her nose, hold it for a second and then slowly release it through her mouth.

"For that you'd kill a woman." Stavros raised his hand and it morphed into a giant black paw complete with razor-sharp claws.

Toni froze in place and blinked, but the image didn't change. Her breathing quickened again.

"No. He didn't want her dead. He just wanted her." The man clutched at his leg and tried to pull himself away.

"What does this man look like?" Stavros asked. He didn't move position, and his very stillness was intimidating. He was like a jaguar toying with his prey. Toni found the image unsettling.

Paul shrugged. "He didn't come himself this time. Sent another guy. Strange-looking dude. Spooky too."

"What does this mystery man look like?" Stavros asked once again.

"Tall, dark hair, good dresser. Always in a suit."

Stavros swore long and low. Toni had the feeling he knew who Paul was referring to. Was Stavros involved in what was happening to her?

Toni crept closer, needing to understand what was going on, why this mysterious man was targeting her. Stavros jerked his head in her direction. His nostrils flared and the clawed paw disappeared, replaced by a normal arm and hand in the blink of an eye.

Toni felt nauseous. Her skin was clammy. What was going on? The whole world had gone crazy.

"Are you going to kill me?" Paul asked. Toni was wondering the same thing. There was no doubt he was capable of it. Dressed, he was formidable. Naked, his true character was revealed. Stavros was a dangerous predator.

In spite of the seriousness of the situation, Toni's fingers itched to hold her camera, and she cursed the fates that she didn't have it when it was usually close at hand. The play of light and shadow on Stavros' skin made him look primal and fierce. All the muscles of his body were delineated to perfection. He was hunter and protector. With his hair flowing down around his shoulders and his square jaw tilted to the side, his face was masculinity personified. The images she could capture of Stavros would rival anything she'd ever done. No, scratch that, they would be the best work she'd ever do.

Stavros picked up Roy's gun and flowed to his feet, his movements fluid and smooth. He held the gun in front of him and Toni held her breath. "No. I'm going to let your boss do that when you don't deliver. And, trust me, by the time he's done with you, you'll wish I had killed you."

He turned and walked toward her, leaving Paul yelling after him.

Toni ignored the man and focused only on Stavros' face. He looked calm but determined. He stopped in front of her, reversed his hold on the gun and handed it to her. She took the weapon. It felt heavy in her hand. Roy would have used it on her if he'd had half a chance. "Go inside and pack up your things. It's no longer safe here."

Toni did her best to ignore the fact he wasn't wearing any clothing. "We need to call the police." That was the sensible thing to do.

Stavros shook his head. "The police can't help you. You're dealing with something beyond your wildest nightmare."

"But you can help me." It wasn't a question, but he answered her.

"I can." He tucked a lock of hair behind her ear. "I will. I won't let anyone hurt you."

"Who are you?" she whispered.

He shook his head, wrapped his arm around her shoulders and led her toward the house. She kept her gaze away from the two dead bodies as they made their way to the front door.

Paul groaned and called after them, begging them not to leave him. Toni stumbled, but Stavros kept her moving forward.

"It's locked," she told him. "I went out through the bedroom window."

Stavros raised his hand and she heard the locks unlatch. "Now it's open." He turned the handle and pushed the door open. The living room light came on by itself. She gasped and stood there, trying to process yet one more impossible thing.

"I'm going crazy," she muttered. "It's the only explanation."

"No." He placed his hands on her shoulders and squeezed. "Not crazy. Pack up your things and come with me. I'll explain everything once I have you safe."

She could do this. It wasn't like she had much choice. No way was she staying here with two dead bodies and an injured man outside. Still, she couldn't help but ask, "What about the guy in the yard?"

Stavros shrugged. "He has his cell phone if he wants to call for help. I don't think he'll contact the authorities. And I'll be surprised if there's a trace of any of them left here by morning."

Toni shivered, stepped inside and hurried into the bedroom. She carefully set both guns down on the bed before turning on the bedside lamp. She looked longingly at the bed. What she really wanted to do was crawl under the covers and pretend none of this had happened, but that wasn't an option.

Thankfully, she didn't have much stuff to pack. She was used to traveling light when she was on the road. It didn't take her long to stuff everything into her duffle bag and carefully place both weapons in an outside pocket. Then she went to the kitchen and packed up her laptop and cameras, placing them carefully into their protective cases.

When she was done, she rinsed off the few dirty dishes and set them in the drain tray on the counter. Then she threw what little food that remained into a box. Once she left here, she wasn't coming back, not for anything.

Stavros patiently waited while she worked, but there was a sense of anticipation, of readiness about him. Whatever was going on, it wasn't over. Not by a longshot.

"You're naked," she blurted. Heat crept up her cheeks and she knew she was blushing. But really, she couldn't ignore the elephant in the room any longer. Stavros was standing naked in the living room like it was no big deal.

And it was a plenty big deal. It was impossible for her not to notice. His hair flowed around his broad shoulders. And the man didn't have a six-pack. He had an eight-pack. She could easily see him gracing the cover of any magazine. And he'd never have to be airbrushed. He was perfection.

"Let's get out of here." He reached for her duffle and slung it over his shoulder. "We'll take your car. You won't be coming back here." Stavros lifted the box of food and tucked it under his arm. He raised one eyebrow in question when she hesitated.

Okay, so he was going to ignore the fact he was naked. If he could, then she could too. Toni took a deep breath and glanced around the room. Nothing of hers remained. She couldn't help but feel that her life had irrevocably changed. Whatever was going on, she needed to get to the bottom of it, needed to understand how her life had gone from normal to crazy in the span of a few hours.

And right now, Stavros was the key.

It might be smarter to run back to the city and catch a flight home to Maine, but deep in her gut, Toni knew the problem would only follow her.

No, as much as she might want to flee, she had to stand her ground and fight whatever storm was coming her way.

She squared her shoulders, slung her camera bag over her shoulder and grabbed her laptop bag. "I'm ready." She turned off the lights and strode past him. She paused on the porch long enough to lock the door before heading to her car.

The sedan she'd rented at the airport was still sitting where she'd parked it the day she'd arrived. Stavros opened the trunk without the key. Toni ignored that little tidbit. The man was Houdini, not seeming to need keys for anything. She set her bags next to the duffle and the box.

"Do you have a purse?" he asked.

She shook her head. "My wallet is in my camera case." She rarely bothered with a purse considering she was always dragging around her camera bag or a knapsack. She dug her car keys out of her bag and clutched them tightly in her hand.

Stavros closed the trunk and then went around to the driver's side and opened her door. Paul must have heard them, because he called out again. She glanced toward the backyard. He was bleeding heavily from his wound and that would attract all sorts of critters.

"You can't help him," Stavros told her. "He signed a deal with the devil and the devil always collects."

A shiver went down her spine. Why did she have a feeling Stavros meant what he said literally and not metaphorically?

Toni had to angle her body to fit between the car and the open door. Stavros held the door with both hands, his fingers curled over the top of the frame. "Toni."

She paused before sliding into the vehicle. She looked up and he leaned down and kissed her. Her toes curled and her body heated the moment he touched her. He slanted his mouth over hers, tasting and tempting, taking and giving.

Toni knew better than to go down this road again. Stavros had proven he could blow hot and cold. She really didn't need any more complications in her life right now. But she couldn't help but respond to his ardor.

He cupped her face, stroked his thumbs over her cheeks, curled his fingers around her neck. His tongue stroked hers in a sensual slide. Her knees went weak. She moved to get closer but the car door was between them.

Like a dash of cold water, reality reared its ugly head. Toni pulled away. "We have to stop."

Stavros' eyes were dark pools of passion, but he nodded his agreement. He stepped back and waited while she slid in the driver's seat. When he shut the door, she took a deep breath. "Get a grip on yourself," she muttered.

Stavros climbed into the passenger seat. Still naked. Toni started the car and pulled away from the cabin. "Where are we going?" she asked.

"My place. Just turn right at the end of the driveway."

Hades was not happy. Those three inept humans had had one job and one job only. Bring the girl to his demon. Still, it wasn't a total loss. He had two new souls to torment and another on the way.

He motioned to his demon, the one he'd used to negotiate with the humans. "Go and collect the remaining human for me." He was almost dead, his blood seeping the ground behind Toni's house. Hades wanted the body claimed before some gator dragged it off.

"And bring me the bodies of the other two as well." Better to clean up his mess than leave any evidence.

"Yes, my lord." The demon bowed deeply and hurried off. The creature's quick compliance and bowing and scraping soothed Hades' temper.

Really, if you wanted something done right, you had to do it yourself.

He stared at the darkened mirror, wishing he could see what was happening. Soon, he'd be able to find them. In the meantime, he needed to prepare. It was going to take quite a bit of power if he hoped to slip out of his realm for a few minutes to kill the woman with Stavros. Maybe the warrior didn't love the woman, but he was protective over her. It would have to be enough.

Hades was tired of this game. Tired of those infernal immortal warriors. He hated losing, and he hadn't won a round in this battle. Even when he'd thought he'd won, he hadn't. All the warriors were alive and well and six of them were happily mated.

Hades growled and headed toward the door of his chamber. He stepped out in the hallway and quickly transported himself to the very depths of his domain. This is where the nastiest and most powerful of his creatures dwelled.

He motioned to the one nearest to him. The ten-foot tall skeletal creature lumbered toward him. Hades felt the demon's resistance, but the creature had no choice but to obey. Hades laughed and caught the demon by the throat. "Your purpose is to serve me, and I've decided you can best serve me by dying." With that, he opened his mouth and began to suck the life-force out of the demon.

Power flowed into Hades. It felt incredible. He'd made do with weak demons for too long. This was how he was supposed to feel. Unbeatable. Invincible.

When the demon was totally drained and no more than a shriveled husk, Hades dropped the body. Then he motioned to a demon cowering in the corner.

Chapter Five

Stavros knew Toni was confused. Hell, he was confused. He'd never expected to run into someone like her during his self-imposed exile here in the bayou—a woman who stilled the restlessness inside him, who completed him in a way he'd never dreamed possible, a woman he wanted in his life forever.

And when he said forever, he meant it. Immortality made that a very real possibility.

Neither of them spoke on the drive from her cabin to the one where he was currently living. He'd called on some of his power to clothe himself on the drive over. Not all the way, but he was now wearing a pair of leather pants. He figured it was the least he could do. He probably should have done it sooner, except there was a part of him that liked the way she looked at him when he was naked. In spite of her best efforts, he knew her gaze had kept coming back to his bare chest time and time again, and lower.

Even now, his cock was swollen with need. It went beyond the mere physical. No other woman would do. Only Toni.

She pulled the rental car to a stop in front of the cabin and turned off the ignition. The light was on over the door. He'd remembered to use his powers to turn it on just before they turned into the driveway. The silence grew even louder.

Stavros sighed, opened his door and climbed out. What he had to tell her wasn't going to be easy for her to understand or accept. In fact, it might have her reaching for her phone to contact the authorities. And while that wouldn't be a problem in the long run—not with his powers fully restored and the money he now possessed—it would be a nuisance.

Toni slammed her car door shut, not bothering to get her bags from the trunk. "You finally ready to tell me what this is all about?" She brought up short and stared at his legs. "You're wearing pants." It came out like an accusation.

"I thought it would make you more comfortable."

She shook her head. "Where did you get pants?" Her voice rose with each word she spoke. "This night just keeps getting crazier." She threw her hands in the air. "I mean, first there are three men who want to either kill or kidnap me for some unknown reason. Then I see a gigantic jaguar, which is impossible. Then you're there, totally naked, in the same place the jaguar was only moments before. Furthermore, you seem to know the unknown man who wants to harm me." Her chest was heaving by the time she finished her rant. Her hands were balled into fists by her sides and her entire body trembled.

He thought about reaching out to her but figured she wouldn't want him touching her right about now. She was right. This was a lot for her to take in. It was a lot for anyone. And it was all his fault for paying special attention to her.

"I'm an immortal shapeshifting warrior." Better to get that out upfront.

Her blue eyes widened and she took a step back. "Ah, okay." She reached into her back pocket and then stopped. Looking resigned, she took another step toward the car.

Stavros figured either she'd forgotten her phone, it wasn't charged or she couldn't get cell service out here. Either way, he was grateful. "I'm not crazy," he assured her.

She nodded but didn't look convinced.

He raked his hands through his hair, knowing what he was about to do might send her running and screaming into the night. He reached for the opening of his pants to remove them and then decided what the hell. He imagined them gone and they were. Once again, he was naked before her.

"How did you do that?" Her mouth was open and she was staring at his blatant arousal. His cock flexed beneath her heated perusal.

"I can do all kinds of things," he told her. "And I wasn't lying when I told you I was a shapeshifting warrior." He turned around so she could see the tattoo that graced his back. "I am the jaguar, and it is me."

Facing her once again, he spread his arms wide. "Watch." He embraced the changed and allowed the jaguar to slide from inside him. His body became long and lean. His head reshaped and his jaw elongated. Huge fangs sprang from his gums. Sleek fur took the place of skin and paws replaced hands and feet. The man was gone, replaced by the jaguar.

Stavros faced Toni. She was staring at him, her face pale. "Holy shit." She took a step back, stumbled and landed on her butt. He hurried toward her, concerned she'd hurt herself.

She was going to die. That was Toni's first thought when the massive cat leapt at her. She threw up her arms to ward him off even knowing it wouldn't do her any good. It certainly hadn't helped the men who'd come to her home, and they'd had a gun. Her weapon and theirs was locked in the trunk of her car and of no use to her.

When deadly claws didn't rake over her skin, Toni peeked out from behind her arms. The cat was sitting next her, calmly waiting for her to acknowledge him. She peered into eyes she knew. There was no denying they belonged to Stavros.

"This isn't possible," she whispered, even though the evidence to the contrary was right before her eyes. The cat lowered his head and butted it against her arm. The gesture was so much like a housecat that she automatically reached out and scratched him behind the ears. The jaguar began to purr. Realizing what she was doing, she yanked her hand back.

Okay, so maybe Stavros was telling the truth. Unless she was having some sort of hallucination, an out-of-body experience, or her mind had lost its grip on reality, the only truth was the one sitting in front of her.

"You really are the jaguar."

The cat chuffed his agreement.

Toni swallowed hard and reached out to touch the amazing creature once again. No, not a creature. Stavros.

The jaguar's fur wasn't really black. It was covered in dark rosettes that enveloped his entire body, making him appear to be one solid color unless you were as close as she was to him.

His breath was warm on her face as he chuffed again.

"Okay, I believe you."

The cat stood and flicked his tail as he walked several paces from her. The play of muscles beneath his sleek coat of fur had her wishing for her camera. But she didn't think he'd appreciate it if she jumped up, got her equipment and started snapping photos. Better not to anger the shapeshifting warrior.

And, yeah, it was going to take her a while to wrap her brain around that one.

Stavros began to shift once again. Only this time, instead of morphing into a cat, he became a man once again. Thankfully, he was wearing those leather pants he'd worn earlier. Not that they were much of an improvement. They clung to his muscular thighs and slender hips like a well-fitting glove.

She looked away from the prominent bulge in the front of his pants. Now was definitely not the time to be thinking about sex, no matter what her libido wanted. His bronzed chest was once again on display. A smattering of dark hair spanned between his two nipples before thinning to a line that ran down his midsection and disappeared behind the waistband of his pants.

"Toni." His rough voice sent a shiver of longing through her. She suppressed it and met his black gaze.

"So you really are a shapeshifting warrior?"

He nodded. "An immortal. A warrior of the Lady of the Beasts, a goddess few in the world remember."

That much was true. Toni certainly had never heard of her. "What are you doing here?" It seemed strange to her that she'd run across such a being in the bayous of Louisiana. Maybe the rainforest of South America near some ancient ruins. That would be easier to believe.

She started to laugh and slapped her hand over her mouth. It didn't help.

She'd obviously lost it. Nothing in her life made sense.

Stavros looked concerned, and there was nothing she could do to reassure him at the moment. She was clinging to her sanity by a thread.

He scooped her into his arms as though she weighed nothing at all and carried her toward the small home. She held on to him, needing something to ground her on this crazy night. Maybe she was in shock. Fine tremors wracked her body from head to toe.

He carried her inside and kicked the door closed behind him. The place obviously had a woman's touch. It was evident in the little touches. The pillows on the sofa, the glass bowl on the table and the pictures on the wall.

Did he live here with someone?

He sat on the sofa with her on his lap and held her against his warm chest. "I'm sorry. What happened tonight was my fault."

She sat up straight, resisting the urge to lean on his strong shoulder. "I don't understand. You didn't hire those men to harm me, did you?" It seemed unlikely since he'd rescued her. Nor did he match the description that her potential kidnapper had given Stavros.

He shook his head and his long, silky hair brushed his shoulders. "No. But my interest in you has brought you to the attention of Hades."

She knew her mouth was open, but really, things just kept getting stranger and stranger. "Hades? As in the devil?"

Stavros frowned. "The Greek god of the Underworld."

Toni had a million questions, but for now, she just went with the flow. "Why would he be interested in me?"

"Because I am." Stavros stood and placed her gently on the sofa. She'd die before she'd admit that she missed his solid presence under and around her. When she was in his arms, she felt protected. Safe. And that was a myth. They had no real connection other than their few meetings, even though Stavros had saved her life.

He hunkered down in front of her and placed his hands on the sofa on either side of her hips. He gazed at her, and she could see sorrow reflected in his eyes.

"This all started five-thousand years ago."

Toni had a feeling she wasn't going to like this story one bit. "Go on."

"The gods of Olympus were at war with the Lady. They are power hungry, never content with what they have." He stood and began to pace the confines of the small room. He reminded her of a jaguar she'd seen at a zoo years ago when she was a child. She'd always thought it unfair to cage such a majestic beast.

"We fought," he continued. "Battle raged. In spite of our prowess in battle, we were losing."

"We?" she asked. Were there more of him? It boggled the mind.

Stavros flashed her a smile that made her pulse jump and her nipples tighten. "I am one of seven warriors. There is Roric the white tiger, Marko the bear, Leander the lion, Arand the wolf, Phoenix the phoenix and Mordecai the serpent."

The way he said the last name with a slight growl of displeasure told her there was another story there. "So there are seven shapeshifting immortal warriors." Even saying that aloud sounded crazy. But crazy was her new reality.

Stavros nodded. "Yes. The Lady cast a spell on us when she realized we could not win." He began to pace again. She watched him prowl around the room, the tension increasing with each passing second. "We were trapped in our animal form, but we were saved from Hades. He was unable to take us to Hell. Instead, he sent some of his demons to watch over us in this realm and took the Lady back to his domain and imprisoned her for five-thousand years."

This was like something out of a fantasy novel. Come to think of it, hadn't she skimmed a graphic novel with a similar storyline the last time she'd visited her favorite comic shop in New York?

"Then Hades came up with a new plan. He wanted the power of the Lady's warriors to help him take over the world."

This sounded like the plot of a B-movie. She leaned forward, resting her elbows on her knees. She was a sucker for a good B-movie. "What happened?"

"Because of the spell the Lady had put on us, Hades could not free us. But somewhere in the world there was a special woman for each of us, one who could free us after thousands of years of captivity. So Hades had his demons build a carnival with a very special ride—a carousel where we seven warriors were displayed. The carousel was hidden from the regular carnival goers, but it drew the women, one by one, and we began to be set free."

"Holy crap." This was incredible. It was hard to believe it was all true, but it was either believe the story or check herself into the psychiatric ward at the nearest hospital for evaluation. And she wasn't willing to do that.

Stavros straightened, hands on his lean hips, lost in the past. As she watched, he shook off the memories. "Once we were released from our captivity, Hades had twenty-four hours to kill us or convince us to come over to his side."

"What did you do?"

The look he sent her was filled with anger. "I escaped and spent many years in the remote rainforests of the world."

"And the woman who freed you?" No, she wasn't jealous at all, merely curious. At least that's what she told herself. She ignored the burning in her gut as she waited for him to answer.

"Hades thought she was dead, but she was saved and lived. I watched over her for many years."

"And the others?"

He waved away her question. "It is enough for you to know we defeated the god and the curse. As a consequence of the bargain Hades made with the Lady, the god cannot harm any of us or the chosen mates of the warriors."

Wait, did he say mates? "Some of the warriors have wives?"

Stavros smiled and she curled her toes. He was lethal to her senses when he was rough and serious. When he smiled, he was irresistible.

"Yes, the rest of them have mated. Four of them with the women who freed them, and two others with women who played a part in our defeating Hades."

Wow. That was a story she'd love to hear someday. But she needed to get back on track. "What does any of this have to do with me?"

When Stavros came to crouch in front of her once again, she knew she wasn't going to like his answer. His smile was gone, replaced by a solemn expression that had her shivering once again.

"Hades is a vengeful god and he feels cheated. He cannot harm any of us or the Lady."

"You already told me that," she reminded him.

Stavros trailed his fingers over her forehead and down the curve of her cheek. "He will harm anyone who is important to me. That is how he plans to take his revenge. He already tried it with two of the women before they were mated to my fellow warriors."

That didn't sound good, but Toni still didn't understand. "I get that, but what does it have to do with me?"

"Ah, Toni." Stavros leaned in close and nuzzled her neck and her ear. Tingles raced down her arm and her pussy began to throb. She could feel the heat pouring off his big body and smell his unique masculine scent. "Hades knows what you mean to me."

"What I mean to you?" She knew she sounded like a parrot, but it was impossible to assimilate everything coming at her so quickly.

He nipped her earlobe and then laved the small sting. Toni's breathing increased and she clutched at his shoulders, scoring them with her short fingernails.

"Ah, Toni. Hades has discovered my biggest weakness. You. There is nothing I won't do to protect you, to make you mine."

Then he kissed her.

Chapter Six

Stavros knew he should slow down. He'd thrown a lot at Toni, including how he felt about her. But he couldn't help himself. He needed to kiss her, to touch her, to reassure himself she was still alive and safe. He'd almost lost her tonight.

At first, she didn't return his kiss. She was motionless beneath his touch, not responding but not pushing him away either. Just when he decided he needed to pull back and give her time, her lips moved beneath his.

He caught her soft moan in his mouth and pushed his tongue between her parted teeth. She tasted sweet and warm and welcoming. He was quickly becoming addicted to her kisses.

He placed his hands on either side of her hips to keep from dragging her down onto the couch and ripping off her clothes. A pounding need to claim her raged inside him. The jaguar part of his nature wanted him to get on with things. But the human part knew he had to take things slow. Toni had been through a lot tonight. It was a miracle that she was letting him kiss her at all.

Her tongue tangled with his. Her breathing quickened and the rapid pounding of her heart echoed in his ears. He inhaled and the spicy scent of her arousal tickled his nostrils.

Toni wanted him.

In spite of everything he'd told her, the entire shocking story, she wanted him. He wouldn't have been surprised if she'd pushed him away and tried to run. That would probably be the most sensible thing to do.

Maybe he should take her somewhere else, somewhere safe and leave her alone. Maybe Hades would forget about her if he did so.

But deep in his heart, Stavros knew there was nowhere in the world that was safe from Hades' far-reaching grasp. And he could not leave Toni even if he wanted too. She was his heart.

He was no longer acting intelligently, but going totally on instinct. He slanted his mouth over hers, tasting and teasing until it was no longer enough. The others had told him he'd know when he met the woman meant to be his mate. He hadn't believed them.

He did now.

Stavros wrenched his mouth from hers. Toni's eyes were half closed and filled with passion. Her chest rose and fell rapidly. Heat rolled off her silky skin. She was wearing a tank top, which showed off her strong, slender arms to perfection.

"Yes or no." His cock pounded in time to his heartbeat. He wanted Toni more than he wanted his next breath, but it was her choice. "If you say yes, you're mine." He knew he should explain it better than that, but it was taking everything inside him not to throw her over his shoulder and drag her into the bedroom. It was the closest thing he had to a lair. Clichéd, yes, but that didn't lessen the intensity of his feelings.

Toni belonged to him. Was his to protect. And he would do so, no matter the consequences. Walking away from her was no longer an option. He knew what he had to do.

Toni swallowed the lump in her throat that threatened to choke her. The way Stavros looked at her made every cell in her body stand up and sing. Oh, she wanted him. More than she'd ever thought it possible to want a man.

But he wasn't a man. He was a shapeshifting immortal warrior. And she was human. That couldn't work. If she slept with him, he'd eventually leave her like everyone else in her life had.

For once in her life, she didn't care. Sure, there was heartbreak in her future, but she knew that making love with Stavros would be more than she could even imagine.

He was staring at her, his bare chest covered in a light sheen of sweat. The muscles of his shoulders were bunched, his body tense. His eyes were black pools of myriad emotions. She couldn't read all of them, but the one she recognized was need. He wanted her and she wanted him. It would have to be enough.

"Yes."

Toni didn't know what she expected, but his slow smile wasn't it. And wow, was he hot when he smiled. It made him look younger. He had an ageless quality about him, but there was something old in his eyes. Of course, he'd lived longer than she could even imagine.

Stavros stood and stared down at her. "You won't regret this."

She kind of was already. The sex would be hot, but she was afraid he'd ruin her for any other man. Before she could think to change her mind, he pulled her to her feet and swung her into his arms. He kissed her again, and she forgot all her doubts. Rational thought didn't stand a chance against his kisses.

She knew he was walking, could feel the play of the muscles in his chest as he carried her into another room. She glanced around when he laid her on a bed. The bedside lamp was on and illuminated the space. The room was sparse, but the bright yellow paint on the walls and the pretty lamp and vase on the nightstand gave every indication that this was a woman's bedroom.

"Who lives here with you?" The question came out sharper than she intended. She wasn't jealous. Not at all. But she didn't want to be the other woman.

"I don't live here." He took off her shoes and dropped them to the floor. "This place belongs to Arand's woman. It was her grandmother's home." Stavros rolled off her socks and tossed them away.

"Oh." Really, what else could she say? Glad you're not a cheating bastard would certainly upset the mood.

He reached for the opening of her jeans and slowly pulled the zipper down. "I do not have any other woman," he assured her.

It was a good thing she wasn't afraid of him, or his dark scowl would scare the pants off her. She almost laughed at her turn of phrase when he pulled her pants down her legs and tossed them aside.

She blinked and he was naked again. That was some trick he did, making his clothing appear and disappear on command. She licked her lips as she gazed at his perfect form. He growled low in his throat and it was so much like a jaguar it startled her. It was a little frightening, and if she was being honest, sexy as hell.

He knelt on the mattress by her feet and crawled up the bed until he was hovering over her. Heat radiated from his big body. They were inches apart but not touching. "I want you naked. I want to see your bare breasts, to cover them with my hands."

She felt like fanning herself. It was growing hotter in here with each passing second. Reaching down, she grabbed the hem of her shirt and dragged it up and off. She wasn't wearing a bra, hadn't bothered with one after her shower earlier this evening.

His eyes narrowed and he licked his lips. He looked dark and dangerous looming over her. Her pussy clenched in response. Stavros inhaled deeply and slowly smiled as if he knew how her body reacted to him.

Stavros cupped her breasts with his large hands, plumping the mounds. "Beautiful." He rubbed his thumbs over her distended nipples, wringing a moan from her throat. She arched up, wanting more of his touch.

He growled again, leaned down and lapped at one pebbled tip. His tongue was slightly rough, and the stimulation sent a stab of pleasure racing to her pussy, making it throb. Toni moaned, threaded her fingers through his hair and dragged him closer.

He purred. Honest to God purred. She cried out, unable to stop herself. It was like having a warm, wet vibrator attached to her nipple.

Her eyes practically crossed when she imagined what that might feel like if he explored her pussy.

As if he could hear her thoughts, Stavros released her breast and began to kiss and lick a hot path down her torso. He tongued her belly button, flicking in and out of the small indentation. He nipped at her hipbones, letting her feel his teeth. Not enough to hurt, but enough to drive her arousal level through the roof.

She writhed and moaned beneath him, trying to encourage him to hurry, but he would not be rushed. By the time he knelt between her thighs and spread them wide, she was ready to throttle him.

He inhaled again and she had to ask. "Can you smell my arousal?"

He licked his lips and her pussy clenched in response. "Oh yeah." The way he said it left her no doubt he was telling the truth. Toni had no idea just what he could do. He was immortal and a jaguar, but what did that all mean? Enhanced senses obviously.

And then he dipped his head between her legs, and she no longer cared. All she knew was she wanted more of the way he was touching her. He stroked that amazing tongue of his over the slick folds of her pussy. She forgot to breathe when the tip flicked the tiny nub of nerves at the apex.

And when he closed his lips over her clit and sucked, she lost her mind.

Toni grabbed fistfuls of the covers beneath her to anchor herself in the sensual storm engulfing her. She'd never felt anything near this before. Stavros owned her body, playing it like a master.

Her breasts ached for his touch. Her mouth yearned for his kisses. Her skin craved his caress. But there was no way she wanted him to stop what he was doing. He teased her clit with his tongue and then gently sucked on it.

Toni thrashed her head from side-to-side as she struggled to breath. She was so close.

When he rimmed her opening with his finger, she went wild, arching upward. Stavros gave her what she wanted, pushing not one but two thick fingers inside her. Her pussy clamped down around him. God, that felt incredible.

He pulled his fingers almost all the way out and then thrust them deep again. Toni pumped her hips, encouraging him to finger fuck her. He growled and the vibration shot through her clit.

Toni screamed as she came. Her entire body spasmed, and she felt the hot release deep in her pussy. Her cream coated his fingers, but he kept pumping them in and out until she was completely wrung out. Only when she collapsed against the mattress, totally spent, did he stop.

He withdrew his fingers, brought them to his mouth and sucked. She shuddered and he immediately stretched out beside her and pulled her into his strong and warm embrace. It felt incredibly right to snuggle up against his hard chest.

Stavros knew his cock was going to explode any second now. He could smell Toni's sweet arousal on his fingers, taste her sweet and spicy flavor on his lips. She was perfection.

But she wasn't quite his. Not yet.

He brushed his fingers through her hair, frowning when he realized it was still braided. Taking his time, he pulled off the elastic band holding it together and slowly unwound the braid. He purred with satisfaction when he threaded his fingers through the thick mass. Her hair fell below her shoulders in a thick curtain. He could spend hours playing with it.

But another time. If he didn't get inside her soon, he was going to disgrace himself. He started to turn her so he could finally get inside her, but she pulled away from him. He missed the warmth and weight of her body immediately. She fit against him like she'd been made especially for him.

She shook her head and he froze. Was she telling him no? As much as it might kill him, he would never force her to do anything she didn't want to.

Toni placed her hand in the center of his chest and rose up on her knees beside him. "My turn."

Stavros was surprised the top didn't come off his head when he realized her intent. A small, sultry smile played at the corners of her lush lips. And when she brushed a kiss against the center of his chest, he thought his heart might burst from his body.

"Just lie there and relax."

Was she crazy? There was no way he was going to relax. Not with her tongue flicking his flat nipple. He groaned and curled his hands into fists to keep from reaching for her. He sensed this was important to Toni. She needed to assert herself, and it was up to him to let her have her way.

Yeah, he was a giver all right. It was such a hardship to lie here and let her touch him. She grazed her hands over his broad chest and then moved lower. Her mouth followed. She kissed a path down the center of his chest, following the thin line of hair all the way to his belly button.

He moaned when she nipped at his flesh. His jaguar roared inside him, the creature stretching and preening beneath her arousing hands.

His cock was engorged, the head purple and damp. His hips jerked when her lips traced the turgid length from tip to base.

"Toni." Her name was little more than a growl. He couldn't take much more of this. His balls were heavy and tight and practically ready to crawl inside him.

"Mmm." The little humming sound she made drove him crazy. He wanted her to make it while her mouth was sucking his cock. Every muscle in his body was stretched tight with the effort it took him not to grab her and roll her beneath him. Or better yet, put her on her hands and knees and fuck her from behind.

Yeah, that would work.

He roared when she closed her warm lips around the head of his dick. He reached for her, unable not to touch her any longer. He clutched her hair and pulled her closer. She laughed and opened her mouth wider, taking him deeper.

Heaven. Surely if such a place existed, this was what it must be like. Toni licked and sucked his hard length, using her tongue to tease the sensitive underside when she pulled back to the tip. She gripped his shaft and dragged her tongue around the sensitive head before flicking it over the slit.

He growled again, unable to stop himself. The animal part of him wanted his mate and wanted her now. No more waiting. But he also didn't want to stop her. What she was doing to him was incredible.

Toni wrapped one small, strong hand around him and pumped. At the same time, she took the head of his cock into her mouth and sucked hard.

Stavros' breath was coming in ragged gasps. He wasn't going to be able to stop. "I'm coming," he warned her.

She sucked him harder. He felt his eyes cross and his balls clench. Then his release rocketed up his shaft and out the tip. His entire body convulsed with pleasure as he came. And Toni, sweet, sexy Toni, sucked and licked and took everything he gave her.

Stavros lost all sense of reality, lost in his own personal heaven. His big body shuddered and then relaxed. Toni released his cock, looked up at him and smiled.

If he didn't already love her, he would have fallen hard for her in that moment. She looked like the cat who'd gotten the cream. The image made him smile.

A sense of foreboding hit him like a sledgehammer. There was no time to waste. He had to protect Toni and he had to do it now.

"Do you trust me?" he asked. Stavros knew he was asking a lot from her. Toni didn't trust easily.

She hesitated and then nodded. His heart swelled and he reached out to her. "Come here." He dragged her over him until she was straddling him. His cock, hard and ready once again, brushed against her stomach.

She seemed surprised and her eyes widened. "Really? You just came."

He smiled. "I'm not human, sweetheart. I can go all night."

She closed her hand around his shaft and pumped. "Is that so?"

A sense of urgency was driving him. He wanted to take his time but felt the clock ticking. "Take me inside you." This had to be her choice.

Toni lifted up onto her knees and maneuvered until the thick head of his dick was pressed against her slick opening. She hovered over him for a long moment with him poised at her entrance.

Just when he thought he'd have to take over, she began to lower herself onto his shaft one slow inch at a time. He stroked his hands up her thighs and over her hips, settling them on her tiny waist. It was ridiculous how much smaller than him she was. She was tiny, but she certainly wasn't fragile. Delicate but strong.

She gasped as his big cock filled her, but she kept going until she was sitting on his groin. Neither of them spoke. Stavros stared deeply into her expressive blue eyes. He wanted to look into those eyes for the rest of his life.

Her breathing quickened and each inhalation made her breasts sway in a tempting manner. Her nipples were taut and red. He licked his lips and sat up. Toni gasped when his shaft sank deeper into her wet depths. Opening his mouth, he took one pert nipple inside. She clutched at his shoulders. Stavros shuddered, loving her touch.

He moved from one damp tip to the other, kissing and licking her breasts. Toni began to move, raising herself an inch before dropping back down onto his shaft.

Stavros rolled and Toni gasped when she found herself flat on her back with him buried deep. She blinked and stared up at him.

"Put your arms around my neck and don't let go." She didn't hesitate, locking her hands at his nape. "Trust me." He had to do this, had to make sure Hades could never harm her.

Stavros began to fuck her, slow and steady, building up speed as he went.

And she was with him all the way, arching her hips up to meet him, offering herself freely.

The scent of sex permeated the small room. He loved the way she smelled, sweet and spicy and some unnamable perfume that was uniquely Toni. She stroked his shoulders and back and then gripped his butt, digging her nails in.

He fucked her harder and faster. His balls drew up tight once again, a telltale sign he was close to release. Toni threw her head back and moaned. Her lips were parted, her eyes closed and her skin flushed. Beautiful. She was everything to him.

He thrust again and again, angling his pelvis so he brushed her sensitive clit. Her eyes flew open and she called out his name. Her pussy clamped around his cock and he roared.

As he came inside her welcoming heat, Stavros placed one hand over her heart and released his life force into her. A brilliant light exploded and then a rainbow of colors showered down all around them. Toni cried out and came harder, convulsing around his throbbing erection.

She shivered and grabbed hold of his shoulders. Stavros shuddered, his big body shaking as he shared his seed and his life force with her. He sensed the moment he'd given her enough and pulled back. The light disappeared, taking the brilliant colors with it.

Stavros collapsed on top of her, covering her entire body with his. Protecting her. Toni was his now. But would she want him when she learned what he'd done?

She shivered beneath him and he angled himself off her enough so he wasn't completely crushing her. It wasn't easy. He didn't want to move at all.

Her face was pale, her eyes slightly glassy. "I feel different." She put her hand on her chest, covering her heart. "What did you do to me?" He hated the tinge of fear in her voice.

Stavros sat up and braced himself for her reaction.

"What did you do?" she asked again, this time louder.

He swallowed hard and faced her, knowing whatever her reaction, he'd do the same thing again. Whatever it took to protect her. "I made you immortal."

Chapter Seven

Toni was sure she'd misunderstood what Stavros had said. "You made me immortal?"

He nodded. "Yes. To protect you from Hades." Stavros reached out and touched her face, rubbing his thumb over her rosy cheek. "Now he can never harm you because you are a part of me."

Okay, she was really getting freaked out now. Her body was humming with satisfaction from the most amazing orgasm of her life, but she couldn't relax and enjoy it. Her skin still tingled from where a shower of colored lights had fallen around them. And her heart—that organ felt different. Powerful yet light. She felt as though something inside her had been stripped away and replaced. And if Stavros was to be believed—and at this point she had no reason not to believe him—that something was her mortality.

Toni raised her hand in front of her and studied it. She didn't look any different. At least not that she could see. "I'm not going to become a jaguar, am I?"

Stavros shook his head, his expression unreadable. Toni buried the small disappointment. It might have been cool to be able to shift into a big cat. And she wasn't seriously contemplating this, was she?

There really was no choice. She had to consider the fact he was telling the truth, that she was now immortal. How did she feel about that?

Before she could decide, the atmosphere in the room changed. The light from the bedside lamp grew dim, as though something was sucking power from it.

Stavros leapt from the bed, all sleek and fluid grace, landing lightly on his feet. He was now wearing pants and holding a four-foot sword in his hand. She blinked, but the sword didn't disappear. The blade gleamed, and she had no doubt it was lethal. The jaguar tattoo stared back at her, the cat's expression fierce. But she didn't fear the jaguar any more than she feared the man.

Her heart skipped a beat. In spite of everything, she trusted him.

"Whatever you do, stay behind me," Stavros instructed. Toni grabbed the blanket from the top of the bed and wrapped it around her. Too bad she couldn't conjure clothing out of thin air like he could. She had no idea what was happening, but she knew she didn't want to be naked and any more vulnerable than she already was.

An inky-black circle appeared in the corner of the room. With each passing second, it grew larger and larger and seemed to suck most of the light from the room. Toni rubbed her eyes, but it didn't disappear. She wasn't seeing things.

A rush of pure menace slammed into her, and she scooted back on the mattress before she stopped herself. The hell with this. No way was she letting Stavros face whatever this threat was alone. She briefly wished her gun wasn't tucked away safely in the trunk of her car.

She slid from the bed and took a step toward Stavros. He never took his gaze off the swirling black hole, but she knew he sensed her movement.

"Stay back," he warned her.

"What is it?" She had to know. It looked like some dark portal. She shivered as another wave of menace slammed into her.

"Not what. Who." Stavros held the sword hilt with both hands, the blade angled in front of him. "Hades has come for you."

Up until that moment, Toni realized a small part of her had doubted Stavros entire story in spite of everything she'd seen and experienced. But no more.

Before she could ask Stavros any questions, a man stepped from the dark depths of the portal and it collapsed behind him, winking out of existence. He was tall with dark hair and midnight-black eyes. There was a cruel twist to his lips, which was echoed in his eyes. His face was all angles and planes. There was nothing soft about him. He wore a suit that had obviously been tailored to his lithe, muscular frame.

"Hades." Stavros called the man by name. No, not a man, a Greek god.

Toni felt slightly lightheaded. She took a deep breath and then another. She'd been holding her breath and that wasn't smart. An honest to god— No, scrap that. This guy was the real deal.

Hades looked more like a CEO than a god. His shoes gleamed, his shirt was crisp and he even had a pocket square in flaming red tucked in his breast pocket.

"Warrior." The god inclined his head at Stavros and then turned his attention to her. Hades pinned her in place with his dark gaze. There were nightmares in those eyes, endless suffering and fear. In spite of her determination to be brave, Toni shivered as a sense of dread filled her.

Hades smiled as if he knew the effect he was having on her and was pleased by it. Toni straightened her shoulders and glared back at him. Hades chuckled.

"I've come for your little friend," Hades informed Stavros.

Stavros shook his head. "You can't have her." And then her warrior smiled. "In any event, you're too late. I've already claimed her. Toni belongs to me."

The possessiveness in his voice sent a shiver down her spine. Her skin went clammy and she felt slightly ill. What did he mean that she belonged to him? She belonged to no man. She liked being single. Liked her life as it was. It was one thing to sleep with Stavros, but that was all it was—sex between two mutually consenting adults.

She was lying to herself. Somehow, someway the jaguar has sneaked beneath her barriers and into her heart. Damn him.

Red fire blazed in Hades' eyes. The fires of Hell.

Toni clenched her fists and stepped closer to Stavros, not so close she would impede him if he needed to swing that scary-looking sword, but close enough for him to know he wasn't alone. She might fight with him later, but right now they were united against a common enemy.

Hades hurled a bolt of lightning at her. Toni screamed. There was nowhere for her to go, no way for her to avoid being hit. It was instinctual to throw up her hands in front of her. It was a puny defense at best, and she knew she didn't have a hope in hell of surviving. But the deadly blast never touched her. It seemed to ricochet against an indivisible barrier and deflect back at the god.

Hades was thrown backward and crashed into the wall, crumbling the plaster as his body punched a huge hole in it. He seemed dazed for a moment. He swore and shook himself. The flecks of plaster disappeared from his suit, leaving it pristine once again.

"What have you done?" Hades demanded.

"I've shared my immortality with her, my life force. She is part of me now. And more importantly, I am part of her." Stavros' smile made her shudder. Right now, she wasn't sure who the most dangerous man in the room was.

Holy hell, the whole immortal thing was real. And she had to stop using any sayings with the word *hell* in them. But it was hard to comprehend the idea that she was now immortal. Stavros had given her that. And all because he wanted to save her from Hades.

"And since I am a part of her, you cannot harm her," Stavros continued. "If you try, you are the one who will be destroyed."

Hades clenched his hands at his sides, threw back his head and roared. Glass shattered and the furniture rose in the air before slamming back to the floor. He didn't look so suave and sophisticated now. No, now he was the all-avenging god.

"Why?" Hades demanded. "Why do you warriors share your power with these human women? You barely know her, yet you give so much to her. Why?"

It was obvious to Toni by the way he said the word *human* that he didn't think much of them as a race.

Stavros shook his head. "If I have to explain it, you'll never understand."

"Tell me," the god demanded. He was panting hard and, if she wasn't mistaken, smoke was seeping from beneath the cuffs of his sleeves and the hem of his pants.

"When you love someone, you'll do anything in your power to keep them safe, even if that means sacrificing yourself."

Toni was dumbstruck. This was the first time in her life a man had told her he loved her, and he hadn't really told her at all. He'd told Hades.

Stavros had gifted her with part of his immortality to save her. That was easier to believe than the fact that he loved her. But Stavros wasn't the type of man to lie. He would always tell her the truth.

He loved her.

She played that over in her head, trying to get used to the idea.

Hades spoke in a language she couldn't understand, but she didn't need a translation to know he was swearing.

Just then, another portal began to form. This one was a swirling combination of brilliant white and darkest black. It formed much quicker than the first one had. A gorgeous woman stepped from the depths of the spinning circle and into the room. She was slender, but there was no mistaking the surge of power that preceded her. Her hair was black and fell to her waist. She was also wearing jeans and a silk blouse. Toni wondered who she was.

"Persephone." Hades seemed surprised to see the woman. From what little Toni knew about the Greek gods, she knew Persephone was married to Hades. Or at least that's what the books said. Toni was quickly realizing that they truly knew little about the ancient gods.

Persephone frowned and shook her head. "You just had to come here, didn't you?" She walked over to the dark god, totally unafraid. Toni admired the other woman even if she wondered about her sanity. After all, the guy was the Lord of the Underworld.

Hades flicked a nonexistent piece of lint off the sleeve of his suit jacket and shrugged.

Stavros came to stand beside Toni. He wrapped one arm around her shoulders and pulled her into the curve of his body. His sword was pointed blade down, the tip resting against the floor.

Persephone waved her hand in the air and the damage Hades had inflicted to the room was quickly repaired. The glass jumped from the floor and reassembled itself in the window, the furniture became sturdy and whole again and the plaster repaired itself.

Toni was in awe. That was some skill. Gave an entirely new meaning to the idea of renovation and redecorating.

When she was done, the goddess turned to them. "You'll have to excuse us. We must be going."

Stavros inclined his head to the woman and shot Hades a deadly glare. "We're done. The curse is finally finished."

Hades didn't acknowledge Stavros at all. He simply wrapped one arm around the woman and ushered her into the swirling portal. It disappeared in the next breath, leaving nothing but a residual energy that made the short hairs on her arms stand on end.

The sword in Stavros' hand disappeared. She wondered where all that stuff went. Did he have a home somewhere he sent it to? Or did he have a cosmic closet? There was so much to consider. Her life had completely changed.

Toni moved away from Stavros, turned and faced him. She wished she was wearing a little more than a blanket but would have to make do. She was good at that.

He stood with his hands on his hips, tall and powerful, and—uncertain. She could see it in his eyes. He wasn't sure what she was going to say or do. That was to her advantage.

Toni stared into his dark eyes. They were black like Hades' but so different. Stavros' eyes held the secrets of the night and a sensual promise. She walked up to him and placed a hand on his chest. His heart raced beneath her palm.

"So you love me, do you?"

Stavros tried to gauge Toni's mood, but it was impossible. Her expression was inscrutable, and his own emotions were all over the place. His blood pumped through his veins thick and hot. He wanted to scoop Toni into his arms and drag her back down to the bed. But he wasn't sure of his welcome.

He'd changed Toni in the most fundamental way and without her permission. Not only that, he'd blurted out that he loved her. He knew she wasn't ready to hear that. Might never be. The woman had trust issues, and he'd violated that trust by making her immortal without her permission.

He nodded in answer to her question, not trusting himself to speak yet.

Toni's palm was hot against his skin. She still smelled of sex, of him. His cat yowled his dissatisfaction. The jaguar wanted him to touch Toni, wanted to rub its body over her until it marked her as his own.

She tilted her head to one side, making her hair fall in a thick curtain. "Why?"

"Why?" He wasn't sure he understood her question.

"Why do you love me?"

Stavros couldn't stand their separation any longer. He scooped her into his arms, ignored her startled gasp and sat on the bed, resting his back against the headboard. Cradling her in his arms, he sought to find the words to make her understand.

"I have been alone for many years." The five-thousand years he'd spent imprisoned were the worst of his entire existence. Toni rubbed her hand over his chest as though to comfort him. He caught her fingers in his and brought them to his mouth and kissed each of her knuckles one by one.

"I was created, not born. I came into being exactly as I am—a warrior of the Lady of the Beasts." He sought to share some of his history with Toni. "I have existed since the dawn of time, since the birth of the world."

"That's incredible."

He lost himself in her eyes. So blue, so warm, like the sky on a summer's day. It would be so easy to sweep her beneath him and make love to her. But she deserved to know exactly who and what he was.

"The seven of us warriors lived to serve our goddess. She is kind and benevolent." He paused and gathered his thoughts. "It was a good life until the rise of the Greek gods and goddesses. They were a troublesome bunch from the very beginning."

"And then came the curse," Toni prompted.

Stavros rubbed his hand up and down Toni's arm, enjoying the warmth and the smoothness of her skin. "Yes, then came the war and the curse. I didn't believe we'd ever go free. I think it changed all of us."

"In what way?" Her concern was a balm to his soul.

"When I was freed, I was confused. I watched over the woman who'd freed me. I felt a debt of gratitude to her but nothing more. Eventually, I made my way to the jungles of South America. I gave my jaguar free reign, not sure how to behave as a man anymore. To my shame, I stayed that way for long years until I finally felt the call of the Lady once more."

Toni clasped his face in her hands. There was no anger or disgust in her expressive blue eyes. Only understanding and empathy. "You have no reason to be ashamed. Not after all you've been through."

He swallowed hard. That she would defend him meant everything to him, but he could not allow her to absolve him of his guilt. "No, it was wrong of me." She looked like she was going to disagree with him, so he hurried onward. "I arrived to help the last warrior freed break the curse. We defeated Hades and the rest of my friends found their mates." He paused and took a deep breath. "I didn't think there was anyone for me."

Toni stilled and looked down at her lap. "I see."

"No, you don't see." Frustration rose in him. He was doing this all wrong. "Then I met you." He smiled in spite of the seriousness of the moment. "You fascinated me from the first moment I laid eyes on you. I followed you for several days."

"I knew it. I knew some animal was following me. I thought it was a cougar."

Stavros scowled. "You take too many chances out there alone by yourself."

"So you were protecting me?"

"Yes. No." He dragged his fingers through his hair. Women were confusing creatures. "I wanted to leave. Tried to leave you alone on several occasions, but I kept coming back."

She was pleased by his answer if the smile playing at the corners of her lips were any indication. Stavros hurried on with his confession. "The Lady told me I could gift the woman of my choice with immortality. It was her gift to all of us for what we'd endured. I didn't think I'd ever find a woman to share it with. I'd planned on keeping to myself for the rest of time."

"To protect everyone from Hades." Toni nodded as she spoke and he knew she understood.

"Yes. I wouldn't risk the life of an innocent." He sighed. "Even though I knew it was wrong, I couldn't stay away from you. It was because of me that Hades tried to harm you. And for that, I'm sorry." He slid his hand behind her neck and cupped her nape. He tilted her head to one side and slowly lowered his lips to hers. "But, Toni, I'm not sorry for loving you. And I'm not sorry for this."

He kissed her then like he'd been dying to do since Hades had left. The curse was finally over. A weight he'd been carrying for five-thousand years dissolved beneath the warmth of Toni's lips. She kissed him back with no hesitation. That gave him hope that she would forgive him for what he'd done, how he'd changed her life. That she might give him a chance to prove himself and his love for her.

Hades stepped out of the portal behind Persephone. He'd expected her to take him straight to his brothers for judgment. Instead, they were in his private quarters in Hell. The portal winked out behind them. Hades strode to the liquor cabinet, poured himself a double scotch and drank it all in one gulp. Then he poured himself another.

Once again, those annoying warriors had defeated him. It was maddening.

"It's over, Hades. Tell me you understand that once and for all." There was a note in Persephone's voice, a desperation that made him turn and study her. He wanted to be angry with her for her interference but found he was not.

She was standing in the center of the room with her arms crossed over her chest. Her lips were turned down in a frown. She looked…not mad, but sad. He found he didn't like the idea of her being unhappy.

As much as it pained him to admit it, what she said was true. "It's over."

There was nothing more he could do to the pesky goddess and her shapeshifting warriors. Not unless he was willing to destroy himself, and that was something he definitely wasn't planning on doing now or anytime in the future. He hadn't really needed the warriors anyway. That had been his mistake—thinking he needed anyone else. He'd make another plan better than the last. He learned from his mistakes.

"Oh, Hades," Persephone cried out in distress. "Have you learned nothing? I can already see the wheels turning in your head, concocting another scheme. The power you lost will grow again in time. Can you not be happy with what you have?"

Why would he be content with what he had? There was a place inside him that craved something more. He wasn't quite sure what it was. Come to think of it, he hadn't felt that way during the long years he and Persephone had been together. In fact, he'd quite forgotten the Lady of the Beasts and her warriors during that time.

He threw back the second drink and plunked the glass down on the cabinet. A spark grew inside him. Maybe, just maybe, he understood the warriors and their willingness to do anything for their women. No other woman had ever stirred the feelings inside him that Persephone did.

That was dangerous to him. He really should stomp out those tender emotions and send Persephone away. But he found he didn't want to. He knew she could fill the empty place inside him. He had eternity to scheme and gain more power, but right now, all he wanted was the woman in front of him.

"Come here." He crooked his finger at her.

She shook her head. "No."

Hades stalked toward her, noting the way her body quivered and her nostrils flared. She wanted him. A sense of triumph surged through him. Claiming her as his woman once again would be greater than any victory he could have gained over the puny human race.

He trailed his fingers over her stubborn chin and down her neck until he hit her collarbone. Her breathing increased and she swallowed. "If you keep me occupied, I won't have time to get into trouble."

Persephone laughed. "Only you would be so arrogant, Hades."

He dropped the façade and cupped her chin in his hand. "I miss you, Persephone." He lifted one of her hands and placed it over his heart.

She sighed. "What am I to do with you?"

He shrugged, not willing to ask for what he wanted for fear she would turn him down. He was already weak enough without adding to it. He leaned down, and when his lips were almost touching hers, he spoke without thinking. "Want me."

"Oh, Hades. I do. That's the problem."

He kissed the corner of her mouth and then licked her bottom lip. "It doesn't have to be a problem." He was close. He could sense her weakening toward him. He knew her so well, knew what made her shiver, what gave her the greatest pleasure.

"This is your last chance. I can't go through this again." Persephone gripped the lapels of his jacket. "I mean it, Hades. I love you but I won't be shoved aside in place of your ambition. Not again."

That gave him pause. But he decided the prize before him was worth the effort. Hades had a new plan, and it was all about pleasure and the woman in front of him. He swung her up into his arms and carried her over to the bed. "You won't be sorry," he promised her.

He laid her on the bed, all thoughts of the Lady and her warriors relegated to the past. Persephone was his now and his future.

Chapter Eight

Toni's head was spinning. So much had happened, but the most amazing thing of all had to be Stavros' declaration that he loved her. But could she believe in that love? Everything had happened so quickly. What if he changed his mind? Eternity was a long time.

But when he kissed her, all her reservations slipped away.

Stavros eased his lips from hers and tenderly brushed a lock of hair away from her face. "What are you thinking?"

It was time to be brutally honest. "What if none of this is real? Oh, I believe that you're an immortal warrior and that Hades was just here." And how weird was it to say that and not be under the influence of alcohol or heavy medication. "But what about us?"

His expression never changed, but she knew she'd disappointed him, hurt him on a deep level. She'd come to know him so well in such a short time and caught the telltale way his mouth tightened and his eyes darkened. That gave her pause. They might not have known one another very long, but she knew him better than she'd ever known another man.

"I can only tell you what I'm feeling." He swept his thumb across her cheek. His touch was tender and nonsexual, but that didn't matter to her body, which was humming with arousal.

"I love you, Toni. Now and forever. You're it for me." He touched his chest. "I know it in my heart in a way I've never known anything else."

She swallowed heavily, incredibly touched. Tears filled her eyes, making them burn, but she managed to blink them back. "I don't know what to say or do." And that felt cowardly.

"You don't have to do or say anything. Just stay with me. Give me a chance to show you what we have is real."

Toni thought about what it had felt like when she'd thought Stavros might have to fight Hades. He'd been willing to battle a god to protect her. It didn't get any more real than that.

She'd been terrified something would happen to him. She cared deeply for him. Damnit, who was she kidding? She loved him.

It felt strange to say the words in her head. She said it a few more times and then took a deep breath and said them aloud. "I love you."

Stavros became as still as a statue, not really breathing. Then he exploded into motion and she found herself flat on her back on the mattress, the blanket somehow gone and Stavros covering her with his naked body.

"Do you mean it?" he demanded.

She tenderly stroked his chest and broad shoulders. He was as vulnerable as she was when it came to their relationship. Baring himself emotionally was as new to him as it was to her. "Yes, I mean it. Ever since I first met you, there's been something there, something I've never felt before. I like you. I want to be with you. And for the first time in my life, I can envision being with you fifty years from now." She paused and laughed. "I guess it's going to be much longer than that."

"Much longer." He lowered his mouth and kissed her. No, that wasn't quite right. He inhaled her, as though she was the very air he needed to breathe.

"Toni. Toni. Toni." Her name fell from his lips like a mantra, a prayer. He pressed openmouthed kisses on her neck, teasing a path all the way to her ear. He traced the delicate whorls, sending a shiver of pleasure racing through her. "You won't regret this," he promised before gently tugging on her lobe with his teeth.

"I know." She stroked his firm warm flesh, loving the play of muscles beneath her hands. Stavros was strong, but he tempered that strength whenever he touched her. He treated her in a way no other man ever had, like she was precious and special. "You won't regret it either."

His smile was tender and filled with such love that it almost hurt her to look at him. "I know."

He sat back on his heels and she scrambled onto her knees until she was facing him. He raised one dark eyebrow in question, but she only smiled. She licked her lips and studied him. He really was the most perfect male specimen in the world. And he was hers.

Stavros laughed. "I'm almost afraid to ask what you're thinking. You look like a cat about to play with its prey."

She slowly smiled. "Maybe I am." She skated her hands over his chest, sifting through the crisp hair that covered it. His abs were sculpted bands of muscle. His cock was fully erect and very impressive. She gripped his thick shaft in her hand. As a photographer, she could appreciate the texture of his skin, the darkness of it against the paler skin of her hand. As a woman, she was enthralled with the way his erection heated beneath her touch. She knew what it felt like to have all that untamed power inside her and she wanted that again.

Toni stroked up and down his cock. He was so heavy and hard in her hand. She rubbed her thumb across the flared head, spreading the moisture that leaked from the tip. Stavros groaned and pushed deeper into her hand.

He was just as busy as she was. He palmed her breasts, covering them with his callused hands. Her nipples were taut but grew harder when he teased them with the pads of his thumbs. It was her turn to groan when he tweaked one nipple between his thumb and forefinger.

"I want you, Toni." With his dark hair flowing around his shoulders and his black eyes glittering with lust, he looked more like a barbarian warlord than an immortal warrior. Or maybe there wasn't that much difference between the two. Stavros wanted to claim her and she wanted that claim, wanted to belong somewhere and to someone for the first time in her life.

"Yes." She slid her hands up his chest, locked them around his neck and kissed him. She loved kissing him. He took his time, exploring, teasing, enticing, as though he had all the time in the world. She felt the heavy press of his cock against her and eased from side-to-side, rubbing it with her stomach.

Stavros pulled away from her and turned her so she was facing away from him. "Grip the headboard." His voice was deep and rough. She knew he was close to losing control. She wanted to push him over the edge.

Toni leaned forward and gripped the wooden slat, knowing that her position gave him the perfect view of her ass and her pussy.

His growl sent goose bumps racing over her skin. The jaguar was close to the surface. She glanced over her shoulder and gave him her most sultry smile. "What are you waiting for?"

Stavros' hands trembled. He who had fought battles since the dawn of time, had faced gods and goddesses and other mythical creatures, was shaking over the thought of claiming one human woman as his own.

No, not human, not any longer. She was immortal now. His.

He used his knees to widen her stance, making a place for himself behind her. Her hair was hanging forward over her shoulders, leaving her back bare. Her spine was so delicate. He dragged his index finger over it, fascinated when goose bumps appeared on her skin.

He could smell her arousal and inhaled deeply, taking it into his lungs. He'd never get enough of Toni's unique perfume. He teased a trail up the back of her thighs, drawing a startled laugh from her. She was ticklish there. He filed that away for another time.

He cupped her full ass and squeezed. Toni moaned and pushed herself more firmly into his hands. Goddess, how he loved this woman. In spite of her fears, she'd given him her love and trusted her body into his care. He would take care of both.

Her love was a treasure he would guard in his heart for all time. And her body, well, he was more than ready to give her the pleasure she deserved.

His cock was so full, his balls so heavy he hurt. But it was the best kind of ache in the world. It meant he was alive, not trapped or imprisoned.

More than ready, he pressed closer, allowing his dick to slide between her thighs, rubbing it over the slick folds of her pussy. Her cream coated his shaft and she shimmied her hips so it touched her clit.

Stavros kissed her nape and nipped at the tender curve of her shoulder. He deliberately stroked his cock over her pussy, making sure to rub against her clit. "I want you. Now."

She moaned and shoved her behind toward him. He knew that was her way of giving consent, that she wanted this as much as he did. He gripped his dick in his hand and angled it until the head was positioned just right. He eased inward until the broad head pushed past her initial resistance. Her inner muscles closed around him, and he swallowed hard and gritted his teeth to keep from coming. Damn, she felt so amazingly good wrapped around him, and he was barely inside her.

He braced his hands on the headboard beside hers and flexed his hips, driving himself home in one hard thrust. She gasped his name. She was panting hard, but so was he.

"I love you." He withdrew and then drove back in again, filling her. Every time was like the first, like there was no way she could feel as good as he remembered. And she didn't. She felt even better.

His motions became faster and more out of control with each thrust. He wanted her. Goddess, how he wanted her. Had to claim her. Inside him, his jaguar roared in triumph. Stavros knew time was short. Yes, he would recover quickly, but he wanted Toni with him, needed her pleasure to complete his own.

He wrapped his arms around her, slid one hand up to cup a full breast and the other down until it dipped between her damp thighs. He fucked her hard and fast while fingering her clit and her breast.

"Stavros." He loved the way she screamed his name, the way her pussy tightened around his cock.

"Yes," he roared as he came, his orgasm ripped from the very depths of his soul. Her wet heat continued to milk him as he filled her with his seed. She was his now.

Toni sucked air into her lungs in great gulps. Her body trembled and shook as Stavros pumped into her, his cock stretching her pussy in the most delightful way. She felt the heat of his orgasm and the flood of his semen as he came.

She curled her fingers around the headboard slat and held on for dear life. The bed bucked against the wall, pounding a hard rhythm as he rode them both into heaven. Her body was slick with sweat, but she didn't care. All she wanted was to be close to Stavros.

Another wave of pleasure hit her and she cried out. Her body trembled until it was impossible for her to remain upright, and she leaned forward, resting her head against her hands.

Maybe it was the whole immortality thing, maybe it was because she loved Stavros, but whatever the reason, she'd never experienced sex this intense before. Every sense was heightened to new levels. The puff of his breath against her neck, the rhythmic slap of their damp skin, the musky smell of sex and sweat combined to amp up the experience.

Stavros collapsed, leaning heavily against her back. She started to buckle under the pressure. He swore and pulled her back against him. Somehow, he managed to get them flat on the bed with him still buried deep. Even though he'd come, he didn't seem to be getting any smaller. If anything, he felt even larger.

She felt safe in his arms. That was a new sensation for her, but one she could get used to. Toni turned her head so she could see him. His eyes were closed but they snapped open the moment she moved.

Suddenly, she felt unaccountably shy. "Hey." She almost slapped herself in the forehead. That was the best she could come up with?

"Hey," he returned her greeting. Then he brushed a soft kiss across her lips. He still had one hand between her legs and teased her clit with his forefinger. She jumped and her pussy clenched. Stavros groaned and his shaft flexed inside her.

As much as she wanted to make love again, she also wanted to talk. "So what happens next?" Duh, that was even less intelligent than the last thing she'd said. With her pussy squeezing his cock, there was only one thing he'd be thinking about—more sex.

But Stavros surprised her when he eased away, pulling his erection from inside her. That made her entire body spasm and tremble. He eased onto his back and pulled her into his arms so her head was pillowed on his shoulder.

"As much as I want to think you were talking about sex, I know you weren't," he teased. He reached out with one long arm, snagged the discarded blanket and pulled it over her. She placed one hand over his heart. The steady beat anchored her. She tilted her head back so she could see his face.

"No. I meant what do we do from here? Where do we go?" A thought occurred to her. "Where will we live?" There were so many details, so much she didn't know about his life.

"We go wherever we want and live wherever we chose." He rubbed her back in a soothing manner. "Time is something we have plenty of."

That was a hard concept for her to wrap her head around. "But where do you live?" She really wanted to know.

"I really don't live anywhere. For five-thousand years, I was imprisoned. Before that, we wandered the earth with the Lady of the Beasts, stopping wherever we chose."

"We can stay at my place in Maine," she assured him. After all, the guy couldn't have much money. When would he have earned it?

He smiled and played with a lock of her hair. "I have an apartment in New Orleans."

She perked up at that. "I've always wanted to spend some time in the city. I'd planned on a few days there once I'd finished my photo shoot."

Stavros looked more relaxed than she'd ever seen him. The tension that usually surrounded him was gone. Because the curse was finally done. She couldn't imagine thousands of years of being cursed. She shuddered and he frowned.

"Are you cold?"

She shook her head. "No, I was just thinking about the curse."

That quickly the tension was back. She absently began to rub his stomach, wanting him to relax once again.

Stavros didn't speak of the curse but continued their conversation. "We can go anywhere in the world you desire. I can take us there in the blink of an eye."

"Really?" Toni sat up and grabbed the blanket when it fell to her waist. Stavros grabbed the edge of the blanket and tugged until she released it. She tried to be mad with him but couldn't. He looked so pleased with himself when her breasts were bared once again.

"Really. I am an immortal warrior. Now that I have all my powers back and you are a part of me, I can transport us both wherever we wish to go."

"That will certainly cut down on airfare." She'd have to cut corners where possible, at least until they figured out a way for Stavros to earn a living.

He frowned. "Is that a problem?"

"Ah, no. Not a problem."

He caught her face in his hand and stared at her until she caved. She couldn't resist the plea in his dark eyes, and if they were going to be together for eternity—and how weird was that—then honesty was important.

"I have enough money to support us until you figure things out. I mean, you've been imprisoned for thousands of years, are used to running around as a jaguar." A strange expression crossed his face, but she forged onward. "Face it, you don't exactly need money to survive as a big cat. You could catch your own meals, sleep in the trees. And I'll shut up now." Damn, in her experience, men didn't like being called out on their work, or lack of it. And she'd practically accused the guy as living like an animal. But he was one, or at least partly.

Nervous butterflies fluttered in her stomach and she clenched her hands. Why hadn't she kept her mouth shut?

Then Stavros did the most amazing thing. He threw back his head and began to laugh. Not a light chuckle, but a deep-down belly laugh. He laughed so hard tears began to roll down his cheeks.

Okay, now she was starting to get annoyed. She crossed her arms over her chest and tapped her fingers on her upper arms. He noticed the gesture and swiped at the tears. It took him several tries and some throat clearing before he could speak.

"You think that was a joke?" Toni admitted to herself that she was a little hurt by his attitude. She'd been offering to support him and he'd laughed at her.

Stavros immediately sobered and caught her hands, bringing them to his lips. "No, I don't think it was a joke," he said in between kisses. "I think you are the most amazing woman in the world."

That made her feel marginally better.

"The world has not changed so much since time began. Men are meant to take care of their women."

"Hey." She pulled her hand away and thumped him lightly on the chest. "I can take care of myself."

"And me." He smiled and squeezed her hand. "But you don't need to worry about money. I can take care of you."

She narrowed her gaze. "It's not illegal, is it?"

He chuckled again. "No, it's not illegal. The short version of the story is that one of my brethren was released decades ago. He started a company and made us all shareholders. He invested in oil and minerals because we know where to find all the world's wealth. He also invested in computers and technologies."

Toni knew her mouth was open, but there was no containing her surprise. It had never occurred to her that immortal warriors would adapt so well to the modern world. She'd underestimated him. And she wouldn't do that again.

"So you're doing okay?" That was probably an understatement.

He nodded and smiled. "There is an account in my name with millions." He frowned. "Or is it a billion?" He shrugged. "I haven't paid much attention to it. Mordecai handles the details."

Toni felt lightheaded and swayed. "Millions?"

"At least."

Stavros didn't seem fazed by that amount of money, but she was practically hyperventilating. "You're rich." It came out more as an accusation than a statement.

"Does that matter?" He lifted her onto his lap and wrapped his arms around her. "What is mine, is yours."

"I can't contribute that much."

Stavros shook his head. "You give me something more valuable than money—love and acceptance."

Her heart ached and her insecurities melted away. How did he always know the right thing to say to ease her worries? "You're one in a million, you know that?"

He gave her his sexiest grin. "More like one in a billion."

She started to laugh, but it was quickly smothered when he kissed her. She was breathless when he finally released her. "Again?" she asked. His cock was pressed hard against her hip and she recognized the gleam in his eyes.

"Again. And again. And again."

She feigned tiredness and sighed. "If I must." He tickled her sides and she began to laugh as he rolled her beneath him and slid home. They both moaned and Toni wrapped her arms around her warrior. "I can see you're going to be demanding."

"You can't fool me," he reminded her. "I can smell your arousal."

Toni laughed again and arched her hips. "You can't fool me either. I can tell when you want me."

"I always want you. I love you, Toni."

"I love you too."

Then he proceeded to show her just how much.

Epilogue

Toni sat next to Stavros on a luxurious leather couch that was the color of dark chocolate and stared at everyone else in the room. She'd gotten to know them all over the past few days and liked the women very much. The men were all like Stavros—gorgeous and intimidating.

"Will you be staying in New Orleans for a while?"

Toni turned to Sabrina. It was her living room they were all gathered in. Well, hers and Arand's. When Stavros had told her he had an apartment in New Orleans, she hadn't expected it to be one of several in a grand old Victorian in the French Quarter. The group owned two houses that sat alongside one another, and there were enough apartments for everyone, even though some of the group didn't live in the city but were visiting.

"Probably," she answered Sabrina's question. "I want to take some photos of the city, and Stavros and I still have to decide what we want to do after that."

"Are there any more of those puff-pastry things you made?" Arand asked Sabrina.

"I'll get them," Sabrina told him. Arand blew her a kiss and went back to conversing with his friend. Sabrina turned back to Toni. "Excuse me. It's better to keep them well fed so they don't get into trouble." It was said in such a wry manner that Toni laughed.

She took a moment to sit back and stare around the large, comfortable room. There were three sofas creating a cozy seating area and two large wingchairs as well. The colors were all earth tones and the furniture was large to fit such big men. The artwork on the walls was vibrant and beautiful, all created by Sabrina herself.

It was really amazing when Toni thought about it, and she hadn't stop thinking about it since they'd arrived in the city. That she, Toni Richards, was sitting in the same room as a bunch of immortals and was one of them. Furthermore, some of the women she'd met were famous in their own right.

Aimee was a graphic artist and had created her own graphic novel, which coincidentally was the same one Toni had seen at the comic shop in New York. Her mate was Roric, the white tiger, and he kept a close eye on her.

Then there was Kellsie Morris, who Toni had recognized immediately. The woman was a big star among the horror movie crowd. Toni was a big fan. Kellsie had been very kind to her when Toni had gushed about her movies. And Marko, her bear of a mate, had seemed pleased by Toni's praise. And that was a good thing, because he was one dude Toni didn't want to get on the bad side of. He was huge.

And then there was Leander, the lion, who was mated with Araminta, a romance author. Toni couldn't wait to read her books. Tilly owned and operated a popular coffee shop in New Orleans and she was mated to Phoenix, who was an actual phoenix. That boggled the mind.

But it was Mordecai, the serpent, who was the most dangerous of the bunch. Toni knew that deep in her gut. She also knew that Jessica, a talented jewelry maker, had him wrapped around her little finger. Mordecai was also the one who'd invested and made all the money for the warriors.

They were an incredible group and she was among them. She grabbed her glass of red wine and took a large gulp.

"Are you all right?" Stavros asked.

He looked concerned, so she smiled. "I'm fine. It's just a lot to get used to."

"We are all family now," Roric informed her as he eased down beside her. The rest of the room went quiet and all eyes turned to Roric. "We have beaten the curse once and for all. It is done. It is now time to live our lives."

Everyone in the room, including Toni, raised their glass and toasted Roric's pronouncement. Then everyone was talking again and, as the evening progressed, Toni began to relax and really enjoy herself.

"You should drop by the coffee shop tomorrow," Tilly told her. "Jessica and Sabrina will both be there. And I know the other ladies are planning to do some shopping while they're in the city. We could all hit the shops together."

Toni still couldn't get over the idea that they'd all dropped what they were doing in their busy lives to come and meet her. She'd expected the third degree, after all, Stavros was their friend. But they'd all been nothing but kind and accepting.

"I'd like that," she told Tilly. "What time?"

"About ten. That way we can get some shopping and sightseeing in before lunch. Plan to be gone until at least supper time." Tilly seemed to sense some of what Toni was feeling, because she smiled. "We ladies have to stick together. After all, no one else knows what we're going through or how to deal with an immortal warrior when he's cranky."

Toni started to laugh, and that caught Stavros' attention. He wrapped his arm around her and frowned at Tilly. "Don't tell me you're spreading tales about me already?"

Tilly just smiled and sauntered away. Stavros turned to her. "Should I ask?"

Toni shook her head. "Probably better not to." She took his face in her hands, unable to stop the flood of emotion filling her. "I love you."

His smile was the slow, sexy one she loved so much. "I love you too. Thank you for making my life complete."

"The pleasure is all mine." She met him halfway and they kissed amidst the laughter and teasing of their friends.

About the Author

Once upon a time N.J. had the idea that she would like to quit her job at the bookstore, sell everything she owned, leave her hometown, and write romance novels in a place where no one knew her. And she did. Two years later, she went back to the bookstore and her hometown and settled in for another seven years.

One day, she gave notice at her job on a Friday morning. On Sunday afternoon, she received a tentative acceptance for her first erotic romance novel and life would never be the same.

N.J. has always been a voracious reader, and now she spends her days writing novels of her own. Vampires, werewolves, dragons, time-travelers, seductive handymen, and next-door neighbors with smoldering good looks—all vie for her attention. It's a tough life, but someone's got to live it.

N.J. enjoys hearing from readers, and she can be reached at njwalters22@ yahoo.ca. You can check out her web site at www.njwalters.com.

To win the battle for his soul, he may have to sacrifice the woman who set him free.

Night of the Tiger

© 2013 N.J. Walters

Hades' Carnival, Book 1

Aimee Horner lives and breathes her career as a graphic novel illustrator, but she never expected it would invade her dreams. In recent months, worsening nightmares have pulled her into the darkest corners of Hell.

On a rare night out with friends at a traveling carnival, she finds herself strangely drawn to an abandoned carousel adorned with vividly exotic animals. One steed, a massive white tiger, is a temptation she can't resist. The moment she climbs upon him, her world changes forever.

More than five thousand years ago, Roric and his fellow shapeshifting warriors were imprisoned in their animal forms, a last-ditch effort by the goddess they served to save them from the horrors of Hell.

With one special woman's touch, he has a chance at freedom and redemption—but the clock is ticking. If he is still alive in twenty-four hours, the spell will be broken, and Hell will have no claim on his soul. The only hitch is his blazing attraction to Aimee. If only he could trust that she isn't merely a distraction sent by Hades—luscious bait to lure him from his mission.

Warning: This book contains an ancient curse, an imprisoned goddess, a graphic artist and the hot shapeshifting immortal warrior who turns her life upside down while they battle Hades and his minions for their immortal souls. There is also plenty of hot sex between the heroine and her hot, shapeshifting warrior. Just saying.

When the devil wants a deal, there's no bowing out gracefully.

Mark of the Bear

© 2013 N.J. Walters

Hades' Carnival, Book 2

At twenty-nine, Hollywood scream queen Kellsie Morris is acutely aware the clock is ticking on her career. Luckily, the one big role she needs to pad her retirement fund has just come through—the story of an immortal, shape-shifting warrior trapped in a carnival run by the Devil's minions.

When Kellsie arrives on set, she can't resist climbing aboard an amazingly realistic carousel bear—and finds herself flung into a world where the horror is real. As real as the heat radiating off the half-naked hunk in her arms.

Marko has waited an eternity for the chance to free his goddess, the Lady of the Beasts, and his fellow warriors from an ancient curse. But once he lays eyes on Kellsie, he knows to the bottom of his soul that his purpose is to protect her life.

But in this hellish game, it's the Devil's move. And there's no predicting when and where the final, brutal stroke will fall—and which lover will pay the ultimate price.

Warning: This book contains a heroine who's a screamer—in and out of bed—and a warrior who gives a whole new meaning to "method". After reading, please use caution when standing up. Your knees may be weak.

When this wolf comes knocking, there's no turning him away

Wolf at the Door

© *2014 N.J. Walters*

Salvation Pack, Book 1

When Gwendolyn Jones inherits a Tennessee cabin from a great aunt she never knew, she quits her job and follows her dream to write full time. Meeting a stranger in a local cemetery isn't a risk she normally takes, but she needs the information on his flash drive for an article she's writing on werewolves. Later that night, when two honest-to-God werewolves come knocking on her cabin door, they're definitely *not* Photoshopped.

Jacque LaForge is on a mission to retrieve a flash drive before it endangers his pack. He never thought he'd find a mate, but the chemistry between him and Gwen is unmistakably off the charts. Now to convince her he's only trying to protect her from his vengeful former pack—led by his own father.

Gwen's first instinct to flee only gets her a smashed car and a concussion. She wakes up in a dangerous new world she never thought existed—and in the arms of the one man who stands between her and certain death.

Warning: Contains a sexy werewolf and his small pack of friends, a paranormal writer who really didn't believe such things existed—until now—and a completely dysfunctional family who are out to kill them both.

37324503R00153

Made in the USA
San Bernardino, CA
15 August 2016